No Kiss for the Devil

Adrian Magson

Also by Adrian Magson from Crème de la Crime:

No Peace for the Wicked

No Help for the Dying

No Sleep for the Dead*

No Tears for the Lost*

*also published in unabridged audio

First published in 2008
by Crème de la Crime
P O Box 523, Chesterfield, S40 9AT

Typesetting by Yvette Warren
Cover design by Yvette Warren
Front cover image by Peter Roman

ISBN 978-0-9557078-1-0
A CIP catalogue reference for this book is available from
the British Library

Printed and bound in Great Britain
by CPI Cox & Wyman, Reading, RG1 8EX

www.cremedelacrime.com

About the author:

Adrian Magson is a novelist and freelance writer, and lives with his wife Ann in Oxfordshire.

www.adrianmagson.com

As ever, huge thanks to Lynne and Jeff and everyone at Crème for their faith and support.

To Christie Hickman, for correcting my mistakes so kindly without drawing blood – and for making me a better writer in the process.

To Parvinder Bassi, MRCVS, a kick-ass vet, for your expertise, your patient explanations and good neighbourliness. Cats rule.

And to PC Dan Hopkins, Thames Valley Police, Banbury, for your kind help and information.

This is for Ann.
Ace muffin maker and sidekick.

The woman arrived in a black VW Golf GTi.

Her approach was watched by a man on the deserted fourth floor of an anonymous office building just off London's Euston Road. As the vehicle turned into the car park below, he took out a mobile and pressed a button. He allowed it to ring once before cutting the connection.

The woman who stepped out was tall, with blonde hair, neatly cut. Smart suit, dark court shoes. Professional. A flash of white slip peeped from beneath the hem of her skirt as she reached in for something on the passenger seat. When she ducked back out, she was holding a burgundy leather briefcase with a shoulder strap and gold buckles. She turned to look up at the seven-storey building, hand raised to shield her eyes against the setting sun, but the man knew she wouldn't be able to see him from down there.

A movement behind him showed in the reflection from the window.

"Boss?" the newcomer said.

"She's here." He spoke in careful English, trying to flatten his tongue and get the words out of the base of his mouth where he felt his origins always betrayed him. "Are we still secure?"

"Yes. Nobody will bother us."

"Good. Take her to the basement. Get her briefcase."

The other nodded and moved away. Moments later, a snatch of conversation echoed along the corridor, then faded. Elsewhere, silence returned as the building emptied for the day.

The man, known as Grigori, walked over to a desk, the only item of furniture in the room. On it was a cardboard folder, a touch telephone and a plastic in-tray. The last two were covered in dust.

The folder contained everything he had needed to know about the woman: name, age, background, friends, past jobs, past loves… past everything.

He fed it into the mouth of a portable shredder on the floor beside the desk, and watched as the cardboard and its contents turned into strips of spaghetti. As of that moment, its subject ceased to be of interest to him.

Or, more importantly, a threat.

He reached into an inside jacket pocket and took out a sheet of paper and a photograph. The paper was a brief biography, the subject of which was – like the woman downstairs – a freelance reporter. She also had no ties, no close family and no obvious corporate loyalties. Another loner.

He studied the photo; it might almost have been the same woman. Not as thin, perhaps, but the same blonde hair and pale skin. The same look of self-reliance.

He returned to the window as the driver of the Golf mounted the steps to the front entrance. Graceful, he thought idly. Elegant, even.

But a dead woman.

She just didn't know it yet.

1

"You'll have to leave your car down here." The constable was a vague, hunched shape looming out of the darkness. Up close he looked cold, wet and miserable, and clearly in no mood to argue. His gesture indicated which way to go. Behind him, the lane disappeared into the dark, then re-emerged beneath a distant glow of arc lights, vehicles and movement, the area beyond it lost in the vastness of the Essex countryside. Radios crackled unseen, the voices snatched by the wind and lost in the night air.

It was starting to rain again.

Riley Gavin climbed out of her car and locked the door. She walked away without waiting. If the constable wanted her car moved he could come and get her.

She wished she'd put on a thicker coat and more suitable shoes. But the officious phone call that had dragged her from bed at three in the morning had neither warned her about the prevailing conditions nor given any details of why she was needed. It had simply urged her to come, and given her careful directions on how to get there. The lack of information had left her with a feeling of dread, overshadowing any thoughts brought on by her instincts as a freelance reporter.

She trudged up the lane towards the lights, skirting the pot-holes and ruts she could see, fingers mentally crossed against the ones she couldn't. It had been raining on and off for three days now, a persistent autumn deluge, and the topsoil was spongy and heavy, incapable of absorbing any more water.

Two men splashed past going the other way, carrying metal cases and muttering about the weather. Both were shrouded from head to toe in white protective suits. Another figure followed, this one in a uniform and peaked cap, dancing across the uneven surface in the wobbling wake of a torch. He unravelled a roll of scene-of-crime tape as he went, replacing a strip fluttering brokenly amid the bushes bordering the track. He ignored Riley, too intent on his task and keeping his footing on the treacherous surface.

"Who the hell are you?" A voice challenged her and she looked up to see another uniform approaching. A torch beam hit her square on, the glare painful on the eyes.

She put up a protective hand just as another voice called out flatly from over by the lights, "It's all right. Miss Gavin? Over here."

Riley stepped round the constable and decided they must have called out the awkward squad. Or maybe it was the foul weather making them all tetchy. She found herself alongside a tall figure in a yellow slicker and black rubber boots. He held out an arm to prevent her going too close, and kept himself between her and the focus of lights on a fold in the ground.

"Sorry about this," he said, and introduced himself. She recognised his voice from the phone. The spread of light gave her an impression of high cheekbones, a confident chin, and a lick of hair plastered across his forehead. His eyes were hidden in pools of shadow. "DI Craig Pell. We need you to make an identification."

Riley's stomach lurched at the idea. When he had called, other than giving his rank, name and directions, he had rung off without elaborating. Now she had an instant foreboding.

Pell checked that her hands were empty, then handed her a white coverall suit. It was the same garment worn by SOCOs – Scene of Crime Officers – to preserve the integrity of the scene. He helped her into it, awkward when she stumbled against him and he had to grab at her shoulder to stop her falling. He mumbled an apology and snatched his hands away as if he'd been stung.

4

Riley wondered if he was always so clumsy.

Once she was zipped up he handed her some overshoes then turned and called out to a figure hunched in the hollow. There was an answering grunt and Pell took Riley's arm and led her forward.

The scene was nightmarish. They were standing on the edge of a wide, shallow ditch bordered by a tangle of coarse bushes. A canopy had been erected to cover the immediate area, and the ghostly glow of lights gave the canvas the appearance of a large lampshade. The man below was hunched over something on the ground, but Riley couldn't see what it was.

"Tread between the tapes," Pell instructed her. "Stop when he tells you. Don't touch anything you see and don't take anything out of your pockets."

Riley stepped down carefully, feeling the ground soft and slick beneath her feet. She came to a stop when the hunched figure raised a hand. He was muttering to himself, and when he stopped and turned his head, she saw he'd been talking into a small voice recorder. He clicked it off and beckoned her closer, moving crab-like to one side and indicating where she should stand.

2

Riley had seen dead bodies before. It was never pleasant, whether death had come by natural or other causes. Each time, she had to steel herself to remain detached. It was never easy, but in the main she reckoned on being able to hold it together long enough to not make a fool of herself.

She had a feeling that this one might be different.

The forensics officer was watching her, eyes in dark pockets of shadow cast by the arc lights. He wore a white suit and overshoes like the others, but exuded a different kind of aura. Heavier somehow, as if weighed down by authority or responsibility. He didn't seem too pleased to see her.

"Take it slow," he said flatly. He glanced past her at Pell and lifted his eyebrows momentarily before adding, "Do you recognise her?"

The woman was lying huddled in the bottom of the ditch, her legs bent and her feet together, shoulders slightly hunched. She could have been asleep or even posing coyly, except that her hands had been taped together at the wrists, the material cutting deep into the skin. Her face was pale and beaded with moisture, wet strands of blonde hair plastered against her skull. Bruising showed on her cheeks and down one side of her throat, and one ear lobe was ripped, a faint stain of red showing where an earring had been torn away.

Riley guessed the woman was not much older than herself, maybe in her mid-thirties, although it was impossible to be sure. She wore a plain dark jacket and skirt, with the hem turned up on one slim thigh to reveal a flash of white silk. Her shoes had been shiny once, but like her lower legs were now smeared with mud. Her fingers were bare, although the glint of a watch showed in the intrusive glare of the lights. Her hands looked well cared-for, the nails varnished with a blush of pink, and were splayed out as if somehow wanting to be distanced from what had happened to her body.

Riley forced herself to look back at the woman's face, passing over the slack mouth to the half-open eyes. They contained no discernible expression, simply two darker areas in an otherwise bloodless skin. But Riley fancied she could see a pleading glint deep inside.

Her gut heaved and she swallowed hard.

"What was done to her?" she asked finally, eyes on the taped wrists. It was the first thing she could think of, familiar with images from Belfast to Baghdad of torture victims found tied up, as if death alone was not enough.

The forensics man didn't answer immediately, but gave her a studied look. He shook his head. "It's too early to tell."

"Anything?" It was Pell, shifting about at the top of the slope, restless for an answer.

It was Riley's turn to shake her head. There was something horribly, chillingly familiar about the woman's face. But she wasn't about to commit herself to these men without a moment's thought. Whoever the dead woman was – had been – she deserved more than that. If Riley got it wrong, the idea of some thoughtless copper blundering upon an unconnected family with terrifying news was something she didn't like to contemplate. As she looked beyond the glare of lights, trying to make the connection to where she might have seen her before, she noticed two other figures in the background beyond the canopy, standing against a gleam of polished metal half concealed in the bushes. As her eyes acclimatised to the change, she recognised the shape as a small car. The men were checking under the bonnet.

"Why me?" she queried, to buy herself some time. "What made

you think I'd know her?"

The car the men were examining had been driven with considerable force into the ditch and beyond, burying its nose into the undergrowth and churning up a burrow of earth as it went. As Riley's eyes became accustomed to the pattern of light and dark, she was beginning to realise that the crime scene was far more than just this woman's body.

"Are you saying you don't know her?" Pell was plainly having to hold himself in check.

"I don't think so. It's hard to tell. Is the car hers?" She guessed they must already have an idea, unless the car was stolen, of course. Or rented. The question remained, though: out of all the inhabitants of the greater London metropolitan area, why had Pell called her?

"Yes." He beckoned her back out of the ditch, holding out a hand to help her up. He let go as soon as she was on safe ground, as if prolonged contact might be misconstrued. When she was standing alongside him, he produced a plastic evidence bag and angled it so she could see the contents.

"This was found in the foot-well," he explained. "You might not have known her, but she seems to have known you."

Riley studied the bag. Inside was a single square of yellow paper. A Post-it note, common in every household and office in the country. In spite of a smear of moisture on the outside of the plastic film, there was no mistaking what had been written on the paper in bold handwriting.

It was her own name and telephone number.

3

"I don't understand it." Riley was slumped in the passenger seat of Pell's car, holding a cup of coffee. It was lukewarm and sweet, like stewed caramel, but a welcome distraction from the scene outside. She was still wearing the white SOCO suit, and in spite of the lightweight fabric she felt hot and constricted, as if swathed in cling-film.

"It's never easy," Pell replied. His tone was of one who had been here too many times.

The car smelled of dog and damp. Sweet wrappers and wet-wipes were crushed haphazardly into the door pockets, some tumbling out on to the floor around her feet. An ancient pair of men's trainers lay in the foot-well, faded and curled like dried banana skins. The two available cup-holders were jammed with polystyrene mugs, each filled with rubbish. A mobile skip, office and taxi all in one, she thought.

"You don't believe in cleaning, do you?" she said.

"I don't have the time."

Outside, the night and the weather and the dark continued, interspersed with the comings and goings of the forensic and search teams combing the area around the body.

Riley stared through the windscreen, wondering how long it would be before the press showed up. Not long, if their usual contacts were on the ball. Journalists had a nose for a story and –

Journalist. Her stomach went ice-cold as her thoughts suddenly fixed with glaring precision on the awful realisation that Pell had been unwittingly right; the dead woman had known her.

She kept her eyes to the front in case Pell interpreted her expression. She needed time to think it through.

The dead woman's face had looked vaguely familiar, yet without that spark of absolute recognition. It was like seeing a celebrity in the street, but not being sure. It hadn't helped that, down in that hollow and under the glare of the lights, any notable characteristics had been flattened, leaving a uniform blandness like a shop-front mannequin.

Now she knew who she'd been looking at, she felt sick.

Pell had taken a phone call moments after getting into the car. From what little he'd said, she knew he'd been hearing confirmation of the dead woman's name and details. She got the impression it hadn't come as a surprise.

"Turns out she was a journalist," Pell muttered finally, half to himself. "Name of Helen Bellamy." Under the dull glow of the interior light, his face was less angular than she'd first thought outside, but still with a determined quality, as if hewn from a lump of wood but with the edges softened. He was also smooth-shaven, and his eyes were surprisingly dark, perhaps with Latin origins. With the hood of his slicker down, she saw his medium-crop hair was peppered with grey. Late thirties, she guessed. "A journalist like you," he added heavily. He drummed strong fingers on the steering wheel, a tattoo of frustration. "You sure you don't know her?"

"I… may have met her. But that's all." Riley had to force the words out, aware that any deliberate lies now might come back to haunt her. She hoped Pell hadn't picked up on her hesitation.

"She could have got your name for business purposes, I suppose." He didn't sound convinced, as if randomness simply didn't happen. His tone was reinforced by the expression in his eyes as he turned to watch her. "The thing is, why would she have it on her? Did you have a meeting arranged… maybe to work on something together?" He let a few beats go by, then said flatly, "Did you know her or not?"

"If I knew her so well that we were going to work together,

10

I think I'd have remembered by now, don't you?" Riley was irritated by his probing, as if he was reluctant to extend his investigation much beyond the close confines of this car. Right now, all that her memory would give her of Helen Bellamy was a vague image of an elegant, willowy woman, friendly and self-assured. A freelance reporter like herself. No more, no less.

"Do you know anyone else who might know her, then?" He was clearly trying a different tack. "Circle of friends, work colleagues, boyfriends… girlfriends?"

"No. I'm sorry."

"You're in the same profession."

"Pell, I know lots of journalists, but none of them particularly well. Like you and other coppers – you're not all best mates, are you?"

He pulled a face in wry acknowledgement. "Good point."

"Why," asked Riley impulsively, "do you think her hands were tied?"

"We don't know yet," he admitted, echoing the forensics man. "She had been restrained and possibly hit, that's all we can tell right now." He shrugged. "Amounts to the same thing in my book. The tape on her wrists might have been to subdue her while they were on the move. You didn't get that from me, by the way."

"Of course." She focussed on the dashboard, trying to process the image of Helen being alive but restrained, unable to free herself or offer any resistance. The idea was macabre. Awful. "You don't normally drag people out to crime scenes in the middle of the night – especially journalists. Why couldn't this have waited until the morning?" She waited, but he didn't answer. "Particularly as you had an idea who she was before I got here."

Pell opened his mouth, then shut it again. The expression in his eyes was indecipherable. If he had any ulterior motives, he was keeping them to himself. "She was discovered just after midnight by a man walking his dogs. He said the car definitely wasn't there earlier in the evening at ten o'clock, when he last came by, so it must have been dumped after that time. That's borne out by a residue of warmth on the engine block. We're still trying to narrow down the timing."

"I see."

"I needed quick confirmation of her ID – from you if I could get it – so we could back-trace her movements."

"You knew I was a journalist?"

"One of the SOCO team recognised your name. He'd read your stuff. He's a fan. I figured it was worth a try calling you. We've got a hell of a caseload at the moment and we need all the shortcuts we can get." He scrubbed at his face with his fingers, suddenly looking bone-weary, as if any energy he'd been harbouring until now was seeping away with the approach of daylight. Riley guessed he had broken with procedure by calling her in at this stage and was now regretting it. His next words confirmed it. "I'm in deep shit if my boss knows I did it."

Riley felt a flicker of sympathy, and glanced across to where the man in the forensics suit was stepping carefully around the edge of the ditch, pointing a large flashlight at the ground. "Is that why he wasn't very friendly?"

"Yes. I had to lean on him to let you in."

"Will he tell anyone?"

"No. He owed me a bit of a favour. Now I owe him a bigger one."

Pell eventually let her go, with instructions not to publish any-thing and to call him if she thought of anything relating to the dead woman. In spite of a reluctant smile, which softened his face considerably, the implications behind the first instruction were clear: her name on a piece of paper at the death scene meant that Riley was far too close to this case to be allowed any leeway as a reporter.

She climbed out of the white suit and returned to her car. As she drove away down the track she passed other vehicles, some with interior lights on behind misted windows. Crime-scene members snatching a quick break in an attempt to dry off and down some refreshments. As she hit the main road, more cars were arriving and heading up the lane. Probably the press pack, all vying for an exclusive on the story. That was going to make Pell even more unhappy.

She checked the dashboard clock, surprised to see it was already gone five. A pale dawn was nudging through the heavy clouds like a wash. With the arrival of daylight, the investigators would be able to get a clear scan of the surrounding area. She didn't envy them the hours to come. For once, she was relieved not to be part of the press melée.

She pulled in at the first lay-by and dialled a number. The recipient wouldn't thank her for waking him this early. But circumstances warranted it.

What she hadn't told DI Pell was that she was aware of one person who had known Helen Bellamy a lot better than she did. Just a few months ago, Frank Palmer, a former military police-man, now a private investigator, had for a brief while been close to Helen. Work had thrown them together by chance and something had clicked. During that time, Palmer had gone around with a soppy smile on his face. Then circumstances and the pressures of their respective worlds had tugged them apart.

The other thing she had avoided telling Pell was that she had met Helen a couple of times, although both occasions were fleeting, and there had been no time to gain more than the briefest of impressions. Frank Palmer liked Helen, which was good enough for her.

The phone rang four times before switching to Palmer's voice-mail. She didn't leave a message; she couldn't trust herself not to sound like the voice of doom. Instead she switched off and thought about what to do next. Sooner or later, Pell and his colleagues would unearth something to show that Palmer had known the dead woman. When they did, they would descend on him like vultures on a corpse. Ex-army man, a bit of a loner, private detective and security consultant, for which some would read bodyguard and therefore no stranger to violence; they'd salivate and find plenty of precedents for making all the wrong assumptions.

She wondered what Palmer's reaction would be when he heard.

She dialled another number. This one was in Finchley, north London. It rang twice and was answered. She said simply: "I'll be with you in forty-five minutes. Can you trace Palmer? It's urgent. There's been a murder. He knew the victim."

The man on the other end sounded not the least bit surprised at being called so early in the morning with such news. "Will do," he replied, his voice plummy and rich. In the background she heard a high-pitched electronic two-tone and the purr of another phone. "I'll get some croissants and coffee on the go."

"Good idea. Make it strong, will you? I need the hit."

She switched off the phone and headed towards Finchley.

4

Donald Brask listened intently while Riley explained what she had seen in the dark wetness of the Essex countryside. He sat with Buddha-like stillness, absorbing her words like a sponge, his plump chins clustered above a shimmering silk dressing gown and fat hands clasped over his stomach. A mug of coffee and a croissant sat untouched beside him, forgotten in the shock of her revelations. For once, Riley had stolen a lead on a breaking story before one of Donald's contacts in the Met had been able to drop a whisper in his ear.

As her long-time agent, she knew he had grown to rely on her professional approach. She never over-glossed a story no matter what the circumstances, and always stuck to the facts. It was something she had heard him lament on long and loud about a couple of his other clients who could be relied on, as he'd put it acidly, 'to turn a cow-pat into a Fabergé egg – with trimmings.'

"I don't think Palmer had seen Helen Bellamy for a while," she concluded, after describing the crime scene. "A few months, maybe. But we need to find him and let him know before anyone else does."

Donald pursed his lips. "He's a big boy. He'll know how to handle it."

"True. But a thing like this?" Frank Palmer was something of a contradiction. He was probably the most irritatingly laid-back man Riley had ever met, with a tendency to underplay most situations like a sloth on Valium. But he was also the most loyal and committed friend she'd ever encountered – and the toughest. Show him a friend in peril, and it was like lighting the blue touch-paper.

The danger, she reflected, was if the police treated him with even the remotest hint of suspicion, based solely on the fact that he had once had a relationship with Helen Bellamy, or if they pushed him too hard in their questioning.

Donald grunted and waved a vague hand. "I've called, but he's not answering."

"He's not on a job through you, then?" Riley knew that Donald Brask occasionally used Palmer for the kind of specialist skills reporters didn't possess. Palmer's background in the Special Investigations Branch of the Royal Military Police had trained him in what Brask sometimes referred to as the dark arts – skills he had used to good effect to help Riley in her work, where danger had threatened something more concrete than a volley of abusive language or a threat of court action by a disgruntled subject.

"Not this time. He must be on a surveillance job."

As they were both aware, when Palmer was on an assignment, he gave it his all – including turning off his phone to avoid distractions. Whether performing close-protection duties for a client or their family, or running surveillance on a questionable employee or business contact, he simply dropped out of touch until he was able to surface again. The ability to completely focus on their needs was what made him so valued by his circle of clients.

"What have you got on at the moment?" It was Donald's signal to return to any work in hand. Riley was under no obligation to take on the assignments he passed her way, but when she did, Donald could be every bit as engaged and committed as Palmer.

"Not a lot." Donald knew exactly what she had on. He had a mind like one of his computers and could keep track of several reporter clients and their assignments – and give them any data backup they needed. As he liked to boast to editors when the occasion demanded, he was as capable of in-depth research as

16

any reporter and better than most. "I've got two follow-up stories to look at," she added, "which you know about."

He nodded. "And?"

"They can wait." She paused, wondering how to approach this one. "I had a job offer yesterday. I was going to talk to you about it."

Donald reached for his coffee, an interested glimmer in his eye. He always delighted in something new, and the bigger the better. If it was obscure, he loved the challenge; if it involved people of note, he couldn't wait to set the wolves running. Getting a head start over the opposition was all part of the game, and made his day that much brighter. "Do tell, sweetie. Is someone trying to poach my ace reporter?"

She smiled. He wasn't joking. Donald believed in protecting his turf like an ill-bred alley cat. "I don't know yet. I'll let you have full details as soon as I can."

"I'd appreciate that. Did they give you an outline?"

"It was an email asking if I'd be interested in pitching to do a profile piece. It's for a business journal."

"Who's the subject?"

"They didn't say. Someone big, though. The fee scale is better than good and syndication is mine to deal with. It's a rush job, apparently. I've got a meeting to discuss it later today."

Donald looked sceptical. "If it's a rush job, sweetie, someone somewhere has dropped it like a hot, flabby turd." He shook his jowls in disapproval. "Still, it's up to you. I wonder if anyone else was up for it? I could ask around, see who might have turned it down." It didn't seem to have occurred to him that Riley might be insulted by the suggestion that she had not been first in line for the assignment.

"They didn't say." Riley knew what was bugging him, and it wasn't the possibly dubious aspect of the assignment. There was very little Donald didn't know about in the reporting field, and the likelihood that a high-profile job had come up without appearing on his radar was remote. If there was one thing likely to sting his professional pride, it was the idea that he might have missed something newsworthy.

"I was thinking," she continued, before he could get all bitter and twisted. "In between looking at this job, I might take a background look at Helen Bellamy."

"Why?" Donald's tone lifted a notch. He looked at a clock set in a chunky piece of quartz on the sideboard. "The nationals will have scoured off the best meat by now. Even if the police get lucky and come up with anything, it'll be old news by tomorrow."

Riley knew he was right, but something else was bothering her. There had been an edge to DI Pell's demeanour which she couldn't put a finger on. It wasn't as if he was dealing with a random murder – the fact that he'd called her out to the murder scene was an indication of that. Usually the police preferred to keep the press as far away as possible until they had something to say or unless they needed media co-operation in turning up witnesses or locating a missing person. She was pretty sure this wasn't one of those cases. Pell had been too guarded, and the more she thought about it, the more she felt he'd been holding back something important. The answer might be staring her in the face.

And there was the Palmer connection, which she couldn't ignore even if she wanted to.

"I've got to do something," she replied. "When Palmer finds out what happened, he'll be all over it like a tiger shark. I can help give him a head start."

Donald nodded, recognising the futility of arguing with her. She and Palmer worked well together, each very capable in their separate disciplines. Palmer was tough and resourceful, with all the directness his army training had given him. All were elements which had proved useful in the past. He was also a first-class investigator. Riley was equally direct in her own way – alarmingly so, with her own personal safety often taking second place to a story – but she was steady and relentless, even under pressure.

He was almost envious of their relationship, and had sometimes wondered what would happen if one suddenly found the other's life at risk. This could be as close as he got to finding out without either of them being the victim. He felt sorry for anyone who came under the spotlight for Helen Bellamy's murder. Especially if they came up against Frank Palmer.

"How will you handle it?"

"I'll see if I can back-track her last assignments. Helen was really committed to her job. Palmer once told me she left him sitting at a restaurant table to go interview someone she was after. Maybe something she was working on went horribly wrong."

"You don't know that. It could have been pure chance. It happens. Maybe she met up with the wrong man."

Riley shook her head. "I don't think so. The whole thing looked so… deliberate. She was working, I'm sure of it."

Donald gave a lengthy sigh. She was probably right. Not all reporting jobs involved nice, civilised interviews over glasses of wine or cups of tea. There were times when all the usual rules went right off the board. It took someone with Riley's instincts to realise it.

Then he remembered something, and rose from his chair. "Actually I may be able to help you. I believe I have details of her last couple of jobs."

Riley was surprised. "I didn't know she worked through you."

"She didn't. She normally used a Brussels agency. But a couple of assignments came my way with her name attached, so I agreed to use her." He waddled through to his office, a large, converted sitting room full of computer equipment, printers, scanners and telephones, which formed the hub of his agency. He ran his fingers across a keyboard and gave a grunt of satisfaction as several lines of text appeared on the adjacent monitor. He moved the mouse and a printer hummed into life on a nearby shelf. He took out the single sheet of print and handed it to her. It contained the name and address of a business magazine publisher near Covent Garden. "The editor's name is David Johnson. I'll tell him you're on the way. He owes me a couple of favours. It could be a dead end, but it might turn up something useful."

"What about Frank?" Riley folded the sheet of paper and slipped it into her pocket. "I'd like to let him know about Helen before the police pile in on him."

Donald agreed. "He'd rather hear about it from you than some faceless copper plodding through an address book. I'll ring round, see if I can trace him. If I hear anything, I'll let you know."

Riley left Donald's Finchley house and drove straight towards the West End, joining an already growing stream of traffic. It was still early, but by the time she arrived at Covent Garden the business community would be buzzing. She still had no clear plan in mind, no idea why she was contemplating looking into this, other than her instincts as an investigative reporter. All she knew was she needed to get the ball rolling. Whatever had happened to Helen Bellamy, she had to do more than stand by and wonder. She knew Palmer would feel the same.

Traffic soon reduced her progress to a crawl, and she reached down and hit the speed-dial key for Palmer's mobile. A part of her was hoping he wouldn't answer until she had some information about Helen's last job from the editor she was going to see. Anything she could come up with might help, she tried to tell herself, no matter how vague. Anything that would give them some direction – some hint as to what had happened in Helen's final hours.

She was almost disappointed when Palmer picked up on the second ring. She felt even worse when he drawled in a cheerful, mock-American accent down the line.

"Frank Palmer. A man for all seasons. I have the talent if you have the money. How may I help you?"

5

"You're late." Alex Koutsatos, the proprietor of MailBox Services, a mail forwarding business, waited impatiently on the doorstep of his shop as a delivery driver heaved a large cardboard box out of his van and dumped it on the pavement. The van usually arrived at six, before most of the surrounding businesses were open and Koutsatos still had the street more or less to himself. Now it was nearly nine and he was already anxious. Too many around here were interested in other people's business. Deliveries often attracted attention, and attention was something he and his customers preferred to avoid.

"Mains burst in Aldgate," the driver muttered shortly, and held out an electronic pad and stylus for a signature.

Koutsatos scribbled as directed and waved the driver away. He would have to leave the splitting up of the parcel until this evening now, when it was quiet. Maybe even tomorrow. This was a bigger consignment than usual, and couldn't be rushed.

Of mixed Armenian and Ukrainian parentage, Koutsatos had done many things in his life, most of them confined to the darker recesses of his memory. Born in a charity hospital in the northern Black Sea port of Odessa, his life had been at an all-time low and his prospects zero, when he had been shown how to gain entry to the UK. The papers, he had been assured, would pass the closest inspection – for a while. As he had discovered later, this was because the original owner, a predatory homosexual on holiday from Glasgow, was now buried in an unmarked grave in Tangiers.

In return for the freedom, independence and a home in London, Koutsatos had agreed to assume a Greek name and to set up a mail forwarding shop in the capital. There was one major condition involved: he would be called on from time to time to assist in the movement of papers, parcels and, just occasionally, people.

Koutsatos dragged the box inside the shop. It was heavy and he was soon out of breath. Fortunately there were no customers around. He had just enough time to check the contents and make sure the labels were included. He worked in silence, using a lethal-looking fisherman's knife to slice through the heavy-duty tape and bindings. He found the packing list and made up five of the largest bundles, putting them to one side. These would be collected by a motorcycle courier for onward delivery to Heathrow. He never studied the contents of the packages, and had never queried – out loud, at least – why they were so important. But once, a careless slash of his knife had ripped into one of them, and he had disposed of the damaged item carefully in the yard behind the shop, in a small brazier.

Somehow the idea that a few magazines could be so important had never ceased to amaze him.

Ray Szulu stood outside the Arrivals exit at Heathrow's Terminal Four, holding a cardboard sign. He was engaged in a silent battle of wits with a security guard in a suit and a couple of armed policemen. He'd been hanging about for nearly an hour now, waiting on a delayed flight, and was getting annoyed. Being stared at by a couple of uniforms with guns wasn't so much of a problem – he'd been there before many times – but the pushy suit's attitude was getting him down.

"You've got a double pick-up," his control had told him over the phone two hours earlier. "Outside Terminal Four, not inside, right? Don't be late." The man's Nigerian accent had rumbled over the airwaves like crushed concrete falling down a wooden chute, making it hard for Szulu to pick out every word. God knows, he thought sourly, what anyone else made of it. He'd just about caught the description and names of the two passengers, and the central London hotel they had to be taken to, before the call had ended. There was also no explanation as to why he had to wait outside, but he wasn't about to waste time arguing. He suspected they had probably travelled here by car from somewhere else. If so, it was their business.

Szulu worked mostly as a part-time driver for a couple of west London cab firms. He drove limousines when he could get the work, mini-cabs when nothing else offered. And in between he tried to stay out of trouble.

Right now, though, he was being stared at as if he was about to do something illegal. He knew the cops were only doing their job and protecting the masses, but why were they giving him the snake eyes? He wasn't carrying anything suspicious, and he was dressed in a smart suit with a peaked cap, even if the dreadlocks hanging round his collar didn't quite fit the image of a regular driver.

He sighed and took another turn along the pavement, skirting a bunch of inbound tourists waiting for their lift, and a straggly line of luggage trolleys abandoned by previous arrivals.

He passed the security guard, who was trying to look tough and failing, and caught sight of his own reflection in the glass doors behind him.

Szulu was tall, slim and walked with an athletic spring in his step and a roll to his shoulders. It was a gait he'd developed twenty years ago in his early teens, when strutting your stuff was more than just for show: it was survival. Back then he'd been tall for his age but skinny, and therefore still liable to be a target for the wrong sort of attention. So he'd done what all his contemporaries had done, and taken to looking tough. Most of the time it worked, helped by having big, useful-looking hands and a hollow stare. Since then, he'd put on a few pounds and learned a few moves to back up the image.

He shook his head, setting the dreadlocks swinging. The beads clicked quietly, but he didn't notice them any more. What he did notice, though, was the nagging ache in his left arm. It had healed over long ago, but every now and then, warm or cold, it seemed determined to serve him up with an irritating reminder.

He wondered what the security drone and the two armed cops would say if they knew he carried the scar from a genuine bullet wound. The thought made him smile. They might have their suspicions of him because of the way he looked, but that proved they didn't know anything about him.

When he turned he was relieved to see a couple of men standing outside the doors, looking around. Slim briefcases, suits, no coats. He held up his cardboard sign and received a nod in acknowledgement.

Thank Christ, he thought, and smirked at the two cops on his way to the car. "Hang loose, guys," he told them cheerfully. "You doin' a good job."

6

Frank Palmer switched off his phone and stared blankly through the windscreen of his Saab into the thin morning light. He was parked in a south London trading estate, adjacent to a chain-link security fence bordering a series of warehouses and storage facilities.

Until the call from Riley two minutes ago, his attention had been on a distribution depot a hundred yards away, where three shift workers were unloading an Italian haulage truck prior to filling up a fleet of delivery vans. At least one of the men was conspiring on a regular basis to load more than the job sheets called for, and with the co-operation of one of the drivers, was steadily plundering the company of a fortune in electronic goods. Palmer had been hired to find out who was doing the plundering and how.

He'd just returned to England after following the haulage truck all the way from a wholesale warehouse in Italy. The trip had been free of incident: no unusual contacts, no unscheduled stops in lay-bys, and no night-time handovers to other drivers. But at least he now knew where the problem lay.

He glanced up at the mirror and wondered if the face staring back at him really looked that cold or whether it was simply the effects of days and nights of surveillance and a lack of sleep. He ran a hand through his scalp, barely disturbing his scrub of fair hair, and felt the nerves tremor all the way down his neck. Just before his phone rang, he'd been fantasising about coffee, breakfast and his bed – in that order.

Now all that was forgotten.

Instead he had a cold feeling lodged deep in his chest, as if shards of iced water had been pumped into him under pressure.

His brain felt oddly scrambled, and he was having difficulty concentrating on the fact that someone once close to him was dead. And not simply through natural causes.

Murdered.

He watched the men in the loading bay for a few more moments. Mentally, at least, he'd already tuned them off his radar. They would keep. Too greedy to stop their little operation now it was working so well, they would continue for as long as they were allowed to get away with it. If necessary, he already had someone in mind who could wrap this up for him.

He turned the ignition key and pulled quietly away from the kerb. He followed the road through twin lines of commercial units with their shuttered warehouses and darkened office fronts out of the estate to the main road, allowing the speed to build smoothly. Speed: now, that was something else. Speed could help you survive, get you out of a tight spot. Speed could provide a sort of solace, when other things couldn't.

The speedometer surged upwards, charging past fifty with no more effort than the desire to go there. The tyres hissed on the wet road surface, smacking through puddles and fissures in the worn tarmac, and the engine noise diminished to a steady hum, as if it were being gradually drained away and left behind by the increased speed. Street lights became a washed-out blur and other vehicles mere furniture, there momentarily, then lost in the slipstream.

Palmer steered smoothly round a battered mini emerging from a side street, catching a momentary glimpse of a pale, shocked face from the corner of his eye. A truck was slow in accelerating from changing lights; he stabbed the brakes, skimming past a traffic island and a barely-visible cyclist wobbling along in the opposite direction.

He breathed out, his heart drumming, and allowed his speed to drop. His eyes went to the mirror. Not clever, he told himself, his hands tight on the steering wheel. Not cool.

He turned north and found himself thinking about Helen, and what she would have thought of his reaction. He hadn't got to know her that well, in spite of the fact that their relationship had, for a while, been intense in more than a merely physical way. They had discovered in each other a shared preference for risk-taking; Helen eschewed the safety of a salaried job with a national daily and all the perks on offer, in favour of freelance work. Flying solo. Never knowing where the next job was coming from, and no guarantees other than a certainty of her own ability. Even if the story she was going after might take her out over a gaping chasm with no safety net.

He'd once asked her about it, knowing the offers had been there. She had laughed and said nothing, and he'd instinctively known the answer: the lure of danger and the unknown had been too much of a pull. Like another reporter he knew. Like himself. Kindred spirits.

In the end, however, it had not been enough to sustain what lay between them. They spent too much time apart on their various assignments, and it had been Helen who gradually began to pull away. She had still been passionate, still the same person, yet with an increasing reserve as time went by, as though she were gently easing herself out from anything too committed.

Finally, she had told Frank that she wanted to remain friends. It had been like a knife piercing his soul, and probably the moment he had realised just how much she had meant to him.

He surged between speed cameras, opening up the car in brief bursts, wary of cruising patrol cars. All the while a map rolled through his mind in case he needed to cut off and lose himself amid huddled rows of houses or the jigsaw mish-mash of small suburban trading estates.

He reached Uxbridge and parked outside his office. It was on the first floor above a row of small businesses. A dry-cleaners stood on one side, and a large, glass-fronted shop on the other. The latter was currently a photocopier display room, but had already changed use three times in as many months. Palmer lived in hope of it becoming something useful, such as a coffee shop with comfortable chairs and crisply-ironed newspapers for patrons. It would make the times between jobs so much easier to bear.

A plain wooden door with a scarred front led to a moribund pot plant and a narrow flight of stairs. A scattering of mail lay on the bottom step, and he scooped it up. At the top of the stairs stood a glass-panelled door; behind it a single office with a desk, chairs and filing cabinet, and a kettle in lieu of a coffee shop. A computer fan purred beneath the desk, and the air was stodgy with the smell of warm plastic. He had gone out several days ago and left it on by mistake. Riley would have a fit. She might be another risk-taker, but he was certain she was developing a thing about carbon footprints.

The room's appearance was what Palmer liked to think of as lived-in and comfortable, like the jackets he wore. His clothes provided anonymity, a necessity for the kind of work he did. But they also reflected the deliberate distancing of his years spent in uniform – an existence according to Queen's Rules and Regulations. What he had now, he freely acknowledged, was another kind of uniform, but at least it was his by choice. And that choice spilled over into his workplace, where comfort was key and dust was allowed to settle and accumulate over long periods until he felt concerned enough to move it around a little.

He switched on the kettle and made coffee. A large spoonful and three sugars. The milk had solidified so he did without. He slopped some cold water into a pot plant that showed signs of becoming a twig. It had been a present from Riley, who seemed eager to prove that even Palmer could make things grow, given time and regular care.

Another one of her presents was a Rolodex file sitting on one corner of his desk. She had insisted that every PI worth his salt had to have a Rolodex. He hadn't felt inclined to argue – mainly because he'd been quietly pleased at the idea. While he waited for the kettle to boil he fanned the cards, enjoying the clatter as the cylinder spun, the gentle, dry sound echoing almost comfortingly in the room.

He flicked through the mail. Most of it was junk, and he dropped it in the bin. There were two obvious bills and one large, official-looking brown A4 envelope with spidery writing across the front and an older address scratched out in the same ink. Whatever it was could wait. The red message light on his answering machine blinked accusingly, but when the first one turned out to be a call-centre, he switched it off. They could wait too. He was too tired, too strung out to deal with trivia.

The coffee was bitter in spite of the sugar, but Palmer barely noticed. He stared out of the window across the rooftops and breathed deeply until his mind began to settle, to wash off the night-time torpor.

Down in the street traffic was building, lifting the day into a semblance of activity. With it, Palmer was beginning to acknowledge that what had happened in the past few hours had affected him more than anything in a long time. It involved someone he had known and, albeit briefly, cared deeply about.

And now he had arrived at a simple decision.

He was going to do something about it.

7

The power base for Copnor Business Publications was a small, first-floor office in Covent Garden, sandwiched between an outdoor activities shop and a theatrical agency. A plate on the wall in the foyer listed a variety of specialist business and trade periodicals. Riley had never heard of most of them. But the list was headed in bold print by a couple of business journals she knew by reputation, and which she suspected kept all the others afloat. The name of the man she had come to see was at the bottom in small type: **David Johnson – Editor**.

She debated turning round and going to Palmer's office in Uxbridge. It was the natural place for him to go, and she knew he'd be there – if not now, soon. It was where he rested, recuperated and sometimes simply allowed time to drift by when he had nothing more pressing to do.

She shook off the thought. Palmer was a big boy. He needed the space, just as she would in similar circumstances. She had told him everything she knew; now it was best to leave him alone to absorb the news and come to terms with it in his own way.

She walked up the stairs and through an open door. A young woman with a shock of red hair and green-framed glasses was just taking off her coat, head craned to one side to study a pile of printed sheets spilling out of a fax machine. She managed to hang up her coat and scoop up the fax pages at the same time, adroitly switching on her PC and simultaneously dropping a wad of mail on her desk from under one arm. A white plastic prism with the name *Emerald* in green print sat on the front of the desk, facing the door.

She glanced up as Riley entered, and pointed a lime-coloured fingernail towards a doorway to an adjacent room. "Miss Gavin?

David said you were coming. He's in there. Tea or coffee?" Her tone and smile were relaxed and unfazed, and Riley had the impression that if this young woman's day got harder she would probably look no different.

"I'd love a coffee," she said gratefully. Donald's idea of coffee was weak and warm, and she needed a stiff belt of caffeine to get her brain in gear. "Sweet and strong, please." Her head was already tight with tension, and she'd likely have the mother and father of all headaches by mid-morning. But getting through the next few hours wasn't going to be accomplished on wishful thinking and a couple of cold smoothies.

"No probs," said Emerald lightly.

Riley stepped through the open doorway into David Johnson's office. The carpet was worn to threads and stained, but the computers and monitors in the office were state-of-the-art and humming with activity.

Elsewhere the place was something of a glory hole: shelves weighed down by papers, box files and reference books, and the untidy disorder of a serial slob oblivious to the apparent chaos around him. Riley was willing to bet the man could lay a finger on whatever he needed at the drop of a hat.

Johnson was a thin, balding man with a harried air and frameless spectacles cantered to one side as if they'd been put on in a hurry and never adjusted. His tie looked new but was already showing signs of strain, and his dark shirt had the rumpled bachelor's look of just-in-time ironing.

"I'm not sure what I can tell you," he said distractedly without introduction. He waved Riley to a chair by his desk. "Donald told me what you'd seen... a horrible business – I can't believe it." He shook his head from side to side, as if the movement might dislodge the distasteful intrusion of death and danger placed there by the news of Helen Bellamy's murder.

Riley wasn't sure what to say. The only deaths to enter this man's world on a regular basis were probably those of companies dying through mismanagement, or senior executives expiring over one corporate lunch too many.

"We wondered…" she began, then remembered Pell would be annoyed if she talked about Helen's death before the police released the details. "We weren't supposed to tell anyone about this. Can you keep it under your hat for now?"

He nodded warily. "Of course."

"What had Helen been working on recently?"

Johnson looked startled, his eyes jumping behind his spectacles. "What – you think someone she interviewed might have – ?" He stopped as if he found the idea too hideous to contemplate. "Christ, I don't know. I mean, she did a couple of assignments for me, but they were all above-board. That was a few weeks back."

"Were they companies or individuals?"

"Umm… a couple of companies, actually." He paused as Emerald entered with two mugs of coffee and retreated again after dropping a handful of opened and sorted post on his desk, some with yellow Urgent stickers attached. "One was the London branch of a US financial services company under investigation by the Securities Exchange Commission in New York – but that was fairly unexciting stuff. There were no threats or anything because the US directors coughed up to minor fraud in exchange for a deal. Their case probably wasn't helped much by Helen's digging, but it was hardly the sort of thing that would have led to murder. They weren't exactly Mafia figures."

"And the other one?"

Johnson closed his eyes in concentration and scratched his head, dislodging a flake or two of dried scalp. "Similar type of thing, if I recall. That one was across the channel – Brussels. Something to do with a scam on EU funding. Helen did her usual thing, digging into the background until she found someone willing to talk." He gave a wry smile. "There's always someone willing to talk."

"Sounds like she was good at her job."

Johnson nodded, his face relaxing. "Yes, she was. I wish I'd been able to push more stuff her way, but we don't often get to cover hard news. Our core business usually circulates around general commercial stuff: corporate developments, mergers and acquisitions, that sort of thing. It's all pretty low on excitement, really. But Helen, she was like a terrier, in spite of her looks." He looked mildly abashed. "Sorry – don't mean to be sexist or anything, but you know what she looked like. She was successful because the people she went after never saw her coming."

Riley nodded. She knew what he meant: Helen Bellamy, a wolf in elegant sheep's clothing. "So she did all right, then?"

"I suppose. She certainly seemed to be in regular work. She probably had the same problems everyone else does – taking on stories that didn't pay in proportion to the time and effort put in. But she seemed to manage."

"And no problems related to any of her past assignments, as far as you know?"

"Spit-backs from previous jobs?" Johnson shook his head. "None that she mentioned. As for what we gave her, like I said, it wasn't exactly hardcore embezzlement or multinational fraud, where people disappear under a motorway piling." He paused and looked warily at Riley.

"What?"

"Well, to be honest, I got the impression the last time we spoke that she was waiting to land something a bit more heavyweight. She was a bit distracted, which wasn't like her. I got the feeling she was frustrated with the run-of-the-mill and wanted something more. It was odd, really, because her work was absolutely thorough and on the nail. Totally professional. In fact, she got a lot of praise for it. I reckon she was in line for some major assignments eventually, if only…" He shrugged and looked saddened. "Sorry."

"When did you last speak to her?"

"A couple of weeks back. I needed to check some detail about a story she'd done."

"You don't know what this potential job was, though?"

"No. She never said. I think it was still hanging at the time. It was more a feeling I had, that's all."

There was something in Johnson's face; something he wasn't saying.

"What was your impression?"

Eventually, he sighed. "She once said she wanted to do the kind of work that you do."

Riley felt a stab of surprise. "Me? She said that?"

Johnson nodded and gave a weak smile, as if he'd betrayed a confidence. "She said she'd met you and admired your work. I think she felt she could have been doing better for herself."

"She once asked me if I knew anything about oligarchs." The voice floated through from the outer office, inserting itself between them. Riley and Johnson turned to stare at Emerald, who was busy filing a nail, her head bent in concentration.

"Oligarchs?" Riley glanced at Johnson, wondering if the girl was in the habit of joining in on conversations with visitors. He shrugged, evidently used to it.

"Yeah. Rich Russians. Billionaires, trillionaires, whatever they are. Like the bloke who bought Chelsea. She asked if we'd ever covered any of them in the mags. I said no."

"Are you sure?" Riley couldn't think why, but she felt it might be important. It was quite a shift, from mundane business matters to Russians with bottomless bank accounts.

Johnson shifted in his chair. "Em's right. It's not something we've ever done." He frowned, focussing on the possibilities. "I'm not sure why, exactly – they certainly have their fingers in enough pies. And with what's brewing up under Putin at the moment, and his antagonism towards the west, maybe a short series – " He realised what he was saying and looked guilty. "Sorry. Bad timing."

Riley let the thought go. She didn't need the conversation to drift off into the realms of publishing fantasy. "Do you know if Helen had any family?"

Johnson shook his head. "No. Well, I don't know – she didn't talk about them if she did. She came in when she had to, did what was needed and that was it. Like I said, very professional."

"What about that last cheque?" It was Emerald again.

"What about it?" Johnson asked.

"She rang and asked for it to go to a different address. Somewhere down in Hampshire – outside Basingstoke. I've got a note here somewhere." She dropped the emery board and attacked her keyboard with a blur of fingers.

Johnson looked at Riley and flushed. "Sorry... I didn't know anything about this."

"Here it is." There was a buzz of a printer and the girl came through with a sheet of paper. It was a simple payment slip for syndication fees, payable to Helen Bellamy. The address was *Mrs C. Demelzer, Long Cottage, Cotton Hill, Nr Basingstoke, Hants.*

"She rang one day last week," Emerald continued. "Said to hold any outstanding payments and if she didn't come in to collect them by Friday, to make a cheque out to the woman at this address. I sent it off yesterday. You approved it." She stared at Johnson as if daring him to argue.

He blinked back. "Did I?"

Emerald smiled conspiratorially at Riley, eyes twinkling behind her green specs. "Well, not really, but you would have in the end. I mean, why should we worry where the money goes – it's her tax bill, isn't it? And she was always really sweet to me. She said I had real style." She gave David Johnson an arch look and turned away.

Riley bit her lip to stop herself smiling. She wanted to jump up and hug the girl. She held up the piece of paper. "Was this normal? To have payments made out to someone else?"

"Not really." Johnson seemed mildly perturbed by the news, and that someone outside the company was now privy to it. "But we have a whole list of freelance contributors, so one-off payments are fairly common. If she'd asked it as a favour, I suppose Em's right – I'd have said OK." He smiled weakly. "Maybe she owed this person money."

"Maybe. Can I take this? It might be important."

"Help yourself." Johnson prodded at his glasses and stood up. His eyes had strayed distractedly to his PC monitor, and he seemed relieved that the conversation was over. "Anything to help. I mean, Em's right… Helen was a really sweet woman. Such a waste."

Outside on the pavement, Riley took a deep breath of air. Somewhere along the line a young woman with a background in business reporting and a growing reputation had expressed a desire to do something else: the kind of work on which Riley herself had built a career. But was that all she had done – simply longed for a change? A shift away from what might have become mundane and 'safe'? Or had she gone further than that, stepping out of her comfort zone into the world Riley knew, and in doing so, looked at something – or someone – just a little too closely for comfort?

8

Palmer parked his car a short walk away from Riley's flat off Holland Park Avenue and stepped out, glad of the opportunity to stretch his legs. He liked this part of west London; it was just on the edge of busy, but not too frantic to enjoy the ever-changing atmosphere and buzz of an inner-city suburb.

He dialled Riley's number as he walked. She picked up on the second ring and told him to come on up, the kettle was on.

He slid the phone back in his pocket and yawned. Everything was catching up on him; too many late nights and greasy pit stops, too little sleep, too long spent peering through a hazy windscreen. And now this.

He hadn't accomplished a lot since hearing the news about Helen. Sitting in his office, remote from the specifics of how she had died, had merely brought on a rising sense of frustration. Worst of all was the increasing realisation that, in spite of their closeness for a while, he hadn't really known Helen very well. The idea filled him with sadness and regret.

He wasn't looking forward to the next few minutes. Given a choice, he'd have preferred to shut himself off from everyone else and deal with the news of Helen's death in his own way. It was unreasonable and even disloyal, he knew that, because Riley was probably his closest friend and the one person he could turn to at a time of crisis. But years of operating in solitude had made him accustomed to not relying much on anyone else.

Riley was waiting for him on the first floor landing. She looked worried and drawn, and he guessed she hadn't slept well, either. He nodded matter-of-factly and followed her inside. When she hesitated before going into the kitchen, and appeared as if she was about to throw her arms around him, he held up a hand.

"I'm fine. Really," he said brusquely, and instantly regretted it. He knew she must be feeling like hell, for him if not for herself. He reached out for her. "Sorry. Didn't mean it. This is good. But don't tell anyone."

They hugged each other tight for a few seconds, then Riley patted him on the back and slipped into the kitchen, where she clattered around making coffee. He couldn't see her face but he could read the body language. He left her to it, relieved he hadn't stuck to the stiff upper lip. She might not have known Helen well, but she clearly wasn't unaffected by what had happened.

A large bruiser of a tabby cat entered from the bedroom and walked across to greet him. It rubbed against his legs just long enough to make contact, then turned away and sat down to clean itself. Palmer smiled. The cat was a feline self-set, having adopted Riley on a whim, but alternating between her and a granite-featured old Pole named Grobowski, downstairs. While Riley made do with calling the animal Cat and stocking standard feline food, Mr Grobowski shouted a lot in heavily-accented English, called it Lipinski, and fed it heavy portions of Polish cooking which he put together in his kitchen for compatriots at the local community centre.

When Riley brought the mugs into the living room Palmer eyed her steadily, waiting. He knew she'd have questions. Some of them would be disguised as throwaway comments, but she'd still be angling for answers. In his experience, women invariably had the edge when it came to interrogation techniques. It was something passed across at birth along with the DNA.

He didn't have long to wait for the first one.

"You never said why you and Helen broke up."

Palmer sighed. This wasn't something he felt good talking about. Not that he had any reason to feel guilty, but saying nothing wasn't an option. "Actually, we didn't so much break up as move on. When it was over, it was over." He took his mug and stared into it. "Ships that pass, I suppose."

"I know what you mean." Riley sat facing him.

He smiled gently. If there was anyone who understood the transient nature of relationships in their respective trades, it was her. He didn't know every aspect of her private life and didn't pry, but he knew she was still coming to grips with a lengthy split from former army officer John Mitcheson, who was somewhere in America. Palmer knew Mitcheson as a likeable, cool, yet detached individual who seemed hell-bent on ploughing his own furrow, even if that took him away from Riley. But he also knew it wasn't as simple as the divergence of paths: there were questions in Riley's mind over Mitcheson which even Palmer wasn't sure about. Some of those questions concerned just what his moral limits were when it came to doing his job, which was partly centred on private security work. It was the 'partly' which raised some of the most searching questions.

As if reading his mind, she said simply, "Life's a bitch, isn't it?"

He nodded and looked at his coffee. "Do you have anything stronger than this crap?"

"You ingrate. That's best Colombian – grade five. I've got some Kenyan, but it's only a three. I keep it for any girlies who come round." She stood up and went into the kitchen, returning immediately with a bottle of whisky and two glasses, already poured. "You had me worried, there. I thought you'd gone teetotal on me." She put down the bottle and handed him a glass, and took a deep pull of her own to lead the way, wincing as the liquor burned its way down her throat. "You'll have to talk to the police, Frank. A DI named Pell seems to be the lead man."

Palmer nodded and took a sip of his drink. "What's he like?"

"OK. Professional… but I got the impression he's a bit of a rebel on the quiet." She explained about being allowed at the crime scene, a favour for a favour between Pell and his colleague in forensics. "He wants to get results, but he's thorough."

"I'll call him." Palmer twisted his glass, then said, "Tell me about it."

He listened as she went through it, leaving nothing out. She began with the phone call from Pell, dragging her out of bed and into the night, with terse instructions to tell nobody. She described the scene with the SOCO team and the rain-soaked glare of lights, the position of the body, and the way Helen Bellamy's wrists had been tied, the bruising around her face. There was a dull flatness to her voice, the telling as unemotional as possible, and he knew she was finding this the most difficult of all.

He waited until she finished, making no comment. He had switched on the part of his brain that was analytical and calm; the part which his RMP training had instilled in him – the ability to remain detached and objective – seeing the subject of the investigation as no more than a set of facts, events and figures.

"What do they reckon?" he said finally. He meant how did the police think Helen had died.

"Pell didn't say. Or wouldn't. They only wanted me there to see if I could identify her." Riley flicked a hand, indicating her face. "At a guess, I'd say she was hit. Hard. There were marks, but it wasn't easy to tell what they were under the lights. They didn't allow me get close enough to judge."

Palmer's expression was grim. "If she was tied up, it was to keep her subdued. She must have got involved in something. You said there was a car?"

She described how the vehicle was buried deep in the undergrowth, adding to the images in his mind. "It looked like a Golf. Was that what she drove?"

"Yes. An old one." Palmer was puzzled. If the car was found by the first walker who came along, it wasn't exactly well hidden. Why flag up the location in that way? He sat back, unravelling the facts in his mind, slicing and dicing until he had some sense of order. Riley had her way; this was his. He didn't have all the information right now – not even a fraction of it – but it was his way of teasing out all the possible answers until he had something to work with.

The other question was why she'd had Riley's name and phone number in her car. Plans for a girlie exchange of information, perhaps? Or a work thing?

"There's nothing significant about her last assignments," Riley told him, "at least, as far as I could tell."

"You checked already?" Palmer lifted an eyebrow. "That was quick work."

"I mentioned it to Donald and he gave me a lead." She shrugged. "I thought it best to check it out." She explained briefly what she had learned at Copnor Business Publications. "It was standard work. They don't cover commercial frauds or anything like that, unless it has a wider market impact, so they're not exactly into anything murky or overtly criminal. But Helen did let drop that she was hoping to get into something more interesting."

"Like what?" Palmer was surprised. From what he remembered of Helen, she had enjoyed her work.

"The editor thought she was bored with the same old same old. I can relate to that. His assistant said she'd asked recently if they'd ever covered the Russian oligarchs as a topic."

"Rich Russians?" He chewed it over. They were as much in the news for buying football clubs and large chunks of the London property market as they were for their on-off relationships with Moscow. Maybe Helen had stumbled on a juicy story and was testing the water.

"She also rang last week and asked for any outstanding fees to go to a woman at an address in Hampshire."

Another surprise. Helen had centred her life on London, apparently eager to be where the action was. She'd never mentioned anyone outside the capital. "A family member?"

42

"I was hoping you'd know the answer to that."

"We didn't get to that level." He was aware that his voice was probably tinged with regret. "She never talked about herself much," he explained. "But then, neither did I." He held her gaze. If Riley had any thoughts about men's lack of curiosity about the women in their lives, she wasn't saying anything. "It seemed to suit us both. You've done good work. Thanks."

Riley stood up and dug out the sheet of paper Emerald had given her. "Here's the address. We could take a look tomorrow, if you like."

He scanned the details. Helen had definitely never mentioned a connection with Hampshire – certainly nobody close enough to have sent money to. "Why wait?" He glanced at his watch, suddenly taken by the idea of doing something positive. "Like now."

"I can't." Riley waved an apologetic hand. "I've got a meeting this afternoon to pitch for a job. I have to get my glad rags on and act civilised. You know how it is."

Palmer knew. Like Riley's assignments, most of his jobs came along by word of mouth or through Donald Brask. But every now and then, he had to do his own legwork to help things along. The brutal reality was, if freelances didn't pitch, they didn't eat.

"Do you mind if I do it?"

"Of course not. Just don't frighten her, that's all. She could be a frail old biddy with a weak ticker."

He nodded. It was also probable that the woman in Hampshire might not know about Helen's death. Springing the news on her could be disastrous. It was a lesson he'd learned first-hand in the RMP.

He tucked the paper in his breast pocket. He had a sudden thought. "When you were out there last night, did you notice signs of another car?"

"No. It was too dark. And Pell didn't say anything. Why?"

"Because it would have taken two people to get Helen there: one to drive her car, the other to help dump the body, then drive them away. A single man dumping the car and moving away on foot would have been noticed." He was trying to picture the scene as Riley had described it. The car had been left less than two hundred yards from the road. Other than forcing it into the undergrowth, there had been no elaborate attempt to hide anything. Why?

"Why leave her outside the car?" Riley wondered aloud.

Palmer shrugged. "Maybe they didn't care. Or they were interrupted while moving the body and didn't have time to conceal it. I think they took her there in a second, larger vehicle."

"Why larger?"

Palmer knew all about VW Golfs; he had spent enough time in Riley's to know them inside and out. "Because a Golf is hardly the best car to drive around with a body on the back seat. Too easy to see inside. They'd have used something bigger."

"So all we have to do is find the other vehicle." Riley looked sceptical. It would be like looking for a grain of sand – and where did they even begin?

"We'll find something." Palmer twisted the whisky glass in his fingers. Somehow it had emptied without him realising. He put it down on the coffee table and stood up.

"How?"

His face was suddenly dark and stony, as if the complexity of the problem had just hit home. "I don't know yet. But give me time and I will."

9

Long Cottage stood at the end of a neat terrace on the edge of Cotton Hill, a hamlet barely six miles from Basingstoke. Other than a tiny pub, a whitewashed village hall and a scattering of other houses set behind hedges and trees, there couldn't have been more than a dozen buildings in sight, as if progress had passed them by, leaving a remnant of a time long gone.

Palmer parked his Saab and climbed out. The air was cool after the inside of the car, and he eyed the darkening sky with suspicion. The journey down the M3 from London had been a stop-start series of road works, and it was a relief to be out in the open.

He eyed the cottage. It had a small, crumbling brick wall surrounding a neat front garden of herb borders and shrubs. An elderly woman in a baggy grey jumper was bent over a large terracotta urn, stabbing energetically with a hand fork at the contents as if giving the *coup de grace* to some unseen enemy.

Palmer strolled across the road and smiled genially when the woman looked up. "Mrs Demelzer?"

She straightened her back with a grunt and dropped the fork into the urn as if relieved to be done with it. She had silver hair swept back into a tidy bun, round cheeks and a pleasant face, and laughter lines around keen eyes. Palmer was never good with women's ages, but he guessed she was somewhere in her seventies.

"You don't know anything about slugs, do you?" the woman said chattily. "All my years gardening, and the buggers still keep coming. I've tried pellets and stuff, but none of them work."

"Have you tried copper?" Palmer said easily, recalling a fragment of a gardening programme, courtesy of a lengthy surveillance job in his car. "I've heard that works."

She gave him a pitying look. "Is that right? Well, someone had better tell the local slugs, because they haven't caught on yet." She brushed her hands together and used her wrist to push a stray hank of hair off her forehead. "So, what can I do for you, young man?"

"I'm a friend of Helen's. She talked about you, and I said I'd drop by if ever I was passing." He told her his name and wondered if the approach was as lame as it sounded. But short of telling her the shocking truth, which he had no right to do, he hadn't been able to come up with a better reason for being there.

The woman tilted her head to one side and smiled, eyes assessing and accepting him all in one look. "Helen? Oh, that's nice. What's she been up to, then?" She didn't wait for an answer, but turned towards the front door of the cottage. "You'd better come in," she said. "Do you fancy a cup of tea?"

"Helen's a sweet girl. Her mum was my best friend – ever since school days. She died ten years ago, but Helen always kept in touch, bless her."

They were seated in the warmth of the cottage's tiny front room, with a tray of tea and biscuits on a footstool between them. The room was like an antique shop, with ornaments of every kind packed on to every bit of shelving and flat surface, even overflowing on to the floor. It was clear that Mrs Demelzer had never thrown away a single souvenir she'd been given or collected, no matter how kitsch. Figurines, pots, plates and statuettes, most of them bearing a place name in gaudy script, all jostled each other in a mad fight for space. And Palmer had never seen so many crystal ashtrays in one place before. Maybe the old lady was a heavy smoker.

Mrs Demelzer stared into her cup as if reading something

meaningful in the depths and gave a vague half-smile. "I'm not sure why she bothers, to be honest. We're not related, and it's only because of my friendship with Margaret, her mother, that we ever met. But we sort of rub along, which is nice." Her smile broadened. "She keeps me in touch with the modern world, I suppose."

"Did you see her often?" Palmer could have bitten his tongue at his use of the past tense, but she hadn't appeared to notice.

"Not really. She comes down three or four times a year, just for a short visit. I keep a room ready for her, just in case. The last time was a fortnight ago. I think she needs some quiet time down here every now and then when life in London gets too much for her." She shrugged. "It's always lovely to see her, though, to hear about what she's doing. She's forever on the go, looking for the next story. But that's the thing with young people, isn't it? You have to keep on top of things, or they find someone else to take your place."

"They?"

"Well, your employers. It's all so cut-throat these days." She sighed regretfully. "Still, Helen seems to manage. Although…" She paused and gave him an uncertain look.

"Although?" Palmer waited.

"Well, when she was here before, about a month ago, she was really excited. She'd picked up an assignment to do a story – an exclusive, she said. Nobody else had got a sniff of it. I asked her what it was about, but she wouldn't say. It was all hush-hush, apparently, and she wasn't allowed to divulge anything. I thought it was silly – I mean, it's not as if I'd know anything about it, living down here. I don't exactly trot off down the pub every evening and gossip, do I?"

Palmer forced himself to be patient. Was this something important she was about to reveal, or had it been one of Helen's other normal jobs she was excited about? "But that sounds good, doesn't it? Exclusives are hard to come by." Even as he spoke, he began to feel a trickle of unease. Knowing the nature of Riley's work, he was aware that one of the big problems about so-called exclusives was that by their nature, they often entailed risk. Had Helen taken on too big a risk for the chance of a headline story?

"Well, if you say so, dear. But the next time I spoke to her, she sounded a bit down. She'd been away for a brief holiday, but it didn't seem to have done her much good. I asked what was the matter, but she just said it was pressure of work. It was so unlike her. The last time I'd seen her down like that was almost a year ago, I think it was, when she broke up with her boyfriend." She smiled at the memory. "I was hoping it would go the distance, that one. But Helen... well, she's not the sort to settle down. Not yet, anyway. A bit like her mother, I suppose: footloose and fancy free."

Palmer shifted uneasily, disturbed by a flush of sadness. It was a mere flicker, but Mrs Demelzer caught it and eyed him in surprise, as if a switch had been thrown.

"It was you, wasn't it?" she exclaimed, then nodded without waiting for his reply. Reassured, she rattled on. "God, I must be having a senior moment. Frank. Of course. She lost her old briefcase... it got damaged. That's right – and the new one you bought her had a shoulder strap and nice gold buckles. It was very smart." She squeezed her shoulders upwards in a gesture of enjoyment, eyes shining. "She was so pleased with that briefcase, you've no idea. She uses it all the time, cramming it with all sorts of stuff. Well, she loves being busy, doesn't she – although I've no idea what she's doing at the moment."

Palmer waited, desperate to push the questions and get away from here. This suddenly didn't look as if it would lead anywhere useful. Whatever Helen did when she was down here was unconnected with her work. And if she had sent money to her friend, so what?

Then the old lady gave him a lead in. "Still, I suppose you'd know more about that than me, wouldn't you?"

Palmer thought his hold on the cup would snap the handle. "Why do you say that?" he asked casually.

"You mean you haven't seen your post?"

Palmer shook his head. "I've been abroad."

"Oh. Well, that explains it. She rang me a few days ago. Said I'd be getting some money, and not to bank it but spend it on something nice. That was kind of her, wasn't it?" She frowned. "I didn't want to take it, to be honest, but Helen can be very obstinate when she wants to – just like her mother used to be. I'll probably use it to decorate her room, which will be honours even, don't you think?"

Palmer nodded. "You weren't a diplomat by profession, were you?"

She laughed outright. "Good gracious, no. I'm far too blunt. Anyway, the cheque came – from a place in London. She also asked me to bundle up any bits of paper she'd left in her room from her last visit. Doodles, they looked like to me – the sort people do when they're on the phone a lot, like Helen always is, even when she comes down here. So I did what she asked: I went through her room and put everything in an envelope. Even the scraps in her wastebasket. Well, they were no good to the dustman and I didn't want to throw out anything important by mistake."

Palmer went still. "Did she say why she wanted them?"

"Not really. I assumed she'd mislaid a jotting or something, and needed to find it. She was always making notes of one thing or another."

"What did you do with them?"

The old lady gave him a wary look, as if he was simple. "Well, I did what Helen asked, of course. I put them in an envelope and sent them to you."

"Me?" Palmer was stunned.

"Yes. A big brown one. I used an old one from the council... some mailing they did about recycling. You should have received it by now." She picked up the teapot. "Would you like more tea?"

By the time Palmer drove away from the cottage, his mind was in a spin. He felt guilty for not having told Mrs Demelzer about Helen's death. But to have done so would have set off a train of action and reaction he would not have been able to explain. It was best to leave it to the police family liaison people. They were trained for it.

He thought about the briefcase, which the old lady said Helen had been so pleased with. Helen was the complete journalist and writer, virtually living by what she could carry: notepad, digital recorder, mobile phone – actually, ditch that, he remembered; she had a new Blackberry which did all of those things. She'd shown it to him one evening, when they'd been out for dinner. Later, as they were saying goodnight – Palmer had a late-night surveillance job – Helen had placed her briefcase on the ground by his car. He'd forgotten about it and driven off, mashing one corner with a rear tyre. Fortunately, nothing else had been damaged, and buying her a replacement was the least he could do. He knew she liked black, but all he could find of a similar make was burgundy. It was lightweight leather with gold fittings, and she'd been thrilled with it. He could still recall her comment afterwards.

"Frank," she'd teased him with a gentle hint of sarcasm. "Where on God's earth did a man like you find a leather brief-case light enough not to pull a woman's arm out of its socket?" She had followed it with a comment about his idea of luggage being an army issue kitbag made of canvas with a rope handle.

"Actually," he'd replied, feigning wounded pride, "I got it in a little place off Bond Street. I'm not a complete Philistine."

By the time he was back on the M3 heading towards London, Palmer was wrestling with two major questions. The answer to one could be in the large brown envelope sitting among the junk mail on his desk. The envelope Helen had asked Mrs Demelzer to send him, even though it was months since they'd seen each other. Exactly why she'd done that was a mystery.

The other question was less likely to be answered so quickly. It concerned Helen's burgundy briefcase with the gold fittings; the portable office that held every detail of her day-to-day work. If it had been in the car with her, the police would have known everything about her within minutes. There would have been no need to call Riley out in the hopes of an early identification.

So if it wasn't in the car, where was it?

10

"Miss Gavin? This way, please." The speaker was a slim, balding man with the colourless air of an academic. He was of medium height and build, and wore a plain grey suit with a maroon tie and black shoes. He was holding a clipboard and had appeared from nowhere within seconds when Riley approached the frosted-glass reception desk of the modern hotel in Bloomsbury. It was a few minutes before two o'clock.

"You will be meeting with our Mr Richard Varley," the man informed her. Varley was the name on the email Riley had received. Without introducing himself or giving Riley an opportunity to ask questions, the man turned and set off down a corridor towards the rear of the hotel.

He stopped in the entrance to an open lounge area and indicated a figure sitting in one corner. There was nobody else in the room. "Please." He smiled briefly, then turned and walked away.

Riley crossed the room and watched as the man in front of her rose to his feet. He was well over six feet tall, with impressively broad shoulders and large hands, and she wondered if he was a former sports professional turned businessman. He was striking rather than good looking, with high cheekbones and tanned skin. He was dressed in a beautifully-cut suit, with a colourful silk tie and white shirt. The clothes hung well from his large frame, and Riley guessed he was in his early forties.

"Miss Gavin. How nice of you to come. Richard Varley." He spoke with an American accent. He stepped forward to meet her, his hand engulfing hers completely. His touch was warm and dry, like his smile, and he had very white teeth and dark, friendly eyes. She noticed with approval a faint lemony tang in the air around him. "Would you like some tea?" he asked, and gestured to a tray on the table behind him.

"Yes, please."

Even as he poured, Varley studied Riley openly. He seemed unabashed at her noticing. When he'd finished pouring, he gestured at the milk and she nodded assent. He slid the cup towards her and sat back to continue his study.

Riley began to bristle under this scrutiny. "Do I pass muster?" she said. With the events of the past twenty-four hours, the last thing she needed was some crummy business type on the trawl for an easy pick-up.

He looked surprised and shook himself. "My apologies – I'm so sorry for staring, Miss Gavin. It's just that I get to meet with so many people in the course of my work – and most of them are guys." He shrugged and gave a sheepish grin. "I'm just enjoying the change, that's all. Please don't be offended."

Riley picked up her cup and sipped the tea, uncertain if he was toying with her or not. She'd met plenty of men who had made similar if not more blatant approaches, most of them with less charm and a less ready display of embarrassment. She chose to give Varley a chance before deciding that a predatory eye was sufficient reason to throw away the assignment. "What did you want to talk about?" she asked.

He reached into a briefcase by his side and produced a magazine. It was glossy, colourful and high quality, and carried the title *East European Trade* in bold type across the top. He passed it across to her.

"The people I represent are committed to providing high-quality, fully-verifiable ethical material for this journal. It's monthly, on subscription only, and aimed at decision-makers in government, finance and international business. It has a high cover price, but that's reflected by the level of information they specialise in." He smiled openly. "Actually, it's pretty boring stuff

– about east-west trade, mostly – but they have a target audience that deals in billions – trillions, even – so the quality and nature of what goes between the covers is very, very influenced by the readership." He shrugged. "And that works the other way round, of course."

"Sounds heavy," Riley commented. She flicked to the inside cover page and read through the information about the publishers. Ercovoy News Press was new to her, but this wasn't her usual area of operations. They listed editorial offices in London, Madrid and Brussels – all P O boxes, she noticed – and a production office at Atcheveli 3-24, Sokhumi, Republic of Georgia. "Is this where you come from?" She was surprised; he sounded so all-American.

"Hell, no." He chuckled good-naturedly. "I'm an army brat, originally from the deep south. My dad was a career officer, so I guess you could say I'm from all over. I've always loved Europe, though, so I'm pleased to be based here now. I'm the editor-at-large. The production office is purely a base for collating the material."

"I see."

"We like to think," Varley continued, steering her back on-track, "that what we publish has high-impact potential. Our coverage is often of subject material most people won't have heard about on the usual wires."

Riley nodded, ignoring Varley's excited sales patter. He talked like an MBA marketing clone, although he seemed genuinely less over-the-top zealous than some. She scanned the pages. There was an article on mineral exploration in Kazakhstan; the results of a study into reducing pollution in the Caspian and Black Seas; a profile piece about a member of the Turkish parliament who was also one of the country's biggest shipping magnates; a debate on the threat of aggressive cross-border trade from the bullish emerging Chinese markets, and the need for manufacturing investment and infrastructure across the states of the former Soviet Union. Boring and worthy, she thought. But presumably someone somewhere read it, and if Varley was right, some would set their political or commercial agenda accordingly.

"Is this for European content only?"

"Not at all. The content is slanted towards Eastern Europe purely because that's where the bulk of international investment is heading right now. But it's read by government departments everywhere, so we try to reflect that, too. By everywhere, I mean the US, Europe, China, India, the Middle East – and Westminster, of course." He raised open palms. "Like I said, this gets seen by some very key people. And the content is also *about* some very key people."

"Odd, then, that I've never heard of it. Or of Ercovoy News Press."

He smiled easily. "Well, because it's aimed at such a specialised market, it doesn't get to appear on the newsstands... but we're hardly alone in that respect."

Riley nodded. She had worked for a few titles which were not available on the street and which most people had never come across. She put the magazine down. Reading it now would be like wading through treacle. "And you want me to contribute?"

"That's right. Over the coming months, we're featuring a series of articles on movers and shakers in the east-west socio-industrial area. People who matter today, but also those who will matter tomorrow. In five, maybe ten years, a lot of the big hitters right now will be gone. Their places will be taken by men and women only just starting out. It's a very fast-moving field, and our readership needs to know who these people are and where they're headed. Some will be well-known, others are lower-profile, maybe because they're still building their power base and finding their place in the market. Either way, we aim to highlight those people and shine a little spotlight on them."

"Good or bad?" Riley suggested.

He chuckled good-naturedly. "Well, I guess some of these guys don't get to the top by being altar boys, do they? But we're not here to dish the dirt." He waved a hand. "Not unless it needs dishing, anyhow."

"Really? And who decides that?"

He lifted an eyebrow, his expression open. "Actually, that's a good question. I guess we all do. We've profiled some questionable people before, no doubt about that. But exposing them has probably only been a matter of time. Sooner or later everyone comes under the spotlight, right?"

"OK. But why me? This isn't the kind of material I normally handle. There are plenty of people with much more expertise in this area."

"True." Varley scratched his cheek with a large thumb. It made a rasping sound in the quiet room. "But you come highly recommended."

Riley waited, but he didn't enlarge on it further.

"May I ask by whom?"

"Actually, I don't recall. Does it matter? Your name came up. You have a solid reputation, your background checks out, so we decided to add your name to the pool of contributors – which is pretty impressive, I might add. You'd know a lot of the names… although confidentiality agreements mean I can't tell you who they are until they complete an assignment and it goes public. We work with good people, believe me." He reached into an inner pocket and produced an envelope. "And to lay out our intentions, so to speak, we make a point of offering a signing-on fee." He handed Riley the envelope, which she opened. "That's an indication of how serious we are."

The envelope contained a cheque in four figures made out in her name.

11

Riley didn't know what to say. She wasn't aware of any publishers who would come calling with cheques this size up-front – at least, not in the field she normally covered. Nor would their approaches be quite so open-ended. On the other hand, she knew a little about most other publishers, if not by reputation, then by product. And of this one she knew nothing.

"Do you have a particular assignment in mind?" She slid the cheque back inside the envelope, waiting for the inevitable catch.

He smiled. "As a matter of fact, we do." He reached into the briefcase again and produced an opaque plastic folder an inch thick, bound by tape. He passed it across to her. It was heavy.

"The name of the person we'd like you to profile is in there," he told her, "along with a great deal of background information culled from various reliable sources." He waved a hand. "Of course, you'll want to check the details yourself, although I can tell you, it's absolutely accurate. There's a detailed brief inside the folder and the deadline is three weeks from today." He lifted his shoulders in apology. "I'm sorry to hit you with such a tight one from the get-go, but I'm sure you'll do a good job. We got let down on another piece and decided to bring this one forward." He shrugged. "It happens. But I guess you'd know that."

"Of course. When do you need my decision?"

A flicker of a shadow crossed his face, then was gone almost immediately. "Well, I was hoping you'd be able to give me that pretty much right away, Miss Gavin. May I call you Riley?" He raised a hand without waiting for an answer. "But, hey – maybe I'm rushing you a bit. And you've probably got things to finish off. Could you get back to me inside a day or so?" He dipped his fingers into a pocket and pulled out a business card. "Maybe you could ring me on that number? I'm in London for about a week, then I have to travel on business."

Riley looked at the card. It held his name and a telephone number. No business address. She waved the envelope containing the cheque. "And if I decide not to take your offer?"

He shrugged affably. "That's your decision – and your cheque to keep." He lifted his eyebrows and looked suddenly boyish. "Uh... in the meantime, maybe we could do dinner."

Riley tried to gauge whether he was serious or simply trying it on. He was undoubtedly an interesting man, and seemed to have an abundant supply of self-confidence. But she'd only just met him. Was dinner all he was after, or did he want to extend their putative business relationship beyond trading on the written word?

Before she could reply, his eyes slid past her shoulder and his face became serious. Riley turned her head. The balding man who had met her at reception was standing in the entrance to the lounge. He gave them both a brief smile, then turned and walked away without a word.

"Riley," said Richard Varley, getting to his feet and picking up his briefcase. "I'm afraid I have to be going. My associate needs me to deal with something." He thrust out his hand and held hers for a long moment, towering over her. Then he let it go and stepped past her.

Ten minutes later, Riley was in the back corner of a coffee shop, holding a large latte and scanning the contents of the heavy folder Varley had given her.

Her initial reaction back at the hotel, given Varley's wandering eyes and the fact that she'd never heard of the magazine, had been to ignore the lure of the unusual signing-on fee and give the job a miss. Now she saw who the profile target was, she was beginning to wonder if she shouldn't go straight back and dump the papers – and the cheque – in Varley's lap.

She had no first-hand reason to think that billionaire retail giant, industrialist and party benefactor Muammar 'Kim' Al-Bashir, was anything other than above-board. There were whispers of heavy-handed reactions whenever journalists delved too deeply into the Egyptian-born businessman's background, aided by a private army of no-nonsense security guards to discourage further probing. Added to that were friends in very high places and a ruthless thirst for revenge on those who dared cross him.

But a quick glance at this file showed that it contained material which wasn't exclusively business gossip – although there was plenty of that. Included were pages of detail and much anecdotal reportage about the man. Her initial impression was that it had been compiled by someone with a very organised approach to gaining the maximum effect from every word – in a very readable style.

Another journalist?

Riley pondered on this for a while, uneasy at the idea that someone else had already worked on this project. If they had ducked out of the assignment before her, as Donald Brask had so pithily suggested, maybe she should ask who... and why. Then she noticed something even more interesting.

In addition to the commercial information in the file, which must have been difficult enough to collate – knowing what little she did of the subject and his ways – there was information of a purely personal kind: the kind which delved into the biggest no-go area of Al-Bashir's life.

His wife, Asiyah.

Riley wondered whether this wasn't simply courting disaster for the sake of it. Taking on a known litigant of biblical proportions, a man with his own security force and the confidence to use it, was not likely to go unnoticed. Nor would it do her reputation much good if the detail contained in the file turned out to be erroneous, misguided or even downright malicious.

She picked up the copy of *East European Trade* and took out her mobile. She had promised to let Donald have details of the publisher involved. She didn't want to get into a discussion with him about this just now, so she took the easy option and texted him the details instead.

As for Al-Bashir, she toyed for all of five seconds with the idea of tossing the assignment aside. Even if she was going to tell Varley to get lost, maybe a more detailed look at the file first wouldn't do any harm.

12

Palmer sat at his desk and picked up the large brown envelope. It was bulky but light, and he soon saw why. Ripping it open, he tipped out a miscellaneous collection of sheets from spiral note-pads, sales receipts from various shops, discarded sheets of A4 plain paper, a holiday postcard showing a slice of blue sea and a rocky coastline, and even a couple of envelopes addressed to Helen at her London home. Mrs Demelzer hadn't been kidding when she said she'd put in everything she could find.

Among the papers were two or three strands of blonde hair. Palmer placed them gently back in the envelope. He wasn't sure if it was his imagination, but he thought he detected a faint hint of Helen's perfume, too. He breathed deeply, forcing himself to relax and concentrate on the papers.

Most of it was, as Mrs Demelzer had said, jottings and doodles, random notes, some scribbled through and illegible, others circled or underlined. Exclamation marks and stars appeared regularly, but their placing had more to do, he guessed, with points Helen might have been reacting to in conversations rather than with any specific words on the paper.

There were several phone numbers. He made a list of them for checking later. He did the same with names, although they were sufficiently vague or common to make identifying the owners all but impossible without Helen's address book, Blackberry or computer records.

His doorbell rang, followed by footsteps on the stairs. He continued reading, surprised to see his own name written along one edge of a page torn from a spiral notebook. It was followed by the words *send photo* underlined twice in a heavy hand, and the word *fourth*. There was no indication as to when the note had been written, nor to whom the photo was to be sent, although he had a good idea. Was it a photo taken of either of them while they were together? If so, he couldn't recall one, or why she should have chosen to send it now, after all this time.

He checked through the pile again. There was nothing. He stared at the wall on the other side of the office. Maybe it was at his flat. If it had been sent there any time in the last week, he wouldn't have seen it. He made a mental note to check the box later, vaguely aware that someone was standing in the office doorway.

"Palmer?" It was Riley, her face flushed from the stairs. She was carrying two large polystyrene mugs of coffee. "What's up? You look like you swallowed a frog."

Palmer swung his legs out from behind the desk and stood up. He took one of the mugs and nodded at the desk. "Take a look at that, will you? See if anything strikes you as significant. How did the meeting go?"

Riley sat down, prising the lid off her mug. "It was OK. I've got a job if I want it. Are you going to tell me how you got on in rural Basingstoke?"

"Later. Trawl through that lot first. I need an objective eye." He wandered round the desk and stood at the window, staring down at the street and sipping his coffee.

Riley did as he asked, carefully studying each item without comment. When she had finished, she sat back. "How did you get this?"

Palmer told her about his visit to Mrs Demelzer. "Helen asked her to send it to me. That's all I know."

Riley nodded and sipped her coffee. "Most of it's meaningless, I'd say," she surmised. "Stuff she was working on, people she was talking to, memos to self… I've got scribbles like this all over – even on my bathroom wall. Except this." She leaned forward and tapped a finger on the piece of paper bearing his name. "Looks like someone was thinking about you recently. Could the fourth be a date?"

"No idea. Possibly. But there's no photo anywhere. I checked."

"There's a postcard."

Palmer picked it up and read the handwriting on the back. It was addressed to Mrs Demelzer and was the usual inconsequential stuff people write when on holiday to those back home. The date on the frank mark was 17, although he couldn't read the month. He shook his head and dropped it among the other papers. "Mrs D must have dropped it in by accident."

"Could Helen have sent something to your flat?"

"Maybe. I haven't had time to check." It was the first indication he'd given that Helen had known where he lived.

"What could it have been – a shot of you two over dinner?"

"Hardly." Palmer stared into the distance. "We didn't exactly get round to photos."

"Well, whatever it was, she must have thought it was important." She ran a finger through the mess on his desk. "Believe me, women don't send ex-boyfriends the dross from their bedrooms. Not unless they're trying to make some obscure point. Did she have your email address?"

"I don't know. Probably."

Riley reached beneath his desk and switched on his computer. "It could have been a shot she took of something, or maybe she scanned it in from a hard copy." She sat back to wait for the machine to boot up, then studied the icons on the screen to call up the email. "Christ, Palmer, you make it so easy for people to access your PC. Don't you have any passwords?"

"You know me," he said dryly. "I'm an open book." He stood behind Riley to watch his inbox fill up. It was mostly spam, dozens of them. He ran his eyes down as Riley scrolled through the list.

She stopped the cursor on an untitled message with an attachment. It was dated five days ago. The sender tag was Hellsbells.

"That's her," Palmer breathed. He recalled them laughing over her email name, which she thought summed her up fairly well. There was no message, just the attachment. Riley clicked on it and waited for it to open. The screen flickered and they were looking at a photo of an office building.

"That's romantic." Riley glanced up at him. "Does it look familiar?"

"Never seen it before." Palmer was puzzled. It was a standard glass-and-concrete panel building, maybe seven floors high, with a pale fascia and a sloping canopy over the entrance doors. A couple of trees stood in circular beds set into a block-paving forecourt, with metal bollards to prevent vehicles parking too close to the glass frontage. It could have been any building from Aberdeen to Zanzibar: functional, unremarkable and built by numbers.

He tried to think what significance an office building might have held for him and Helen. Clearly she had thought it had some relevance. But nothing came to mind. Why was there no accompanying message?

Riley voiced his thoughts. "Would you send anyone a photo of a building without at least a word of explanation to go with it?"

"No. Unless they were expecting it."

"And you obviously weren't."

"No." He sighed, frustrated by the lack of clear answers as to what had happened in Helen's life over the past few days. Yet surely this must have held some special meaning, or she wouldn't have been trying to contact him.

"Unless," said Riley sombrely, "she couldn't add a message in the normal way." She right-clicked the mouse button and a box appeared marked Properties. She studied it for a moment, then said, "I wouldn't swear to it, but I think this photo came from a mobile phone camera. Did she have one?"

"Yes. She got it just before I met her. I'm sure it had a camera.

It did everything but make coffee."

Riley gave him a sideways look, and Palmer knew what she was thinking. He had a basic brick of a model which did nothing but make and receive calls, and which Riley had once commented was heavy enough to double as a cosh if he needed one.

"It's called progress, Palmer. I'm surprised you haven't got one. In your line of work, you'd find it useful, taking snaps of adulterers in their frillies." She moved the cursor and the picture became larger as she zoomed in. A couple of clicks and the area above the entrance moved into the frame. "Got you," she breathed, and moved the cursor to a faint outline of a sign above the doors. It read: **Pantile House**.

Riley opened Google and typed in the name of the building. It came up with ten pages of hits. Many were of buildings with the name Pantile all over the country, including several commercial properties.

"This could take some time," she warned him, after several false starts. "We'll be dead lucky to get a match on the internet. It could be anywhere – or be one of these buildings from a different angle." She tapped her fingernail on the desk. "On the other hand, I know someone with access to a commercial property database. Fancy a trip into the city?"

"Couldn't we email them the photo?" Palmer checked his watch. "We don't have much time."

"Don't worry. The person I'm thinking of works unsocial hours. And he owes me a huge favour." She picked up her mobile and checked her directory. "Won't be a second."

Palmer walked over to the door, impatient to be going. If there was even the faintest of trails, he wanted to follow it, no matter where it led. "Suits me. What else are we going to do?"

A door slammed, the noise intruding over the muted hum of homeward traffic along the Euston Road. It was followed by a faint burst of laughter, the sounds echoing up through the empty fourth floor.

Grigori gave a start. He didn't enjoy having to use this place. But he was obsessive about not leaving a paper trail, which was why he couldn't risk hiring a facility legitimately. Contracts and invoices left a footprint, and remaining invisible in this city for the time being was essential. He was here on someone else's territory, and if he made a mistake, he knew his presence would be compromised. It was one of the reasons he had a variety of names and identities at his fingertips. The man he was specifically trying to avoid was not one to let an opportunity slip by without taking drastic action.

He stood up and stared out of the window. It didn't help that he did not altogether trust the building's supervisor, Goricz, who had arranged access to this empty office. The Serbian immigrant had promised that the lease was frozen pending legal complications, and that nobody would disturb them. But he had dealt with people like Goricz before. If they sold their services to one person for a few paltry pounds, they could just as easily do it to another. It was the nature of the beast.

The office door opened and his assistant, Radko, slipped inside.

"Well?" Grigori switched on the desk lamp.

"I checked the briefcase again. There were some notes, which I burned, and a cellphone. I have someone checking the call log through the service provider. The woman called several numbers over the last few days, one of them more than once." He shrugged. "Could be a friend we don't know about – setting up a date, perhaps."

Grigori nodded. "Maybe. When will we know for certain?"

"That we are still safe? A few hours – tomorrow at the latest. Even then, there's no guarantee that she didn't talk about what she was doing."

"I know. Let us hope she did not. If Al-Bashir even sniffs we are here, he will know why." He stared hard at Radko, eyes bleak. "He has men he can call on. And I know he will not hesitate to use them." He checked his watch. "I want to leave in half an hour."

Radko nodded. "I'll tell the others to be ready."

13

The offices of Crichton, Rutter & Dean occupied the ground floor corner of an office block just behind the south side of Oxford Street. The property consultants shared building space with a marketing company, a film production HQ and a container leasing firm, and were protected by an entry-phone, CCTV and a uniformed commissionaire.

Riley announced their names and the man clicked open the door and showed them through to a reception area with a smart desk and a young woman with a Hermes scarf and a brooding air of boredom. She lifted her chin in query.

"We're here to see Mark Chase," said Riley. "He is expecting us."

Before the woman could respond, a side door opened and a man in his late forties stepped out with a welcoming smile. He was plump and shiny-faced and dressed in shirtsleeves, pinstripe pants and braces, and had a head of glossy hair peppered with grey.

"Riley! I spotted you coming in. Nice to see you again." His tone was relaxed and educated, the greeting enthusiastic. He looked at Palmer. "You must be Frank." He waved a hand. "Ex-RMP, right?"

Palmer smiled back. "And you weren't."

"No, sorry. I was in the Grenadiers for a bit. Managed to avoid you lot, thankfully." He grinned boyishly, eyes sparkling, and ushered them into his office. He sat them down, then slid behind a vast, mahogany desk sinking beneath paperwork and files and a large flat-screen PC monitor. A black and white photograph on a shelf behind him showed a group of men in combat uniform posed against an army truck. Another – this one in colour – showed an attractive woman with dark hair, sand-wiched between two small boys. Riley had met Cathy, Mark's wife, and knew she was fiercely protective of him.

"I'm afraid I haven't got a lot of time," he said apologetically. "We've had a rush visit dropped on us by the Foreign Office. A team of Chinese civil servants want to see some office space, so I might have to drop everything and run."

Riley had explained on the way across town that Mark Chase had been caught on the periphery of a property scam she had investigated a couple of years ago. It had been Riley's word that had kept him out of prison when a former business partner had left him holding suddenly worthless papers. He had been waiting to pay back her kindness ever since.

"Mark," Riley reassured him, "it's good of you to see us."

"No problem." Chase glanced at his watch before turning to his monitor. "You were looking for this building, right?" He tapped the keyboard and spun the monitor round to face them. It showed the picture that Riley had emailed him before leaving Palmer's office. "It's not the greatest picture... poor resolution, I'm afraid. Taken on a mobile – am I right?"

"We think so," said Riley.

"It's fine." Chase shrugged. "Some of our people use them all the time for quick snaps." He pulled the screen back round and tapped the keys again. The photo was replaced by a sharper image taken from a slightly different angle. "Is this the one?" He turned it back so they could see it.

Riley and Palmer both leaned forward and studied the screen. The colouring and detail of the canopy over the entrance looked the same, as did one of the stubby trees set into the ground nearby. This time the name PANTILE HOUSE was clearly visible.

"How did you find it so quickly?" said Riley. "That's amazing."

"Stroke of luck and a good database," Chase replied modestly. "I shoved it out on the net and got two replies within minutes.

Our data confirmed it. Two of our leasing agents had been there recently and recognised it immediately." He grinned. "Lucky it was here in London, though. Anywhere out in the sticks and we'd have had a problem."

"Where is it?" Palmer asked.

"Off Eversholt Street, near Euston. Thirty years old, seven floors, basic commercial property with facilities, parking and part-time suit-and-boot security."

Riley looked blank.

"A supervisor in a serge uniform," he explained. "The rental doesn't allow a full-time presence, and there's minimal electronic coverage. Used to be a DHSS office before it was refurbished, but that was years ago." His eyes drifted to the screen. "I suppose you wouldn't care to tell me why you need this, would you?"

"We don't know yet," Palmer said easily. "The photo was sent to us, but we're not sure why. It could be part of something we're looking into."

Chase nodded. "You're a PI, is that correct?"

"Yes."

"Fair enough. Just interested. Actually, we don't look after this place any more. We handed it to another company as part of a shared management deal. But I can tell you that most of the tenants are solid and have been there for years. All except those on the fourth floor, anyway. They went bust and legged it. We're still trying to sort out the legal situation."

"Did you say the fourth?" Riley pounced on the reference to the floor number.

"That's right. We weren't able to let it, and so far neither have the other company. I doubt they'll do so now, anyway; there's talk of a developer moving in. They'll probably knock it down and start again." He sat back and looked between them with a knowing eye. "You want to get inside, don't you?"

Riley gave him her best winning smile. "How did you guess?"

"Call me perceptive." He scribbled on a slip of paper. "I can't go myself because of this Chinese visit, but if you ring Malcolm Swan, he'll get you inside. You can pretend to be interested punters."

"Can he do it today?" said Palmer.

"Sure." Chase didn't miss a beat. "What's left of it. We often do evening viewings. I'll call him and tell him you're on your way. He works for the other firm, but he's a good mate." He made a brief call and issued a firm request, then hung up. "OK. All arranged."

Riley took the slip of paper along with the address details and stood up. The two men followed. Chase came round his desk with his jacket in one hand and gestured towards the door just as his phone gave three short beeps.

"Damn – that's my call to arms," he said, and opened the door. "Late night for me, with prawn balls all round. Can you see yourselves out?"

"Of course," said Riley. "And we do appreciate this."

He eyed Riley warmly and gave her a quick, no-nonsense hug. "I still owe you big-time," he told her seriously. "And Cathy would kill me if she knew I wasn't taking you to this place myself. Call me if you need anything else?"

Riley nodded and touched his arm. "We'll be fine. Say hello to Cathy for me – and don't mention civil rights to your dinner guests."

They left him to his evening meeting and walked out into the square.

"So," said Palmer, eyeing a darkening sky. "Now we know the where. What we don't know is the why."

Riley looked at him, sensing the hunter in his demeanour. Whatever he might be feeling about Helen's murder, Palmer was beginning to gather strength and momentum from everything they learned. It was almost scary watching the gradual transformation. "How do we find out?"

"The only way there is. We go take a look."

"What about DI Pell?" she reminded him, suddenly remembering the detective. "It would be better if you called him rather than the other way round."

Palmer gave her a dry smile. "Let's do this first. While I'm still free."

14

Pantile House in the flesh – or at least, its equivalent in concrete and glass – looked even less attractive than the photo images had suggested. Squatting in a hinterland of narrow streets a stone's throw from Euston Station, it appeared faded and sad in the evening light, a stark contrast to the newer buildings springing up in the area. The tarmac around the outside of the building was liberally spread with litter and pitted with holes from years of low maintenance and heavy vehicle wear, and the louvred shutters at ground level, indicating a basement, were peeling and drab, in need of a good paint job.

Malcolm Swan turned out to be a lofty young man in a dark suit, striped shirt and heavy black brogues. He was waiting for them outside the entrance, clipboard and mobile in hand. The car park was nearly empty, and an air of silence hung over the building. There were a few lights left on, and the whine of a heavy-duty vacuum cleaner drifted out of an open window.

"I gather you want to take a quick recce inside," he offered eagerly as they shook hands. When his eyes fell on Palmer, he almost stood to attention. "Mark suggested I, um… get you in, then leave you to it." He seemed unconcerned by this strange request so late in the day, and turned to survey the building. "Fourth floor, Mark said. That right?"

Palmer nodded. "That's the one."

"Okey-dokey. In that case, I'll do my clipboard bit with the super and get you upstairs. Then I'll go take a phone call or two. If anyone asks, you're out-of-towners checking out some possibilities." He smiled to take any possible offence out of the comment, adding, "Londoners do office hours." He turned towards the entrance. "Follow me."

They entered a glass-walled foyer furnished with a reception desk, a clutch of chairs and a few pot plants in large tubs. A faint smell of stale polish hung in the atmosphere, and the strip lighting highlighted the need for a coat of paint and a layer of carpet tiles to rid the place of its utilitarian appearance.

Along one wall was a black wooden board listing the tenants in plastic lettering. The names gave no useful indication of their function, consisting mostly of acronyms followed by the universally bland UK or EUROPE. None of them meant anything to Riley or Palmer.

"Small businesses, mostly," said Swan perceptively, eyeing the board. "Some holding companies, manufacturing and distribution admin offices, that sort of thing. Four is empty right across the floor. Now, where is that man?" He cast around just as the lift door opened and a tall, thin individual stepped out carrying a tool box. He was wearing dark blue overalls over a blue shirt and black tie. "Ah, Mr Goricz. There you are."

He made vague introductions all round and confirmed that the visitors wanted to see the fourth floor. Goricz nodded affably enough, but made no attempt to shake hands.

"It's not clean, you know?" he told them, his Central European accent overlaid with traces of east London. "Nobody has been in there for weeks – including me." He seemed impatient to have the viewing over and done with, and moved crabwise towards the lift without waiting to see if they wanted to inspect any of the ground floor.

"No problem, " Swan assured him. "They're here to judge the space, not the dust mites."

On the way up Swan ran through the services and facilities on offer, playing his part to the hilt without sounding over-zealous. Goricz, meanwhile, stared blankly at the light board. Helping to do a selling job on the building's facilities clearly wasn't part of his job description.

The lift stopped and they all exited, at which point Swan, bringing up the rear, excused himself and held up his buzzing mobile. "Sorry – better take this. You folks go ahead and browse around. I'll see you down in the foyer." He looked at the supervisor, who was unlocking the doors to the fourth floor suite. "Mr Goricz, do you want to come down with me? I'm sure we can leave Mr and Ms, umm… to take a peek in private."

The supervisor hesitated, then threw open the door and peered inside. He stepped aside and gestured for Riley and Palmer to go in. As Palmer brushed by him, he was sure he sensed a wave of tension coming off Goricz, and wondered why.

He and Riley waited for the lift to go down again before moving through the empty offices. The floor was covered in drab, brown carpet tiles, with an occasional clutch of telephone wires showing where workstations had once stood. Other than a few empty notice boards on the walls, it was clear that whoever the previous tenants had been, they had left little of value for any incomers to use save for a single desk. This was in the main office, which ran from the front to the rear of the building and overlooked the rear car park.

Palmer walked over and flicked open the desk drawers. They were empty save for a large file drawer on one side, which held a reading lamp with a green shade, the flex coiled neatly around the stem. A plain telephone and plastic in-tray stood on the top of the desk, both covered in dust. Palmer ducked down and checked the surface against the light from the window, then straightened up and looked around the rest of the floor.

Riley watched him moving about. This was Palmer's speciality. He knew more about examining buildings and rooms than she did, and she was happy to let him get on with it.

When he came back and stood next to her at the rear window, he wore a puzzled expression.

"What's up, hound-dog?" she asked him. "You've got your

worried face on."

He shook his head and said loudly. "Looks pretty good. Not sure about the street access, though." With that, he walked back to the door, crooking a finger for Riley to follow. She caught on quickly: now was not the time or place to talk about why they were really here.

When they were out in the stairwell, he turned and said quietly, "For a place that's been empty for ages, the desk is completely dust-free, but the phone isn't. There's a reading lamp in one of the drawers, and the inside felt warm, although it could have been my imagination. But the nearest wall socket switch is in the on position, and there's no dust on that either. The others are all off and haven't been touched for a long time." He opened his hand. He was holding a toffee wrapper with a small dab of brown, sticky substance at one end. "This was on the floor near the door. The toffee's still moist."

"A supervisor with a sweet tooth?"

But even as Riley said it, she recalled the man's words just before they had entered the lift: *Nobody has been in there for weeks – including me.*

15

By nine the following morning, refreshed by a few hours sleep, Riley had completed researching what she could find of Helen Bellamy's life. There was almost nothing of a personal nature.

A schools reunion site yielded some names from a meeting a year ago, but nothing recent. Helen's professional record, which was spread across a wide range of business topics, showed a varied and regular pattern of work, although, strangely, nothing for the last six weeks. But that, she decided, could have been because Helen was working for publications without a web presence. She had worked for a number of small but solid magazines and newspapers, and was clearly building up to a more prestigious future when she had met her untimely death.

She had belonged to one or two journalism or writing-related support groups, but they were also woefully thin on detail. Riley's conclusion was that Helen Bellamy had been a very private person, and had left almost nothing of a footprint, unless it was with people who knew her well. People like Frank Palmer, who appeared to have known precious little.

For a change of pace and atmosphere, she turned her focus on the background, work and minutiae of 'Kim' Al-Bashir, retailer, multi-millionaire, investor and speculator.

Originally named Muammar, after his grandfather, Al-Bashir had decided shortly after arriving in England to call himself Kim – a fact which had earned him the early, taunting tag of 'Johnny English' from both the press and his enemies. Al-Bashir seemed to have developed the knack of courting the former when it suited him, and evidently had no shortage of the latter. Rumour suggested that these enemies stretched from his birthplace in Egypt to the corridors of Whitehall in London, many of them the trampled human casualties from numerous business dealings and his ruthless desire to rise to the top.

Al-Bashir's biggest problem seemed to be his belief that, having bought a large amount of London property during the 1980s, including a chain of household-name department stores with a flagship address and branches all over the country, he should have been riding high in the nation's consciousness and hearts, loved and respected by all.

Sadly for him, this had not happened. As if in compensation, he had surrounded himself with a small army of security men, and the stories of how he dealt with perceived enemies were numerous. He had been investigated many times, and some of his men had been charged with assault or intimidation, but nothing had stuck, confirming the belief among many in the press that, in spite of his claims to the contrary, he had friends in high places.

Yet when it came down to basics, all Riley managed to find was that Al-Bashir – rich, powerful and seemingly paranoid – was no worse than many other rich, powerful businessmen. He had more money than most and, if rumour in the city was true, backers with unlimited resources to help fund his various business ventures. But in that he was hardly unique.

One of those ventures, verified in the on-line city pages of the nationals, concerned Al-Bashir's desire to become a leading player in the telecoms market. He had bid for a share of an imminent release of licences across Central and Eastern Europe, effectively seeking to supply, equip and run the entire cellular network across a vast land base. According to the *Financial Times*, Al-Bashir already had a share in the huge new Batnev satellite system which, once hooked up, would control a substantial amount of mobile phone and wireless connections. It was rumoured that the low cost of the new system would allow him to mop up subscribers across an even wider area, including parts of the Middle East and even sections of the hugely profitable European subscriber base, where users were no longer troubled by brand loyalty.

Riley turned to the folder Varley had given her. She had deliberately left this to one side until she had formed opinions based on her own research. Much of it merely confirmed what she had already discovered, probably culled from the same public domain sources. Al-Bashir, it said, was after some very big fish indeed, and could, if successful, change the face of a large part of the communications world across Eastern Europe.

A note on a single sheet of paper in the file caught Riley's eye. Folded in on itself, it was snagged between two other documents. There was no indication where the information had come from or where it was supposed to fit. Although typed, it read almost like an afterthought.

Apart from the established providers (already bidding), there could be other obstacles in Al-Bashir's way. These amount to a number of previously unidentified wealthy individuals or equal-interest groups with a strong desire to keep control of the market in local hands while taking advantage of the enormous potential offered. Although largely resident abroad, these émigrés (oligarchs?) still command substantial resources and considerable influence in the region from local (state) up to national level, in some cases capable of outstripping bids from the more impoverished national treasuries. Singly or as a group, they should not be discounted.

Oligarchs. Riley sat back. That word again. Coincidence? It must be. She forged on, her thoughts drifting to whether Al-Bashir had considered how unpopular his bid was going to make him if he succeeded. Commercial enemies were one thing and to be expected. But consumer resentment of one man's grandiose schemes was something else entirely, and very unpredictable. If he had thought it through, he was evidently unconcerned by it.

Reading further, she found other disturbing questions coming to the surface. They concerned Asiyah, Al-Bashir's young and beautiful – but rarely seen – wife. A gifted musician and artist from a traditional Alexandrian family, she had walked into his store one day, and by the time she was ready to leave Al-Bashir had proposed.

Some of the press speculation and reports included mention of Asiyah's alleged taste for the high life, free of the restrictions of her family and homeland. But why not? She was the wife of a wealthy man who clearly liked to indulge her. There were reports that he was protective of her, some suggesting to a degree beyond the merely reasonable. One of Al-Bashir's security men had been dismissed for allegedly looking at Asiyah too openly; another had been sacked, subsequently accusing Al-Bashir of having him beaten up for disagreeing with Asiyah over a question of her personal safety.

Yet again, nothing startling, given the kind of life these people led. Mildly eccentric behaviour came with the territory. But press reports fed eagerly on the mundane, turning it as if by magic into something else, coloured and re-packaged for public consumption.

It was only when Riley was well over halfway through Varley's notes that she found the personal detail began to outstrip the commercial. Wading through documents similar to the ones she had discovered, she found additional allegations which, if true, meant Asiyah Al-Bashir wasn't just merely extravagant, but unfaithful, too. If the allegations were false, they were opening up the publishers of the magazine – and by implication, anyone putting their name to them – to legal action. And funded by Al-Bashir's vengeful millions, that would mean personal and professional ruin. But what if they were true?

She read through an impressive looking report prepared by a high-level security company, looking for weaknesses in the detail.

Asiyah, it was stated, had formed a secret liaison with a non-Egyptian national. She had been followed to several meetings in London, Paris and Athens, where compromising photographs had been taken. From the angle of some of the photos, Riley could only surmise that the photographer had been standing on a balcony right outside the woman's hotel room, and that Asiyah was criminally careless when it came to drawing the curtains.

It was bad enough that Asiyah's lover was allegedly Israeli – heinous indeed for the wife of a staunchly proud Egyptian. But there was worse to come – at least, from Al-Bashir's point of view.

His wife's alleged lover was another woman.

16

"You said nobody would come. That we would remain undisturbed here. You guaranteed it!" Grigori's eyes were flat and grey like the early morning sky outside, his voice icy with anger. Emotion had brought an unusual level of colour to his cheeks, but it was not a good sign. He stared for several seconds at the two men before him with all the friendliness of a snake, waiting for an answer. "Well?"

"We don't know why they came, boss. It was not a scheduled visit." His assistant Radko was the spokesman, which was his job.

The man beside him, named Pechov, squat as a dumpster and blank-eyed, seemed impervious to the vitriolic atmosphere. He had the indifference of a junior employee, and chewed rhythmically on a toffee. He remained silent, which was his job.

"How, not scheduled? You said the supervisor, Goricz, would warn you. Yet suddenly, last night, two people come up here and ask to look around. Did we not pay him enough?" He leaned forward over the desk strewn with the papers he'd been working on. "Or perhaps you did not frighten him enough? What happened – is he taking money from someone else?"

"No, boss. I don't think so. It was a genuine visit. Two people – a man and a woman – came with an agent to view the empty floor. It was short notice, Goricz said, and he couldn't turn them away. They were from out of town, and couldn't see the place any other time. They went in, looked round, then left." He shrugged his broad shoulders and gave a soothing smile. "It was nothing, I promise."

"You *promise*?" Grigori's words were coated with sarcasm, wiping the smile from his assistant's face. "Like you promised the Bellamy woman would be dealt with properly? Like you promised we would remain secure in this building? Like you guaranteed the German woman would do what we wanted?"

"The German was not my fault." Radko's face went pale beneath his tan, his eyes flinty with resentment at being taken to task in front of Pechov. But he remained polite, wary. "She was not my choice. As for Bellamy, she is already forgotten. The police have found nothing and nor will they. Her place has been cleared, her briefcase and work records destroyed." He paused for a moment, before adding softly, "As for Goricz, I will deal with him."

"No. You won't," Grigori countered quickly. "If anything happens to Goricz, it will only draw attention to this building – and we still need it for a while yet." He looked his assistant in the eye and said deliberately, "But once we are finished here, I do not expect the Serb or *his family* to see another day. Understand?"

"All of them?" Radko exchanged an appalled look with the silent Pechov. "But here, in London? It would be a huge risk – "

"All of them! If you cannot do it, I will find somebody who can." The statement hung in the air between them, the meaning chillingly clear.

Without another word, Grigori flicked a dismissive hand and turned to the papers on the desk before him as if the men did not exist.

He forced himself to remain calm. He was disturbed by what had just happened. Was Radko beginning to show signs of weakness? He hoped not, for that was something he could not allow. A weak link threatened them all, and would be seen by others as a challenge to his authority.

Several miles away, across London, Ray Szulu drummed his fingers on his mobile and waited. It was gone nine. He was usually up and out earlier than this, but there had been no call yet, and he was still in his skivvies. He was waiting for Ayso, the controller and manager of the mini-cab firm, to give him some work. The limousine company had nothing, he'd already checked that, so here he was again, worrying about earning some money from short drives and wondering if his moans about Ayso's pig-ugly accent had somehow got back to the man. It would be just like him to make Szulu squirm and wait for a job out of spite.

"Hey – Raymond. You comin' back to bed? I'm getting cold!" The girl's voice cut through from the bedroom of Szulu's one-bed flat in what she probably thought was a sexy, seductive tone. All it did was set Szulu's teeth on edge.

When he'd first started talking to her yesterday evening in a club in Hammersmith, her voice had sounded husky and alluring, muffled slightly by the driving bass line of the music and the constant hubbub of talk and laughter. And when she'd run her fingertips across his bullet scar, mention of which he'd dropped casually into the conversation the way he always did, because the ladies just ached to know they were talking to a real, live, wounded man who'd seen some action, she'd sounded positively honey-toned and had fluttered her eyelashes as if they were powered by Duracell.

But once outside and on the way back to his place, with her hanging on his arm – his wounded left arm – her voice had turned out to be sharp enough to stop the traffic.

He fingered the slight indentation in his upper arm. It wasn't hurting this morning. Not that he'd admit that to her, of course. As far as the ladies were concerned, the pain was always there, a reminder of how close he'd come to leaving this life and moving on to the next. As usual, he always skirted round what had happened to the man who'd shot him and focussed on himself. After all, he was still here, wasn't he?

"Raymond – you comin' or what?"

Szulu dropped the mobile and made his way back to bed. Work or not, screechy voice or not, he had a reputation to uphold.

Another job would come along sooner or later. Until then, there were other comforts.

Small blessings, as his ma used to say about all of life's ups and downs. Small blessings.

17

"Mr Palmer? DI Craig Pell." The detective walked into Palmer's Uxbridge office, leaving a uniformed officer hovering at the top of the stairs. It was just after eleven and the morning street noise had died to a rumble.

Palmer swung his feet down from his open desk drawer and stood up. He'd left a message for Pell earlier, and the man had called back to say he would drop by for a 'chat'. The speed with which he had done so and the presence of uniformed back-up weren't necessarily significant, but neither was it a good sign.

He offered Pell coffee, but the policeman declined and sat down heavily on one of the hard chairs, thrusting his hands into his jacket pockets. The man's face was all planes and angles, and Palmer guessed he would be the same mentally. A tough cop, he judged, and young for his rank. It meant he was good at his job.

"You say you knew Helen Bellamy," Pell began without preamble. "Would you care to describe how and when?"

Palmer sat down and related how he had met Helen when he was hired by a businessman she happened to be profiling at the time for a trade journal. Palmer was doing a security assessment on the man's factory, and had bumped into her in the company car park. They had exchanged telephone numbers, and from there it had progressed through dinner to more dates, and into what had been a very pleasant relationship, even it hadn't been long-lasting.

"Really? Why's that?"

Palmer shrugged, aware that Pell was looking for clues as to how well he and Helen had known each other. "Work, mostly. Helen was trying to make a name for herself; I was away a lot. At the time, it didn't suit either of us to try for anything more than that." He heard the words and thought how bland and casual it must sound, as if their relationship hadn't been worth more effort.

"At the time?"

"Looking back is easy. We did what we did."

"So it was just fun?"

Palmer felt his face harden. "Come again?" His words fell softly into the room, and Pell shifted uncomfortably and looked away. For a moment, the creak of the chair and the shuffling feet of the officer on the landing were the only sounds.

"Sorry – that didn't come out the way I meant it." Pell admitted. He seemed genuinely embarrassed. "Do you regret the relationship not being more than it was?"

Palmer breathed easily and tried to ignore the not-so-subtle meaning behind the question. "I regret lots of things," he said evenly. "I regret not having been able to help her, if that's what you're asking. But I can't change the circumstances."

"So you last saw her… when?"

"Several months ago. I'd have to check, if you want me to be more specific. But I don't see how it would help with your investigation."

Pell nodded slowly. "So you wouldn't know what she might have been working on recently?"

"No. She specialised in commercial and business matters, that's all I can tell you."

"Fair enough. You were in the Military Police, is that right?"

"Yes." Palmer guessed that the moment he had rung and left a message, Pell would have had someone trawling through the records. It would have been negligent not to. And Pell was coming across as anything but slow to join all the primary dots.

"So you know a bit about procedure."

"I know you have to eliminate everybody, yes."

"What made you come forward?"

Palmer shrugged. "You'd have come across my name eventually."

Pell raised a cynical eyebrow. "Miss Gavin didn't suggest it, then?"

"I'm not sure what you mean."

Pell eased back in the chair and stretched out his legs. "I was up at Paddington Green station when I got your message, sitting in on a National Crime Squad taskforce meeting. Bloody boring, most of it, talking about budgets and targets. It's like being in a call centre. Anyway, I was relieved to get a message that someone had called about Miss Bellamy. It gave me an excuse to get out for some fresh air."

"Glad to have been of help."

"While I was taking the message, a senior suit ambushed me; he'd heard your name mentioned and dragged me to one side. He told me a few things about you – and your friend, Miss Gavin." He stared hard at Palmer. "You know Chief Superintendent Weller?"

"Yes, I know him." Palmer wondered at the small community that was the police service. He had encountered Chief Superintendent Weller on a previous job with Riley. The officer was a member of the Serious Organised Crimes Agency, and was fond of using people involved in cases to get results; of allowing them a certain degree of slack to see what might be stirred up, like sludge on a river bed. It was a risky strategy, but it had worked before and the man had the confidence and clout to use it. "You shouldn't believe everything Weller tells you. He mixes with people who tell lies for a living. It rubs off."

"He says you're quite a team, the two of you." Pell waited, but Palmer refused to be drawn. "For him, that's praise indeed." His mouth slipped into a humourless smile. "Although I got the impression he might have a couple of question marks posted against your name. What's that about, then – past misdeeds?"

"You should have asked him."

"I did. He went all secret-squirrel on me and said it was nothing worth worrying about." He waved a vague hand, drawing a line beneath the topic. "If he can live with it, so can I. Back to the matter in hand. Were you ever in Miss Bellamy's flat?"

"Yes. Several times."

"You know where it is, then?"

"Beaufort Street, Chelsea. Why?"

"Elimination purposes. When were you there last?"

Palmer made a show of remembering. But he was thinking instead of how close he had come to going to Helen's place yesterday, but how other things, like seeing the inside of Pantile House, had intervened. He'd been lucky, by the sound of it. Being found in the wrong place at the wrong time had dropped many people in the dock when they didn't need to be. And the home of a newly-discovered murder victim was about as wrong as it could get.

"Again, several months ago," he replied eventually. "My prints might still be there, I suppose."

"Do you know who she might have started seeing, after you?"

"No. We stopped going out; that was the end of it."

"Did the relationship end on a good note?"

"Yes. Friendly, in fact. It had run its course, that's all. We didn't fall out, if that's what you're asking."

"I wasn't, but thanks for saying so." He studied Palmer carefully, then said casually, "Had Miss Bellamy been in touch recently?"

Palmer felt the air around him crackle. Pell knew something. It could only mean he'd got a look at Helen's phone or email records.

"Actually, she emailed me something a few days ago," he admitted frankly. If he didn't tell them, they'd soon find out. "It was a photo, but there was no explanatory message. I think it came to me by mistake."

Pell glanced at Palmer's PC. "May I see it?"

Palmer nodded and opened his email, then turned the monitor so that Pell could see the screen. The detective leaned forward to peer at the photo, but other than that, showed little reaction. "It's an office block."

"Yes. I have no idea why she sent it. It was probably a mistake."

"Do you know the place?"

"I've never seen it before."

Pell sat back with a sigh.

"OK. What was your initial reaction to her murder?"

"Shocked. Saddened. What do you expect?"

"Angry?"

"Of course."

"Weller described you as being very laid-back."

Palmer shrugged. He wasn't sure what Pell was leading up to, but he had a feeling it could be something he might not like.

"He also added a 'but'," Pell continued, and levered himself out of the chair. He looked down at Palmer for a moment. "A big one. He said you were totally loyal to your friends, and capable of doing anything on their behalf. I was wondering what that meant."

"Like I said, Weller mixes with the wrong crowd. It plays havoc with his imagination."

Pell nodded. He seemed to toy with something for a moment, then said, "Our database is quite good these days. We get stuff turning up on it all the time; some of it's useful, some not. It sits there until someone decides it's no longer relevant. Or until something rings a bell. Literally, I mean. We have this little electronic sound reserved for entries or cases with more than five points of comparison – I forget what the techies call it. Anyway, whenever something similar to an existing entry pops up, the bell rings. It rang this morning."

"How dinky for you. So?"

Pell looked deadly serious. "This isn't for public consumption, so don't repeat it outside this office. But six weeks ago, the body of a young woman was discovered late one night alongside the A12 in Essex. She'd been thrown from a moving vehicle."

Palmer waited, wondering why he'd been made privy to this bit of information. Weller, perhaps, playing his old games of stir the pot to see what was in there?

"She was a German national, name of Annaliese Kellin. You ever heard the name?"

"Never."

"Hardly surprising. She had no family or friends here in the UK. Interestingly, she shared three similar prime characteristics with Helen Bellamy."

Palmer felt the breath catch in his throat. He suddenly knew with absolute certainty what Pell was going to tell him next.

"Annaliese Kellin was a freelance reporter, specialising in business and commercial matters. That was one. When she was found, her hands were tied together." He gave Palmer a grim look, waiting for a reaction.

But Palmer merely said, "Three. You said there were three similarities." Pell hadn't mentioned how Helen had died. This had to be it. He could feel it.

The policeman let out a lengthy sigh that seemed to come from deep within him. "Early indications," he said carefully, "and they haven't yet confirmed which, is that Helen Bellamy died the same way as Annaliese Kellin: of a broken neck and/or strangulation."

"And/or? What the hell does that mean?" Palmer's jaw clenched tight.

"We think," Pell forged on carefully, "that the killer used a stranglehold method, placing the arm round the neck from behind. There was bruising under the chin consistent with someone standing in an elevated position behind and above the victim." He sounded as if he was reading from an official report, and his face showed he wasn't enjoying it.

"She was sitting down?"

"Or kneeling, yes. I'm told the blood circulation would have been cut off, along with the air supply. Then the neck was broken. One of my colleagues is ex-Special Forces. He said it's not as easy as it looks and takes considerable commitment." He paused. "I know it's no consolation, but it would have been quick."

Palmer thought about it. That was just about the most intimate way he could imagine of ending someone's life. You had to get right up close. And killing a woman that way took a special kind of cold-bloodedness.

"You're wrong." His voice was soft but sure, cutting through the charged atmosphere in the room like a blade. He looked right through Pell as if the policeman wasn't there. "If you know it's going to happen, how can it ever be quick?"

Outside on the pavement, Pell breathed deeply and stood for a moment, glad to be out in the fresh air. He hadn't enjoyed the visit, especially the bit when Palmer had looked at him after his verbal blunder. It was like being skewered by the eye of a killer shark.

He wondered at the nature of the relationship between Palmer and Riley Gavin. Riley came across as a hard-nosed reporter, yet with a softness he found intriguing – and attractive. He thought the softness reflected the real person. At least, he hoped so. Palmer, on the other hand, was harder in more ways than one, in spite of his apparent easygoing attitude. His background was clearly that of someone not unaccustomed to death or violence and therefore hardened to it, but he wasn't immune to its consequences.

The contrast made him wonder if there was anything deeper

between them; the attraction of opposites, perhaps?

He walked over to his car where the uniformed officer was waiting, and tried telling himself that he was not secretly hoping that the relationship was purely professional; that he might have a reason to speak to Riley Gavin again.

18

Riley scrubbed at her eyes. They felt gritty after staring at her screen and wading through reams of paper, absorbing thousands of lines of type. Apart from the folder Varley had given her, her own research was continuing to unearth further material, all of which was emerging steadily like a paper fungus from the belly of her printer.

She watched the cat sprawl inelegantly across the carpet as if it had been tossed from a great height, and envied it the lack of stress. What she would have given for a complete reversal of circumstances, for none of the awful news she had been given, and the ability to choose only nice subjects with pleasant endings to work on. Then she told herself that she was daydreaming. If she had wanted nice, she'd have taken up patchwork.

She got up and made some tea. The cat stopped sprawling, its radar on 'scan', and followed her, eyeing the fridge with an intensity which had Riley automatically reaching for a fork.

While it ate, she thought about what she had accomplished so far. With all the reading and the paperwork, she had ended up with little more than fairly strong rumour and a whole host of speculation about Al-Bashir's intentions, and the so-called lifestyle of his young wife. She was going to have to do some more digging.

She picked up the copy of *East European Trade* Varley had given her, which had migrated out to the kitchen on one of her earlier coffee runs. She flicked through it, still undecided about what to do. She either went with the assignment and got her name in this magazine, or she returned Varley's cheque in spite of his assurances that it was non-returnable, and got on with helping Palmer to solve his problem. Given the choice, she knew which she'd have opted for.

Then she stopped. She was staring at the inside title page of the magazine, her face suddenly as pale as the paper she was holding.

I don't believe it, she muttered softly, and snatched up the phone. She dialled Palmer's number. He answered on the second ring.

"I need you to confirm something," she told him. "Have you still got the postcard from the stuff Helen's friend sent you?"

"Sure." She heard his chair creak. "OK, what about it?"

"What's the place name on the back?"

He read it out. "Sokhumi, Georgia. Unusual place for a holiday, unless you're Russian." He paused. "Hang on, there's something written alongside."

"I know," said Riley. She could almost picture the words; they hadn't impacted on her when she'd first seen them. "Helen wrote *Ercovoy*, then *Atcheveli 3-24*."

"I don't get it." Palmer's voice was sharp with interest. She heard the chair creak as he got to his feet. "How did you know?"

"The magazine I got for my new assignment," she told him, "is published by a company called Ercovoy. Their production office is at Atcheveli 3-24, Sokhumi, Republic of Georgia. It's on the Black Sea."

She ran out of words, trying to make sense of the information. How the hell could there be a connection between Helen and her own new assignment? It was crazy.

"She must have gone out there for some reason." Palmer spoke softly. "But why – and why send the postcard?"

"Maybe it was a genuine coincidence. She went out there for a break after getting the assignment and stumbled on the office. Stranger things have happened."

"Yeah." Palmer didn't sound convinced.

"There's something else I found." Riley hesitated, then plunged in. "Some of the research notes for this job I'm looking at."

"What about them?"

"A lot of the notes have been put together at random – as if someone went through a bunch of files and dragged out anything of interest. But some of it has been collated and written up by someone who knew what they were doing. A professional."

The line hissed between them, then Palmer said, "A journalist?"

"It feels like it. There was discussion about Al-Bashir's bid for the telecoms licence in Eastern Europe, most of it very general. But one small entry, like a note to be added later, said his main opposition might come from wealthy Russian émigrés."

There was a longer silence, and Riley wondered if she'd done the wrong thing telling him. It was mere speculation on her part; an attempt to join up dots which might not be connected.

"For émigrés," he said finally, "read oligarchs."

"That word was in the file. It's thin, but… " She sighed, struggling to argue convincingly against her own thoughts and suspicions, and not liking what she was thinking.

"I still don't get it," said Palmer. "If she was worried about something, why didn't she contact me?" He sounded frustrated.

"Maybe she was going to but never got round to it." Riley wanted to drag the words back as soon as she uttered them. Palmer was already feeling bad enough about Helen's death; he didn't need the additional burden of knowing she had been scared enough to consider asking an old boyfriend for help, but had been prevented at the last minute. He appeared not to have noticed, so she continued, "There's something about Helen that struck me." She told him about her earlier research into Helen's publishing history via the internet. "Helen had a steady work rate, with regular jobs going back three or more years, here and overseas. That's good going for a freelance. Some were fillers, where she was probably asked to stand in for staff writers. Others were normal, freelance assignments, which was her bread and butter."

"Like the jobs she did for Johnson."

"That's right. There were probably a few I didn't find, but there were no huge gaps."

"Go on."

"Suddenly, for the last six weeks, nothing. It was like she'd dropped off the map. It was unusual."

The silence lengthened, then Palmer said, "Are you at home?"

"Yes."

"OK, stay there and I'll come to you. Oh, one more thing," he added sombrely. "I just had a visit from Pell."

"What did he say?"

"He told me that Helen wasn't the first female freelance found dead recently."

In his Finchley base, one of Donald Brask's phones purred softly. He reached out to switch it to loudspeaker. The display told him it was Tony Nemeth, a reporter based in Ankara, Turkey. Donald had tracked him down the previous day with an urgent task, on the promise of further work if he came up with anything useful.

"Anthony, dear boy," he breathed softly. "What have you got for me?" He had been disturbed by Riley's information about the magazine *East European Trade*. He had never come across it before, and one thing Brask prided himself on was knowing about all the potential paying markets out there waiting for him and his clients. The other source of disturbance was that he had a bad feeling about it which wouldn't go away.

"It's difficult to say, Mr Brask," Nemeth's voice sounded furred, probably by too many cigarettes and strong brandy. Now it held a tone of regret, even puzzlement. "I went to the address you told me. I had to hire a sea-plane taxi to save some time – I hope you're OK for the fare? I got a good deal, though, from my cousin, Mehmet."

"Of course I'm good. What did you find?"

"It's a big apartment block. But not a nice place, you know? Shit plumbing, rotting concrete, lousy Soviet design – I'm surprised it didn't come down in the last earthquake."

"The devil looks after his own. What else?"

"If there's a publishing company there, nobody knows about it," Nemeth replied succinctly. "It's residential only – and I'm not saying high class, you know? Half the tenants are illegals, the electricity and water don't work every day, the sewers are more often blocked than not… you know the kind of place I mean."

"Actually, dear boy, I'm relieved to say I don't." Donald stared at the ceiling. He'd had a feeling about this from the moment Riley had first mentioned it. Publishing companies weren't in the habit of splashing money around on spec, least of all those in Eastern Europe. Not, at least, the legitimate ones with nothing to hide. He'd decided to check out the place after receiving Riley's text message.

"Lucky you. I took a look at the number you gave me. It looks no more than a crummy flat, like all the others around it. There was nobody in." He paused, then added, "Someone's got an interest, though."

Donald sat up. This could be Nemeth adding some spice to make it look as if he'd come up with something good. "Like what?"

"None of the locals would say much. But I'd only been there half an hour when a car arrived and couple of men went inside. They came out with a pile of envelopes and stuff and took off."

"You think somebody warned them?"

"I don't think so. One old guy I spoke to said it was a regular thing. They come and go at odd hours, he said. He also said none of the local kids go anywhere near the place ever since one of them tried to break in. He disappeared the next day."

"We could do with some of that round here. What else?"

"He called it a party car. Then he spat on the ground."

"Maybe he's asthmatic." Donald was only half joking. He had a growing feeling that Nemeth wasn't the sort to push for a story where there wasn't one. "What else?"

"He clammed up after that. I hinted at cash, but he looked at me like I'd offered to buy his sister."

"What did he mean by a party car? A stretch limo?" Donald tried to picture one of the monster vehicles used by hen-night organisers to carry clutches of drunken women on tours of their favourite pubs. It didn't quite gel. Nemeth confirmed it.

"No. He was referring to the old Communist Party – the Interior Ministry. They used to drive around in big, black saloons with blacked-out windows. The only difference was, this was a black BMW X5 instead. Easy to follow," he added cheerfully. "I got a kid on a motorbike to tail them."

"That was bloody brave of you."

"They drove from the flat to a freight forwarding depot. When the passenger got out, he was carrying a box, all taped up and labelled. I think he'd parcelled up the stuff he'd collected from the apartment along the way."

"Anthony," Donald almost crooned down the line, "if you got the address where that parcel was going, I swear I'll get you so much work, you'll think your feet are on fire."

Nemeth's smile as he read out the address – one of the PO box numbers Riley had provided – was evident in his voice and seemed to beam all the way into the room.

Donald had a sudden, chilling thought. "Wait. You said Interior Ministry. You mean it was a government car?"

"The way they drove around the place, it had to be," the reporter replied. "I'm guessing the old guy spat because he was referring to the Russians. They're currently called the *Federalnaya Sluzhba Bezopasnosti.*"

"What the hell does that mean?"

"It's the FSB to you. They used to be called the KGB."

19

"You should kick this job into the long grass." Palmer was looking grim.

After he had picked up Riley, they had decided to go to Donald Brask's Finchley base for a conference. Palmer had just finished relaying Pell's revelation about the murder of Annaliese Kellin. It had left a charged atmosphere in the room.

"Why?" Although shocked by the news, Riley instinctively challenged the notion of backing off from a job. Any job. "Are you going to let Helen's murder go?"

"That's different."

"Crap," she replied with mild bluntness. "Pell's jumping to conclusions. There might be no connection between the two murders. Annaliese Kellin could have simply picked the wrong car for a lift."

It was Palmer's turn to look cynical. "She was tied up. That doesn't sound very random to me."

Riley shook her head obstinately and glared at him, daring further argument. She'd had the same thought herself. She switched her attention to Brask, who had remained quiet while Palmer was speaking.

The agent held up both hands. "Sweetie, I'm on your side. But Frank's *so* right."

"I disagree. If there's a connection here, it would be better if I was on the inside."

Donald opened his mouth then shut it again. Instead, he changed the subject. "There's something you should both know. The publisher's address you sent me is a post box in a run-down residential block. Most of the flats are empty or used by illegals."

Riley stared at him. "How did you find that out?"

He looked pleased with himself. "Contacts, sweetie. As always, contacts."

"How reliable are they?" Even as she asked, Riley knew that it was a pointless question. The credentials of Donald's various sources of information were impeccable.

Donald, however, seemed unmoved. "Totally. His name is Tony Nemeth. He discovered that at various times of the month, a parcel is collected along with any other mail, bundled and forwarded to London." He studied his fingernails, playing the part of the all-seeing puppeteer to the full. "The package is sent to a PO box in London, which is the same as the editorial office listed in the magazine. That turns out to be a mailing facility in north London." He slid a piece of paper across his desk to Frank Palmer. "I don't know what you can do with this, but I understand the packages arrive courtesy of an Aeroflot flight into the Heathrow cargo terminal. They're delivered to the mailing facility and presumably split up there. I haven't had time to check yet, but I suspect the Madrid and Brussels PO boxes feed into London. They're probably no more than a bit of gloss for impressionable readers."

Riley glanced at Frank, who was staring intently at the ceiling.

"You've lost me," she said. "If this magazine is a hole-in-the-wall affair, how can it pay the kind of money Varley is offering? And who reads it?"

Donald cleared his throat. "Well, to answer your first question, every magazine throughout history which continued against all the odds was usually bankrolled by someone with plenty of money. There's no way round it. As to the readers of this one, by all accounts, there are some very influential people."

"Like?"

"People in the White House... some Whitehall mandarins, and I gather a few copies are read avidly in the halls of the Elysée Palace and some of the darker corridors in Bonn, Rome and

Brussels. It's available on annual subscription, and only then at a high price. It would have to be, because the subscriber base is probably restricted and exclusive."

Riley nodded. "That's what Varley implied. I've never heard of it."

"Perhaps you weren't meant to."

Riley looked puzzled. "I still don't get it."

"I think it's designed," said Donald, "to disseminate information from the East for consumption by eager little eyes in the West."

"The purpose being?" Palmer had returned to earth.

"*Entente*. Understanding. Hands across frontiers, call it what you will. It's not the first one ever published. *Storm* was one, allegedly with links to Soviet Intelligence, but never proved. That was during the sixties, put out via India. *Soviet Time* was another. They served a noble purpose – on the surface."

"Which was?"

"To help spread understanding. To make us feel comfortable in our beds at night."

"And otherwise?"

"Cynics would say they were used to tell us simpletons in the West only what the Kremlin wanted us to know." He shrugged. "The old guard may have gone, but the game hasn't changed. Publications just like it are still around, telling us things the current powers would like us to know without appearing to. They don't have to turn a profit, at least, not in the usual sense, because that's not the aim."

"Especially," murmured Palmer, "if they're run by wealthy individuals with the quiet connivance of the state. Nice arrangement."

Donald nodded. "Smoke and mirrors."

"God, you two are cynical," Riley said darkly.

"True, sweetie. But we're also right." Donald reached across to his desk and picked up another piece of paper, which he passed across to her. "I've done some digging. This lady is a lecturer in Russian and Post-Soviet studies at the London School of Economics. Worth a visit, I think. She agreed tomorrow at two."

Riley read the name off the paper. "Natalya Fisher? Sounds like a ballet dancer."

"She was probably that, too, in her time," he said enigmatically. "She came to the west twenty years ago and married a British scientist. She'll tell you more about the Russian mindset in fewer words than anyone else I know. There's a chance she might point you somewhere useful."

"You make her sound as if she has some special knowledge in this area," said Palmer.

"Well, I suppose she has." Donald beamed, before dropping his bombshell. "In a former life, Natalya Fisher worked for the KGB."

20

Natalya Fisher was a short, plump academic in her sixties with a soft, generous mouth. Dressed in various shades of grey, even her eyes had the quality of wood smoke, settling lightly on Palmer and Riley as the two investigators entered her cluttered office. But her smile was genuine and warm, and sharp with interest.

She indicated two chairs and bade them sit, then surprised them by leaping up and opening a window, before firing up a cigarette. "You have to excuse me," she continued uncompromisingly, waving away a cloud of noxious smoke. "But I have lived with worse things than smoking bans, and I need my nicotine. Please, join me if you wish. Nobody will disturb us here." Her accent was soft, overlaid with a mixture of influences, but echoing her origins a long way east of this dusty, paper-strewn hideaway. She took a huge drag of the cigarette, the tip glowing like molten steel, and sat down with a sigh of pleasure, lifting her legs and waggling her feet as if she had just walked a long way. "Now," she continued, "Donald Brask said you were interested in whatever I can tell you about certain Russians, yes?"

"That's right," said Riley. "Specifically, oligarchs."

"Oligarchs," Natalya queried flatly, "or *mafiya*?" Her eyes flicked between the two of them, the hint of a smile tugging at her mouth. Donald must have given her an idea of what they wanted to discuss, but she sounded sceptical.

Riley waited until the professor's eyes met her own and said, "Aren't they the same thing?"

"No. Not really. But there's an old Russian saying which says that one snowflake never settles far from the other." She inhaled deeply and blew smoke towards the window, where it billowed with startling clarity into the outside air like smoke signals over an Indian campfire. "Put another way, if you discover cow shit in your living room, don't bother looking for sheep."

Palmer grunted. "Another old Russian saying?"

"No," she admitted, and gave him a coy grin. "I just made that up. What I mean is, you shouldn't be too surprised if you find that oligarchs – what you in the west used to call moguls, I think – are viewed elsewhere as not so very different from the *mafiya*." She shrugged. "Same heads, different hats." She shuffled her feet and seemed to go into deep thought for a moment, before stirring. "You have to understand, such men are relatively new to Russia. They came to prominence under Gorbachev and Yeltsin, many with friends – even family – in the old Party."

"The Communist Party?" interjected Palmer.

"Yes. That surprises you?"

"A little. They're hardly soul-mates, I'd have thought."

Natalya raised an eyebrow. "Where money and power are concerned, Mr Palmer, all men are soul-mates. The first oligarchs made their money because they were allowed to, not necessarily because they were clever. It suited everyone to have the appearance of a free market. There were many crooks, of course, and corrupt officials, and they are drawn together like maggots to fresh meat. Then, with new investment from outside, came the others – the modern businessmen. Smarter, politically and financially, they soon realised that without connections, even their money and power could be taken away very easily. Some of them stayed, working with the new administration, others moved abroad, taking their fortunes with them."

"Buying football clubs and big yachts," said Riley dryly.

"As you say, buying their big toys. Many of the early oligarchs were not sophisticated and lost everything. But there are many others who survived." She studied the tip of her cigarette. "In my experience, there are three levels of these people you call oligarchs. Level Three is the lowest. They are rich, with many interests, but not influential enough to be really important. The reason for this is, they don't have the right… mmm… resources."

"Resources?"

"Friends. Contacts. Nothing is accomplished in Russia without knowing people. People with power… people who can provide assistance." She tapped ash from her cigarette into the palm of her hand without apparent discomfort. "Level Two," she continued, fluttering her hand over a waste bin, "are those with lots of money and influential friends. In my opinion, these are the ones who always want more. They work to make more contacts who can help them become richer and more powerful."

"But isn't that how you said most of them got there in the first place?" said Riley. "Through patronage?"

"Most. But not all." Natalya's eyes squinted through the smoke. "With all these things, there are changes; people are moved, contacts are lost… some fall out of favour, which in my country is often fatal. Then there are those I call Level One. They operate in what mountaineers would call rarefied air. They are very few in number, extremely rich, extremely powerful with many friends in high places. They have everything, but they still need to protect what they have. Some are in the east, others have come to the west to live and run their empires in exile… but even these men are missing something that all their millions can't buy."

"What's that?"

"A welcome home." She pulled a face at the blank looks of her two visitors. "All Russians," she explained, "wherever they live, eventually want to go home. A Russian out of his homeland is first of all a man with an aching heart. It pulls him back, even when he knows that going back is the last thing he should contemplate. That is why you will notice many Russians have a darkness around them – a sadness which eats into the soul." She flicked the cigarette butt out of the window with practised ease. "It makes them drink too much and dream of what they used to know. Because in the end, they wish to take their place where they were born."

"Even the oligarchs?"

"Sure. Especially them. Can you imagine, to have all that money, yet not be able to buy a ticket home?" She dusted the front of her skirt and gave her visitors a measured look, as though judging their powers of understanding. "Money in the west does not equate to happiness in the homeland. You think having big yachts or a football club or owning a small island is to warm the heart of such a person? It is playing with money and newspaper headlines only – a sport for bored men, usually trying to impress beautiful women." She smacked a hand against her chest. "But it does nothing to fill up the void in here."

"But going back," Riley guessed, "would mean losing everything?"

Natalya nodded. "For some, yes. But they don't give up, these men. They are like children going home from school." She smiled and raised a demonstrative finger. "What better way to impress your parents than by taking home a big school prize?" She peered at them for a sign of understanding, no doubt as she did with her students in class. "For the *right* prize, parents would forgive almost anything." She smacked a hand on her thigh. "That is the heart of their thinking – a welcome home."

"As well as," Palmer put in cynically, "guaranteeing you don't get a visit from a man with a phial of polonium."

Palmer felt Riley's eyes on him as a sudden silence descended on the room. Nobody spoke for several seconds. If Natalya felt insulted because of her background in the KGB, she gave no sign. But then, as Palmer knew well, the KGB hadn't been known for breeding sensitive souls. All the same, he couldn't help but wonder what special qualities had permitted a former KGB officer to settle in the UK. Maybe she had interesting photos of someone in authority.

He was beginning to worry that they were wasting their time. So far, the conversation showed signs of moving along a separate and slowly diverging path. If all they were going to get were her opinions on the melancholy soul-searching of her exiled countrymen, it wasn't going to help them find out what they wanted to know.

"This searching for approval," he said, to jolly things along. "Would it make them dangerous?"

"All such men are dangerous," she said without hesitation. "But some are worse than others. Those looking for something they have lost inside, for example. What *you* have to decide, Mr Palmer, is which one you are dealing with." She blinked and reached for another cigarette. "And that, I cannot tell you for sure. I hear rumours, but it is not fact. All I will say is, try taking away any of their toys and you will very quickly find out how dangerous they can be." She smiled, amused by the idea, and lit up in a cloud of smoke.

He decided to try another tack. "Have you ever heard of Richard Varley?" He carefully avoided looking at Riley, but was aware of her turning to stare at him. He spelled out the name.

"Varley? No." Natalya frowned at the tip of her cigarette. "I used to know a Varliya, once, but that was Anna – a girl at school. She was good at music, but died young. Her parents drank. Everybody drank. Who is he?" More smoke billowed towards the window.

"That's what we're trying to find out. It's a name we came across."

"But is it a real one?" the professor replied enigmatically and lifted her eyebrows. "Is he rich? What does he do?"

Palmer waited, sensing Riley wanted to answer.

"He's in publishing," she said finally. "Business magazines."

"Ah. Donald said something about that. If he is in magazines, he is not Russian."

"He sounds American."

Natalya shrugged. "Then that is probably what he is. Russians who want to be rich prefer petroleum, metallurgy or real estate. Not publishing."

"I see."

"These men you speak of – these oligarchs – are ambitious. They wish to dominate... to own. They are what critics would call control freaks. They are also of the earth. The earth and what is in it gives them the control... the ownership they crave." Her hand sliced through the smoke like a cleaver. "You have men like this, too, of course. It's not unusual. Just unusual for Russians... until recently, anyway."

"What about the magazine?" said Riley. She produced the copy Richard Varley had given her and passed it across.

Natalya took it and thumbed through it, then turned back to the inside front cover and scoured the publisher's details. She hummed a few times, then flicked through again before passing it back to Riley with a nod.

"I have seen this before," she said. "Is a small publication, but good quality. For where this comes from – Sokhumi in Georgia – very good."

"But?" There was a tone in Natalya's voice which altered the atmosphere in the room.

"But nothing. There have been many like this before. They come, they go. This one is around longer than most. But not very big circulation, I think."

"At a guess?"

Natalya shrugged. "Two hundred copies – maybe three. But not more. Is this the magazine your Richard Varley is running?"

"Yes."

Natalya pursed her lips, her mouth elongating like a duck's bill. Her next words came as a surprise. "I do not think so," she said finally, the statement drawn out but assured.

"Sorry?" Riley leaned forward.

"This publication," the professor said, stabbing a finger towards the magazine, "is good. It has a good reputation. But so does *Caravan Magazine*. You go in caravans?" She looked between her two visitors, but they merely stared back. She shook her head. "Never mind. Is cheap way to take a holiday if you don't mind rudeness of other drivers and thin walls. But this, this *East European Trade*, does not make money for Richard Varley. Or anyone else. Believe me." She patted her chest again. "I know about such things."

"Maybe he has other interests," Palmer suggested.

"Almost certainly." Natalya agreed. "But you must realise these magazines, they are not for direct commercial gain. They are for propaganda." She stubbed out her cigarette. "Is not to make money."

"Yes, I know."

"They are to tell others what you want them to know. No more, no less. The west has them, too. It is nothing new." She pursed her lips again and looked longingly at the cigarette packet.

"But propaganda," said Riley, "is put out by state organisations... like your former employers."

"Of course." She nodded vigorously, unaffected by the mention of her previous life. "And my former employers, as you call them – the KGB – were very good at this kind of thing. In the sixties, they had a single directorate which was bigger in publishing than many western newspapers." She brushed flecks of ash from her knee. "But the KGB is no more, of course."

"Yeah, right." Palmer spoke mildly, the scepticism evident in his voice. "And Vladimir Putin's a boy scout."

Natalya chuckled appreciatively, a twinkle deep in her eyes. "You know the KGB, Mr Palmer?"

He gave her a smile in return. "I had to know a bit about them once, for a while. I wouldn't be overwhelmed if you told me their successors – the FSB – was still doing this kind of work."

"Of course." She nodded in agreement, and with what might have been a touch of pride. "The FSB is responsible for internal security, but also propaganda. Misinformation. It is the way it has always been."

"They haven't changed, then."

Her next words brought a chill into the small, smoke-filled room. "Why should they? If something is not broken, why fix it?"

21

The afternoon was fading by the time Palmer turned south off the King's Road into Beaufort Street. The choke of exhaust fumes had been washed away on a sharp breeze from the Thames, replaced by the tinny, sour tang of the river itself a couple of hundred yards away. Only a few pedestrians were about, leaving him a clear view of the street all the way down to Battersea Bridge.

There were no obvious signs of a police presence, no figures lurking in doorways, and he turned into the block where Helen Bellamy had lived with the easy manner of someone who belonged.

After leaving Natalya Fisher, he'd told Riley he had things to do. He knew she hadn't believed he was going home to a lunchtime nap and a cup of Earl Grey, but she hadn't pressed him for an explanation.

The front entrance was locked, as he'd expected. He pressed one of the buttons on the security keypad and waited.

"Yes?" A woman's voice screeched out of the box, tinny and stressed.

"Police. Sorry to bother you."

"God, haven't you lot finished? OK." The door buzzed and Palmer stepped inside, grateful for the influence of cop shows and easy assumptions wrongly made.

He walked up the stairs, waiting for a door to open, for a head to appear. But whoever had admitted him was clearly uninterested or too busy.

Helen's flat was on the second floor. There was no tape across the door, no signs that the police might have been here other than the woman's comment and Palmer's knowledge of their methods. He waited for his breathing to settle and for the sounds of the building to become familiar and recognisable. If the police – or anyone – were keeping an eye on the place, they wouldn't be far away and Palmer would know it.

He allowed a few seconds to tick by, then took out a 'soft' key and inserted it in the lock. He flexed it gently from side to side, feeling the resistance change as the tumblers moved under the pressure. There was a click and the door opened.

The familiar smell washed over him. Helen's perfume, softly fragrant and warm, still hung in the air. He closed the door and stood still, absorbing the atmosphere.

He suddenly wished he were somewhere else, far from here. A car horn sounded in the street, jolting him. He had to move, to get on with this. The police might decide to come back. He stepped left into the sitting room, and stopped.

The place had been trashed.

In an instant, what should have been familiar was gone. What should have been comfortable was dispersed like smoke. He stepped over a broken picture frame which had been ground into the carpet. A large, dusty footprint showed across the broken glass. A man's shoe.

The photo was of Mrs Demelzer and Helen, smiling up at him, squinting against the sunlight. Nearby, a small vase was in fragments on the floor, and books had been pulled from their shelves, pages opened and scattered like wounded birds. The television lay on its face, the back ripped off, and several cushions were in tatters around the room, foam stuffing littering the carpet like brown soap suds.

The kitchen was the same. Drawers had been emptied, storage boxes up-ended and even the fridge and oven left gaping, like mouths opened in shock. He moved quickly through to the bathroom. The same treatment there, with a snowfall of talcum powder and pills to add to the disarray. He swallowed, remembering Helen's pride in her home. It hadn't mattered that she had spent more time out of it on jobs than inside; it was her sanctuary whenever she needed it. Or had been.

He'd deliberately left the bedroom until last. This had been Helen's inner sanctum. But it hadn't escaped the storm. The bed was ripped, the bedclothes flung across the floor, the wardrobe opened and gutted, with every piece of Helen's clothing tipped out, the shelves laid bare. Drawers lay tumbled upside down, some on the floor, others on the bed, showing the trail the intruder had created. Even the carpet had been peeled back.

Palmer noted the personal effects, the papers, the clothing, the soft and the delicate, the workaday and utilitarian, all tipped out into the light with no respect, no thought for the owner.

He felt the resurgence of a deep, intense anger.

He turned back to the living room. There was no point in looking further. If there had been anything to find, a search like this would have uncovered it.

He picked up the broken photo frame, and fragments of glass fell to the floor, tinkling like mournful music. The back had already been torn off, revealing the white reverse side of the photo. It was dated three years ago, in black ink. And a notation.

Christine D and me.

A slim blue book caught Palmer's eye. It was closed and had been placed on the edge of a coffee table, the positioning out of sync, almost, with the rest of the room. He picked it up and let it fall open.

It was an address book, divided alphabetically, two pages per tab. The tabs were made of coloured plastic. He flicked through it. There weren't many entries, mostly phone numbers and a few email addresses. Helen would probably have had more on her mobile than in here. Some entries had been crossed through in a deliberate, end-of-an-era style, some altered to reflect new numbers or address details.

His own name had a line drawn through from left to right. Not heavy, he noted. Not angry. Simply drawn through. With regret, maybe? He tried not to think about it, and wondered why the police hadn't taken the book with them.

Unless the man who'd trashed the place had found it afterwards.

On an impulse, he checked the G tab. There was one entry, followed by a familiar phone number and Riley's name. Underneath had been written: *Any contacts?*

Palmer stared at it. Helen must have been thinking of calling Riley about work. Johnson was right: she'd been getting restless. It explained why the Post-it note was in her car.

He was about to close the book when he noticed a gap in the pages. The D tab was gone, a ragged edge where the pages had been ripped out. He saw why. An envelope lay on the floor near the coffee table. A friendship card lay next to it, a simple coloured wash with a piece of verse. It was signed *Christine*.

Christine Demelzer.

His neck went cold. The card, the photo and the address book. The intruder had made the connection and removed the details.

In its place he had inserted a folded toffee wrapper to mark the page.

Long Cottage huddled silent and still in the darkness of Cotton Hill. Palmer stopped his car a hundred yards away and stepped out, allowing the door to click shut. He listened for night noises, sounds he was familiar with from hundreds of night-time surveillance jobs, hunched in his car or under cover, listening to nature all around him. All he heard was the wind through the trees and a motorbike engine clattering in the distance. No birds, no foxes. Nothing.

He let the minutes drift by, breathing in the smells carried on the air. A hint of wood smoke, the sweet aroma of cut vegetation, the faintest tang of cooked food.

He left the car and walked along the edge of the road. Once he was close to the house, he stepped on to the verge to muffle his footsteps, his shoes swishing faintly through the grass. He felt as if he was being watched, but pressed on, the feeling familiar. The night could play tricks no matter how experienced you were, and if you gave into it each time you'd do better to stay at home and do crossword puzzles.

He walked down the side of the cottage and stepped over the back gate, which was little more than knee high. The flagstones in the path felt uneven and partially overgrown. He trod carefully, easing his toes forward to feel for obstacles in his way.

The back door was locked. A pale glow of bluish light showed from inside, reflected through from the front room. Palmer walked round to the front and knocked softly on the door.

"Oh, it's you." Mrs Demelzer stood in the narrow gap. She looked wary but calm.

"Sorry," said Palmer softly. "I didn't mean to startle you. You really shouldn't answer your door to strangers without using the chain."

"You didn't startle me. And it's my door." The elderly woman stood aside to let him in. She sounded tired and her shoulders were slumped, as if she had been carrying a heavy load. "I heard about Helen," she said in explanation, and shuffled through to the kitchen. She switched on the kettle, then turned to face him, her eyes moist and accusing. She was rubbing her hands together in agitation, as if they itched. "You should have told me."

Palmer nodded. "I'm sorry. I wanted to, but I wasn't supposed to know."

She sat down at the table and signalled for him to do likewise. In the background, the kettle roared like an old steam engine. She toyed with a fold in her dress for a while, then looked at him with keen eyes.

"The police came. They said Helen's death was suspicious and it was being investigated. They wouldn't give me any details, though, and said I should avoid reading the papers. I think they were being kind. They asked me if I knew anything about Helen's recent movements. Her friends."

Palmer didn't say anything.

"I didn't tell them about the papers I sent you. Or your visit. Was that wise? I mean, I don't really know you. But you were Helen's friend and I know she liked you a lot. She told me not long ago that she was sorry it had ended. She said you made her smile."

The kettle clicked off noisily, a forced punctuation, and she got up to make the tea. Palmer felt as if he'd been kicked in the stomach.

She came back to the table with two mugs and set them down.

"Has anyone else been here?" Palmer asked. He had difficulty speaking calmly. A car rumbled by outside, and he felt the hairs on his neck stir.

"No. Not that I've seen. Why?"

On the drive down, he'd thought about what he could say to this woman. Whatever he told her would be alien to her world, as dark and unlikely as anything she could imagine, set against this picture-perfect cottage and the garden she tended so lovingly. But leaving her here was unthinkable, especially after the way Helen's flat had been turned upside down. Whoever had done that would eventually come here. It was the law of all search patterns: when all the most obvious possibilities have been covered, you start in on the rest.

And Mrs Demelzer's name was top of the list.

"Is there somewhere you could go for a few days?" he asked her. "A friend, perhaps?"

She was no fool. She gave him a knowing look. "Why? Is my life in danger? Something to do with Helen's death?"

"I don't know. It could be." He explained about Helen's flat and how whoever had searched the place now knew her address and what she looked like.

"Really?" She seemed incredulous. "But why would they come looking for me? It was only a greetings card."

"It was enough," he said. "I don't know what he was looking for, but he found the card and made the connection with your address book and the back of the photo."

"But what could I tell them? I don't know anything about Helen's work. It is about her work, I suppose?"

"I think so. She may have got involved in something dangerous. I'm trying to find out what it was."

Mrs Demelzer stood up, the tea forgotten. Her manner was suddenly brisk and decisive. Palmer stood, too. "I'd better go and pack a bag, hadn't I? If you can take me to my sister's house – she lives about ten miles away – I'll be safe enough there for a while. Even if they ask anyone around here, they won't be able to tell them anything." She walked towards the stairs, then stopped and turned to Palmer with a strange expression. "What are you going to do?"

Palmer took a deep breath. "Find them," he said honestly. "Find the people responsible. Who did it, and why. After that…" He shrugged enigmatically. "We'll see."

It seemed to be enough. Mrs Demelzer nodded and patted him on the arm with great tenderness. "I'm glad. I'm sure you'll do what you think best." She smiled with enormous sadness and went to pack.

22

"You've been up to something – I can tell." Riley walked into Palmer's office the following morning and found him at the window, staring into the street. "I rang you several times last night. Your mobile was off." Her voice was deliberately accusing; he'd left her out of the fun.

"I needed an early night."

"Palmer." Riley stared at him, eyes like flint. "You've never needed an early night in your life. Where were you?"

He told her about his visit to Helen's flat, the destruction he'd found and the connection between the card, the photo and the address book.

"What did you do?"

"I moved her out of harm's way. She's safe for now."

"Why didn't you tell me? I'd have helped you. I thought we were working together on this."

"We are. But it was easier to go to the flat by myself. If we'd walked into a police surveillance unit, you'd have been compromised as well. Alone, I had a halfway believable reason for being there."

"Maybe," she conceded grudgingly. "But next time, let me in."

He nodded and toed the carpet. "OK, boss. Sorry, boss."

"Apology accepted." Riley smiled, relieved to see he hadn't lost his sense of humour. Being absorbed in his work was one thing; Palmer without humour was worrying.

"But we do this my way," he insisted, leaving her no room for argument. "Our only line of connection is from Helen through the publishers in Sokhumi, through you to Richard Varley. It's there, but a bit ragged. I want to take a look at him first.

And Al-Bashir. If there's something brewing between them, we need to figure out what it is before we go blundering in." He looked sombre. "Especially if there's a connection with the Russian security services."

"Is that really likely?"

"Anything's possible. If it's big business, the FSB would take an interest. It could be you've walked into a straightforward propaganda exercise and Varley is being used without his knowledge to recruit contributors for that purpose. Helen's death could have been a mistake, or even be unconnected. We need to find out more."

"I can help with that," Riley volunteered. "Varley fancies his chances. I can ask him for another meeting. I'm sure he'll agree. I haven't actually said yes to the assignment yet, so it won't seem unreasonable to want to talk it over."

Palmer looked doubtful. "I'm not sure that's a good idea."

"Can you think of a better one?"

"No."

Before he could think up an argument, Riley took out her mobile and dialled the number on Varley's business card. When he answered, she said, "I'm in. But I need to talk over a couple of things. Any chance we can meet?"

"Of course!" Varley sounded almost relieved. "Great to hear from you. Sure, we can talk. How about lunch today?" He named a restaurant in Curzon Street.

"I'll see you there." She hung up and looked triumphantly at Palmer. "See? Easy."

The restaurant was busy when Riley arrived. Richard Varley was sitting at a discreet corner table at the back, sipping from a glass of water. He looked solid, respectable and at ease, the sophisticated businessman enjoying a lunch break. As Riley followed the head waiter between the other tables, she was aware that the man she had come to see was watching her, and was himself the subject of discreet attention from one or two female diners.

He stood as she approached, and held out a hand. His touch was warm, like before, and lingered just long enough without being overly familiar.

"Riley. Good to see you. May I offer you a drink?"

Riley asked for a gin and tonic and sat down. The head waiter took her order, then waited.

Varley ordered a filet steak and salad and looked innocently across at her. "I usually know what I want, so why waste time?"

Riley kept her eyes on the menu, ignoring the coded statement – if that's what it was. If he was trying to come on to her, he wouldn't be the first, and he clearly felt confident enough, as he had demonstrated at their first meeting. She chose salmon and handed the menu back to the waiter.

"I don't get enough time to relax," Varley said regretfully, and sipped his water. He gestured around at the restaurant. "This is a rare luxury for me, taking time out like this. Thank you for giving me the opportunity."

"My pleasure," said Riley. "But why so busy?"

"Well, our business is all about current events in a changing world. Like yours. Old news is no news. We have a crowded programme of features and specials, and there are lots of eager shareholders to satisfy, as well as a list of high-level subscribers waiting for their next copy."

"Shareholders in Georgia?"

Varley didn't miss a beat. He waved a vague hand. "Hardly any, actually. As I told you before, it's just a base – and it's cheap. We get the printing done at various facilities across Europe, wherever the price and production quality seems best. It keeps down the overheads and avoids local business taxes. It's a struggle sometimes, but we manage. Do you work with anyone?"

The question was so smoothly delivered, it almost threw her. She wondered if there was a reason for it other than to divert her away from asking about the company. She was grateful when her drink arrived. "Nobody special," she replied. "If I need help, I recruit it when I need to – like you." She took a sip. "It keeps down the overheads."

"Touché." He dipped his head in acknowledgement. "Tell me about yourself. Any family?"

"No. I'm what's referred to as a singleton – although I loathe the word. I think it implies a lack of free choice."

He raised an eyebrow. "And are you – single, I mean?"

"At the moment, yes."

"By choice?"

The question was reasonable, but Riley wondered if it was genuine. Or did he already know all there was to know about her background? That prompted thoughts about John Mitcheson, and she shook her head. Now wasn't the time. Instead she focussed on the present, remembering that corporations could find out about prospective employees at the push of a button. Christ, Palmer, she thought wildly, you're making me paranoid. The man's only being pleasant. She wondered where Palmer was and what he was doing. He'd said something about going back to Pantile House for another look round, but Palmer had a habit of not always doing what he'd talked about.

"Riley?" Varley bent his head and smiled, catching her unawares.

"Sorry. There was someone once. We drifted apart."

"It happens." Richard studied her over the rim of his glass. "Where is he now?"

"In the States somewhere. We lost touch."

He nodded sympathetically. "I was married once, but it didn't work out. I spent more time away than I did at home. It wasn't fair on her."

"Where is home?"

"All over. I stopped having papers delivered a long time ago. What's the Paul Young song? *Wherever I Lay my Hat*?"

"I know what that's like. So where is your wife now?"

"In Paris somewhere. We lost touch." He smiled at returning her own line, then said, "I'm pleased you're going to help us with this assignment, Riley. I hate to talk work on such a pleasant occasion, but it would be nice to get it out of the way."

Just as it was getting interesting, too, Riley thought. "That's fine. I just wanted to find out a bit more about the line you want to take on Al-Bashir. He's an interesting man."

"But a dangerous one in court. You read the briefing notes?"

"Yes. How reliable are they? Only, I think you should know, I like to do my own research. It's a thing I have."

He appeared unmoved. "So you should. Although, as you've probably seen, the notes I provided are very comprehensive. I doubt there's anything in there that your own research won't also uncover."

"Quite possibly. So far. But how personal is this meant to be?"

His smile faded slightly. "I don't follow."

"For a business profile, there seems to be a lot of personal stuff about his wife. Is that really necessary?"

Just for a second, Riley could have sworn his genial demeanour wavered a fraction. A hint of a frown touched his brow and he flicked at a crumb of bread on the edge of the tablecloth. "Like I said at our first meeting, we don't.dish the dirt, but if there is any… And who says it's not relevant in this case?" He sighed and waved a vague hand. "I have no brief for Al-Bashir either way, believe me. But if you consider his background, and where he's taking his bid for the network licence, there's almost certainly an interest in how his private life may affect his business affairs."

"In what way?"

"Well, it's not that important to many westerners, I guess, but there are some who think that anything unseemly in his background might have an impact on his backers and local sensitivities."

"Why should they care? It's business."

"True. But it's more fragile than that. If he gets far enough along the route and actually wins the licence, then has to back out for any reason – say, someone with the power to pull the plug doesn't like something about his background – it will leave a massive hole in the project with nobody to fill it. The cost of mounting, presenting, then losing the bid will be considerable. Another bidder might find it impossible to take his place. It could torpedo the whole project for years."

"So you're saying it's better to get the skeletons out of the cupboard right from the outset?"

Varley shrugged. "Why not?" He leaned forward, suddenly serious. "Riley, this entire project has huge implications for the consumer market right across Eastern Europe. It will liberate vast resources for the man in the street, as well as small businesses and governments. You know how the commercial sector has exploded in the Indian sub-continent and in China; this is just an extension of that. What they don't need is a bid that falls at the last hurdle. Because if that happens, it'll be dead for a long, long time to come."

"But it could fail for all sorts of other reasons," she pointed out. "A market crash, ill-health, a change of government somewhere."

He tilted his head from side to side. "Not really. The various governments are right behind it; the consumers definitely want it to go ahead. And there's the technology and science out there to make it happen. If it goes through – either with Al-Bashir at the helm or one of the others – it will be a huge success. But only if nobody rocks the boat *after* the bid is awarded." He lifted his shoulders and smiled, as if suddenly trying to take the heat out of the conversation. "Hell, what do I know? We're only watching the game, not out there playing."

"No," Riley agreed. "We're not." She wondered why the sudden change in tone. Had he realised he was arguing too fiercely?

"Write what you see, Riley. It's all we can ask."

"Even if it turns out bad?"

"Bad for who? Al-Bashir, maybe. Or even the other bidders. I think we have to wait and see." He looked up as the wine waiter approached. "Now, how about another drink?"

Frank Palmer watched from a café fifty yards down the street as Riley and her companion stepped out of the restaurant after their lunch. The area was busy, providing ample cover for him to watch without running the risk of being seen.

The publisher was tall, making him easy to follow in the crowd. As they walked towards the kerb, he placed his hand on Riley's back. The gesture looked natural without appearing over-familiar. A taxi stopped nearby, and Riley climbed aboard. Varley leaned in briefly, then the vehicle moved off, leaving him standing on the pavement for a moment, before turning and walking in the direction of Piccadilly.

Palmer put down his cup and set off after him.

23

Riley climbed the stairs at Copnor Business Publications and found David Johnson still looking confused and harassed in equal measure. She suspected it was his default position. There was no sign of Emerald.

"Hello again," he said with a faint smile. His expression could have been welcoming or wary, it was hard to tell. He cleared some papers off a chair for her. "How can I help?"

"I need to pick your brains," Riley told him, "about the East European telecoms market." After talking to Richard Varley, she had found a number of questions vying for attention, and David Johnson might be the easiest person to provide the answers – or the name of someone who could. She had called him earlier and got him to agree to a meeting.

"What about it?"

"Who's in it, who's trying to get in... what's the potential market size. Stuff like that."

He blinked and puffed out his cheeks, then plonked himself down behind his desk. "Well, the potential market size is huge. Vast. And that's down to the latest round of talks going on."

"Go on."

"Over the last couple of years, there's been a move to put together a loose federation of independent states – a free trade sector modelled on the EU but confined to the former Soviet states and some emerging republics."

"Sounds like trade protection."

"It's a response to the enlargement of the EU, and the drain of their skilled workforce to the west. They're not exactly pulling up the drawbridge, which would be bad for trade, but they are trying to draw local demarcation lines to keep out the commercial rabble."

"That's a tall order. It would be like holding back fog."

"Not the way they see it. The telecoms industry uses a saturation approach, banging up masts everywhere, with competing shops and networks in every town, all to get ten-year-old kids carrying mobiles and texting each other. And what does it do? In a poor country, it starts to direct the local, then the regional economy. Commercial property prices go up, land prices rise and soon everyone is looking for the next cheap deal or the latest cool mobile phone. Crime follows like night after day."

"That's a bit simplistic, isn't it?"

"I'm not so sure." Johnson ruffled his hair with his fingertips. "Look at other economies around the world and you'll see the same thing. It's the thin edge of the wedge. Sure, we're happy with our mobile market because we grew into it. Your average Eastern European – and I'm talking about way, way east – still hasn't seen it."

"I'd have thought some competition would be good for keeping prices down."

"They don't share that view. Remember, we're only a few years down the road from communism and state control. The people with the clout reckon there's only one way of keeping the commercial hordes from ransacking their economies and upsetting the status quo."

Riley thought she saw where Johnson was heading. "Go on."

"What they're planning is to allow a single chosen operator to have sole access to the satellite technology, and effectively bar every other provider. They could do it, too, with the new LEO system."

"What's that?"

"Low Earth Orbit. Mobile phone communication requires LEO satellites to function at their best. They circle the earth very fast – every ninety minutes or so – and feed off lots of other satellites for their signals and coverage. The new federation have just put a new satellite system in place. It's called Batnev. It'srumoured to have the capability of piggybacking signals off far more satellites than ever before – in effect, borrowing capacity from other systems – which means much lower operating costs."

"And lower costs to the users?"

"Exactly. They're working on the theory that it's better to have a million people paying peanuts, but right on time and growing, rather than a smaller number of high-value subscribers struggling to pay their bills and defaulting."

"I see."

"And they'll get them because the extra satellite capacity means they can cover a much larger region than ever before."

"Will it work?"

"They think so – and they reckon they could ring-fence the entire region if they chose to."

"Which would mean…?"

"Locking out every other provider."

Riley stared at him. If Johnson was right, it would give the selected provider one of the biggest consumer markets on the planet. And no competition.

"So who's likely to be in the running?"

He chuckled dryly. "You name a provider, they'll be chucking their hats in the ring for this one. There's already a couple of quiet mergers going on as a result."

"How about anyone who isn't a provider?"

"What – investors, you mean?"

"Yes."

He nodded. "Possibly. They'll need heavy backing, though, because the up-front investment will be considerable."

"How about Al-Bashir?"

Johnson nodded. "Definitely. He's already got a share of the Batnev system. It's not his normal field, but he's got the investors to go with him."

"Like who?"

"Middle Eastern, mostly. They're very traditional, but not averse to risk. And they've got lots of oil money sloshing around."

Riley suddenly saw what Richard Varley had been driving at. "Is Al-Bashir a Muslim?"

"Yes – as are his backers. Their investment rules are a bit rigid, but bringing communications to the masses will appeal to them. The one thing he can't afford to do is upset the more fundamental elements."

"Are there any local investors in the running?"

"Certainly. They've got the money and the interest, even if they're based abroad."

"What's in it for the various states in this so-called federation?"

He shrugged. "Control. They'd have control of the technology release, and I'm pretty sure they'd control prices and even the manufacture of the equipment. With command of the network, they could control all other electronic industries in the region."

"But that's frightening. What does Moscow think of it?"

He pursed his lips. "I gather they're not bothered. They'll get a spin-off benefit, anyway... and Putin's probably happy because it's spitting in the eye of western conglomerates."

"So what would it mean for the eventual winner?"

Johnson puffed out his cheeks again. "God knows. They'd have to give a lot away to the various controlling state bodies, but in return they'd have a monopoly, with no threat of competition and the backing of the regional governments. Most analysts reckon they can't lose."

"Apart from having the federation peering over their shoulders."

"True. But they'll still make a killing. I wouldn't mind having shares in it." He looked at Riley and tilted his head to one side. "You know something, don't you? You've been researching–" He sat up as if he'd been stung. "Christ – *oligarchs*! Is this connected with Helen's death?"

But Riley was already getting to her feet. The more she heard about it, the more she was beginning to see the astonishingly weak link in Al-Bashir's grand plans: his wife, Asiyah. If the rumours were true, it brought to mind David Johnson's earlier comment about his backers.

"The one thing he can't afford to do is upset the more fundamental elements."

Once outside, Riley ducked into a quiet doorway and rang Natalya Fisher. She was lucky to catch her between lectures.

"Miss Gavin," the professor greeted her, coughing wetly. "How is that nice young man you were with?"

"Palmer? He's fine, thank you." It was a reminder that, once again, she didn't know where Frank Palmer was. It was something he'd again managed to avoid telling her.

"How can I help you?"

"The oligarchs we were talking about," said Riley. "Could they out-bid someone like Kim Al-Bashir in a bidding war?"

"Al-Bashir? Al-Bashir the shopkeeper?" Natalya laughed. It produced another coughing fit. When she recovered, she apologised and said, "Of course – if they wanted to."

"But his financial backers have deep pockets."

"So do Levels One and Two, Miss Gavin. They could buy him without even noticing... for, what you call it – small change." She clearly didn't like the man.

"And Level Three?"

"Not so easy. I suppose they could join forces with others. But they would then run into their main competitors."

"The other two levels."

"Precisely. They are like fleas on a dog, these people. The pecking order has its rules." She chuckled. "I am mixing metaphors a little, I think. But people who break the rules rarely survive."

"But if in doing so, they go home with the school prize?"

"Then you have a different situation, Miss Gavin. Then all the rules are changed."

24

Over the years Frank Palmer had followed more suspects than he cared to think about. He'd tracked men and women across crowded city centres and deserted suburbs; through colourful shopping malls and dreary industrial landscapes; he'd followed them through open territory and down arrow-straight motorways – even, on occasion, along cold, wind-swept canals and waterfronts. Following Varley through London proved simple by comparison. At least, on the surface.

After waving Riley off, Varley walked for a while, his long stride easy and assured, a man working off a leisurely lunch before heading back to the office. He seemed to have time to spare, wandering into one or two clothes shops, but emerging without any noticeable purchases. By the time he reached Grosvenor Square an hour had gone by, and Palmer was beginning to think he was wasting his time. Maybe he was a publisher after all, enjoying some free time. Then Varley seemed to come to a decision and flagged down a passing cab.

Palmer did the same and told the driver that he was on a company initiative test, and promised a generous tip if he didn't lose the other vehicle.

"No problem," said the driver disinterestedly, and concentrated on the road ahead.

Varley's vehicle turned north, cutting across Oxford Street towards Marylebone. The journey took a brief turn along the crowded chaos of Marylebone Road, then turned left, skirting Regent's Park and picking up speed. Palmer told the driver to hang back. The leading cab eventually turned north-east, and finally pulled in near a row of shops in Camden Town.

Palmer told his driver to pull over too. Ahead of them, Varley paid off his cab and crossed the pavement, stopping for a moment to look round before entering a glass-fronted shop.

Palmer handed the driver his money and dodged across the street, heading for a café on the other side. He turned once he was through the door and studied the premises where Varley had disappeared.

The shop was called MailBox Services, with a post-box motif on the fascia. It was a post franchise, where boxes of varying sizes could be rented by the day, week or month. The windows were plastered with special offer stickers and a pin-board of personal ads, but Palmer could just about make out the interior. It had two rows of steel boxes, one on each side and a counter at the back, topped by a glass and aluminium security frame.

Varley was standing just inside the door, watching the street.

"You want something?"

Palmer turned. A jowly woman with a shock of coarse hair was scowling at him from behind the café counter, a dishcloth in one hand. Steam was hissing into the air around her head, drifting over a wobbly stack of cups and saucers and misting the glass on a battered display case holding a selection of tired-looking pastries. There was nobody else in the place, which he took to be a bad sign.

He ordered coffee but gave the pastries a miss on health grounds, and chose a seat back from the window, from where he could watch Varley without being seen. He thought at first that the publisher was waiting for someone. But it was soon obvious that he was actually watching his back, scanning the street and the faces of passers-by. Where he was standing, he was masked by a series of posters, and would be virtually invisible to anyone coming along the pavement in his wake.

Palmer felt a familiar drumming deep in his chest. Normal people didn't do this. But then normal people didn't have the training or the need. Was Richard Varley unusually cautious – or something else entirely?

Eventually Varley stepped back from the window and joined a thickset man in a jumper and slacks at the rear of the shop. Palmer assumed he was the owner. They were looking down at something, and Palmer realised that they were discussing a large brown cardboard box by the counter. Judging by the amount of gesticulating going on, Varley wasn't happy. He bent and tore at the cardboard, and took out what looked like a magazine. He checked the cover before flicking through it in an animated fashion.

After a while, the owner turned to the back and shouted something. A woman appeared and both men left the shop. They walked thirty yards along the pavement and disappeared inside a small restaurant. Varley was carrying the magazine he'd taken from the box. The two men sat down and a waitress approached with a pad.

Palmer paid up and left the café, turning left and walking a hundred yards before crossing to the other side. This would bring him back to MailBox Services without having to pass the restaurant where the two men were sitting.

As he stepped inside, he heard the sound of a buzzer at the back. The shop was empty. He looked around and spotted a security camera high on the back wall. It would have a clear view of the shop and all of the mail boxes. That's if anyone was looking.

The woman appeared, feet scuffing heavily on the tiled floor. She bellied up to the counter and eyed him with a tired look.

Palmer was trying not to look at the box on the floor, but from the corner of his eye, he caught a splash of colour inside the tear Varley had made.

"I need to rent a box," he explained. "Do you have a price list?"

The woman stared at him with a blank expression. He repeated the question, and when she still didn't seem to get it, he pointed to the boxes on either side and waved some money in front of her. "How much?" he said.

The penny finally dropped and she began to look. As she ducked her head below the counter, Palmer surreptitiously nudged the large box with his knee. It felt heavy. He nudged it again and something shifted inside. More magazines, at a guess. Lots more.

"Moment," the woman murmured, and disappeared through the door at the rear.

Palmer leaned down and slid a magazine from the box, coughing loudly to cover the scrape of cardboard. It was a copy of *East European Trade*, but with a different cover image from the one Riley had shown him. There was also a stapled pack of labels on A4 sheets just inside the lid. He slid it out. The first dozen sheets bore names and addresses spread right around Europe. Most of them seemed to be in capital cities, many with PO box numbers. The majority of the addresses on the remaining sheets were in the Middle East and Asia; Palmer spotted Egypt, Dubai, Jordan, Iran, Syria, Pakistan and various others. The names of the recipients meant nothing, although he spotted the word *Minister* among many of the titles.

He weighed the magazine in his hand, recalling what Natalya Fisher had said about the circulation run. *"Two hundred copies – maybe three. But not more."*

Yet this box and the list with it contained easily twice that number. Was there a reason for increasing the print run? An increase in business, perhaps? Unlikely.

Someone had scribbled in heavy print across the top of the list: *Issue 1572 & 1573.* The magazines in the box were issue 1572. Palmer replaced the list and slid the magazine inside his jacket just as the front door opened and the buzzer sounded.

It was the shop owner and Richard Varley. They stood in the doorway, staring at him.

25

As soon as Riley got home, she checked the phone directory and got through to Al-Bashir's office. It was a risky venture she was about to undertake, but without it she would always be one step back from finding out some important facts about the man. And sometimes the full-frontal approach worked where guile didn't.

"I'm sorry," the receptionist purred, as soon as she heard Riley's request. "But Mr Al-Bashir is very busy and requires advance notice of interviews. I'll put you through to our media office – I'm sure they'll accommodate you."

"Please don't," Riley purred back. "Tell him it's about his bid for the Batnev network licences in Eastern Europe. I have information which I think means his bid will fail. I'll call back in fifteen minutes."

She called in ten. The woman coolly told her that Mr Al-Bashir would see her the following morning at nine o'clock. She made a note of Riley's name but asked for no other details.

"What you want?" The owner of MailBox Services seemed surprised to find anyone in the shop. He was unshaven and overweight, and in stark contrast to the impeccably dressed man by his side his clothes were uncared-for and worn.

"A bit of service would be a start," Palmer replied. If they'd seen him take the magazine, they weren't saying anything. Which was odd. "Are you the manager of this place?"

"Yes. Koutsatos." The man looked wary, as if he'd suddenly realised that he might have jumped to the wrong conclusion and could be facing someone in an official capacity. Palmer was tempted to play it that way, but there was a risk the man might ask for some proof of identity.

"Well, Mr Koutsatos, I'm interested in renting multiple boxes. I came in looking for some prices. But your assistant doesn't seem to have the details. Maybe I'll get more satisfaction somewhere else." He moved away from the counter. As he did so, he came face to face with Richard Varley. The man was taller than Palmer and broader, and up close exuded a strong aura of vitality and power. His eyes made a brief assessment of Palmer's face, then he stepped aside without a word.

"Wait." Koutsatos reached over to the pile of leaflets and snatched one up. He handed it to Palmer. "I am sorry. She not my usual girl. You come back soon."

Palmer nodded at him and walked over to the doorway. "If you say so." He stepped outside and walked away. As he looked back, he saw Koutsatos frantically manhandling the box of magazines through to the rear of the shop, watched by a grim-faced Richard Varley.

Palmer waited a hundred yards down the road, having snagged another cab. It was fifteen minutes before Varley emerged. But instead of hailing a cab he began walking south.

It left Palmer in a familiar dilemma: either stay in his cab and risk the vehicle being spotted, or hit the pavement himself and hope Varley hadn't played clever and had a vehicle waiting to pick him up a hundred yards down the street.

He chose the latter and paid off the driver. There was still a risk he could be spotted, but Palmer had confidence in his own ability to stay out of sight.

Fifteen minutes later, during which Varley took a couple of elementary detours but made no obvious signs of having spotted him, Palmer knew with absolute certainty where he was going. Sure enough, Varley turned off a narrow street and walked across the car park and through the front entrance of Pantile House.

Whatever business Varley had in the office block did not last long. After five minutes he emerged again, and made his way out to Eversholt Street, where he hailed a cab.

Palmer followed, the procession turning west towards Marylebone, before cutting off south and eventually stopping outside a smart hotel close to Lancaster Gate, across from Hyde Park. Palmer watched as Varley paid off his driver.

But something about the scene wasn't right.

Palmer paid off his own cab and walked towards the park, pretending to be on his mobile. As he turned to allow a couple of nannies and their charges to pass him on a narrow section of pavement, he glanced back to check Varley's progress.

What he saw gave him an instinctive jolt of unease.

Two men were standing outside the hotel. Varley passed almost between them, but they showed no interest in him other than a brief nod. Yet they were scrutinising everyone else very carefully.

To Palmer, it was an eerily familiar scene. Both men wore suits and were pretending to be deep in conversation, friends, perhaps, who had encountered each other by chance. But he knew a security detail when he saw one. The men looked fit and capable, and by their bearing were probably former military personnel. Blond hair and high cheekbones pointed towards origins in Scandinavia or somewhere further east.

As Palmer watched, another man came out of the hotel entrance and walked over to a gleaming black four-wheel drive at the kerb. He tried the door, which was locked, and nodded in satisfaction. He was shorter than the other two and heavier, but clearly of the same mould. As he stood there, three black youths walked past the front of the hotel, eyeing the four-wheel drive. The newcomer ignored them. Seconds later, an older man in dreadlocks and a Rasta hat ambled past, carrying a white kitchen-style jacket slung across his arm. None of the security men gave him a glance.

After a few moments, the third man seemed to lose interest and walked away. He passed the other two and nodded briefly before disappearing round the corner.

Palmer continued walking, certain that brief instructions had just been passed between the men. Of one thing he was growing more convinced: whoever or whatever Richard Varley was, it was doubtful publishing was his first profession. If it was, why would he require a security detail at the hotel where he was staying?

He decided to stay with him. So far he had nothing definite to show for his labours, yet all his inner alarm bells were ringing. The problem was, Varley now knew what Palmer looked like. He needed someone else to take over and get close to him and his men. Someone anonymous.

He knew just the man for the job.

26

Isleworth had changed little since Palmer had last visited the area – this street, in fact – nearly a year ago. Still busy, still wearing that slightly run-down air of too much movement and too little care, it seemed to slump wearily in the evening gloom as if exhausted after a long, hard day.

Palmer's attention was fixed on a Victorian-style villa across the street. A low retaining wall wearing drunken coping stones fronted a neglected garden, which held a rusted motorcycle frame and a discarded kitchen unit with battered fibreboard sides swollen and distorted by rain. A set of broken steps led up to the front door, and the windows were draped carelessly with grey net curtains. A line of buttons and name slots sat on one side of the door.

Palmer checked his watch. So far there had been no sign of movement at the house, and no sight of the man he'd come to see. But he couldn't sit here all evening.

Just as he was about to cross the road for a closer look, a car pulled into the kerb. It was a plain black Mondeo with a cab licence plate on the rear skirt.

The driver got out and walked up the front steps with a spring in his step, scanning the street on either side. He made it look casual but Palmer knew it was anything but. A lifetime of staying one step ahead of dubious friends, unpredictable enemies and the eager reach of the law had given Ray Szulu a set of habits too ingrained to break. He disappeared inside and closed the door.

Palmer left his car and quickly crossed the street. He knew Szulu's flat had a view over the front, and that he would probably look out of the window as a matter of habit as soon as he got in. He ran up the steps and tried the door. It was locked, but ill-fitting, the wood tired and loose. He grasped the central knocker to keep it still and pushed with his shoulder, concentrating on the centre of the door. The wood creaked once, then the lock clicked and the door swung open. Inside, the air was muggy, the atmosphere heavy and dark. He listened for sounds of movement, then walked up the stairs and knocked on the door of 3A.

"Yeah, wha-?" The door opened and the familiar face registered instant recognition. And dismay.

"Hello, Ray," said Palmer, smiling genially. "How's it hanging? I was in the area and thought I'd pop round for tea and cakes."

"No way!" Szulu started to close the door, but Palmer slammed it back, propelling him into the room.

"Not nice," Palmer chided him, and followed him inside, closing the door behind him. He glanced around the room. It was furnished just as he remembered it, with large cushions, a sofa, a couple of armchairs and a CD player, mercifully silent. He remembered how Szulu liked to play music very loudly, even when he had visitors. "Have you decorated since I was last here? It's not very ethnic, if you don't mind me saying so." He was taking a deliberate swipe at Szulu's ability to dip in and out of his Rasta roots whenever it suited him. The man wasn't quite as dumb as he liked to pretend.

"What the fuck do you want, Palmer?" Szulu was rubbing his arm and wincing, his dreadlocks forming a curtain across the side of his face. "You can't come in here like this – I'll call the cops."

"Of course you will. And they'll come running because they so value your safety. Now we've got that out of the way, how about a cup of tea? I'm parched." He turned and found his way through to a small kitchenette. It was surprisingly neat and tidy, with evidence that Szulu knew his way around both kitchen and supermarket.

Palmer filled the kettle and switched it on.

"So," he continued, affably, "how's the driving job?" He turned to face Szulu, who was looking at him as if he'd grown horns. "More importantly, how's the arm?"

"Go screw yourself," muttered Szulu, his voice sliding into a soft Jamaican twang. "And stay out of me place, man. You trespassin'."

Palmer gave him a pained look. "See, that's what I mean. Now you've gone all Bob Marley on me. I only came round to offer you some gainful employment. You haven't gone all fussy about who you take money from, have you? Oh, of course, not – you drove for Lottie Grossman, didn't you? Remember – that wicked old bitch who tried to kill Riley and me?" He turned back to the kitchen and made two mugs of tea, and brought them back into the living room.

Szulu was scowling at the memory of his last encounter with Palmer and Riley, but took his mug and sat down. "What do you mean, employment? You need a driver or a heavy – what?" He'd lost the twang.

"What I need is someone who's street-savvy. Someone who can melt into the shadows and move like a panther. Someone who knows all the moves. A surveillance job, in other words." Palmer took a seat and sipped his tea, waiting for Szulu to catch on and show some interest. "Know anyone like that?"

"You're taking the piss, right?" Szulu looked offended. "I can do that. How much we talking about?"

"A hundred. Cash. Shouldn't take more than half a day. No risks."

Szulu looked suspicious. "Like there's no catch, man. How do I know it ain't gonna turn tribal? Last time I had you and that Gavin woman near me, I got shot, remember? And what was that army nut's name – Mitcheson?" He went back to massaging his arm and glanced towards the door as if the assailant he was referring to was about to come charging into the room.

"Mitcheson's in the States," Palmer told him. "He's got better things to do than follow you around." Szulu had earned his bullet wound after threatening Riley Gavin with a .22 calibre automatic. Her then boyfriend, John Mitcheson, a former army officer, had appeared and calmly shot Szulu with his own gun. Szulu evidently still hadn't quite come to terms with the fact that making threats sometimes brought unforeseen consequences.

"Oh." He seemed to relax a little. "He comin' back?"

Palmer waggled a hand in a 'maybe/maybe not' gesture. "The jury's still out." He smiled. "I could bring Riley round if you like, though. She's joined a gun club since you last met. She uses a .357 Magnum."

Szulu nearly gagged on his tea. "Don't joke, man. That ain't funny. I already apologised to her for that stuff."

"Don't worry, I'm teasing." Palmer looked at him. "Are you on, then?"

Szulu shrugged. "Sure. Easy. But why you being so generous with the dough? Who's the target?"

Palmer rolled his eyes. "Subject, Ray. We refer to it as the subject. A target is something you shoot at. Or someone," he added pointedly.

"Subject, whatever. Who is it? And why the dosh? You could've got me to do this for free."

"Because it's personal." Palmer's face was suddenly serious. "And I believe in paying for talent."

Szulu's eyes widened and he tucked away the compliment for later. Having a man like Palmer calling him talent was rare. But he stayed with the look. He remembered all too clearly the last time he'd seen Palmer with that expression on his face. The man was scary when he got going, and prepared to go through anything. The last time, it had been a psychotic south London gang leader named Ragga Pearl and some former spy gone bad that had set him off. Him and Gavin, he had to admit, they made a good team.

"So who is this person?"

"They. They're a very careful bunch."

"Yeah?" Szulu shrugged again and stared into his tea. He wanted to change his mind and say he was too busy driving, that he'd got a long distance trip to do and couldn't spare the time. But a part of him wouldn't allow it. It wasn't the money, either; a hundred wasn't that good, even for a half day. He wondered about the subject. He knew it couldn't be Ragga Pearl, who was currently a guest of Her Majesty in Wormwood Scrubs. But he'd bet it was someone in the same mould. Otherwise, Palmer wouldn't be interested. In spite of that, he was intrigued. "How d'you mean, careful?"

"The subject's got a security detail on him, twenty-four-seven. He's also what we in the profession call 'risk-aware'. Take street-wise and ramp it up a few notches. He's not the sort of man to treat lightly."

"OK. Sounds cool. What's he do, this bloke?" Szulu took another sip of tea, relaxing at the idea of doing something more interesting for a change than driving people around London.

Palmer took a long time before replying. He seemed to be weighing his words with care. Then he said calmly, "There's a possibility he's connected to the Russian Mafia."

Szulu's tea erupted all over his face.

Palmer approached the side of Pantile House and stopped, checking the area for any signs of movement. He glanced at his watch. It was past nine in the evening and the streets were quiet. He'd waited for ten minutes already but seen nobody. From what Mark Chase had said about the building, there was no twenty-four-hour security watch, and he'd already noted and discounted the position of the nearest street cameras.

He stepped over to one of the louvred vents at ground floor level and gently removed some of the slats, placing them to one side. The opening was covered by a protective mesh grill, and beyond that more slats which could be closed like internal shutters. He waited for a truck or a bus to go by, and under cover of the engine noise, placed his foot against the mesh and kicked it in. After removing the internal slats he slid inside, then replaced a couple of the outer slats to cover signs of his entry.

He waited two minutes, ears taking in the hum of the heating and air-conditioning system, eyes adjusting gradually to the atmosphere. He was standing at the end of a passageway, lit every few feet by a low-wattage overhead lamp. The air was stale and dusty, with the dull lifelessness of a space largely unused and forgotten.

He moved along the passageway away from the vent. At the far end he hoped to find the base of the lift shaft and a stairway to the ground floor, rising somewhere near to the reception area. He skirted a tangle of old Dexion racking, and adjacent to it a pallet of paper bags, their gutted bellies spilling heavy grey dust, remnants of a maintenance programme which, judging by the lumps of solidified cement, had been called off long ago. Everything around it was grey and still. His shoes crunched faintly with the gritty feel of an unswept floor, and he tried to put his weight on the edges of his feet to minimise the noise. He breathed through his mouth, straining for the sound of movement in the gloom.

A fresh pool of light from one of the lamps revealed a puddle of water across the floor. Above it, a dark mould showed in the concrete of the roof support, with another drip ready to fall.

He skirted the puddle, stepping past a pile of empty cement bags, and approached a large square section of aluminium casing. It seemed to grow out of the concrete floor, stretching to the ceiling and eating into the roof of the tunnel like a square, hungry snake. The casing at floor level was scarred and battered, where careless negotiation of the narrow gap with unwieldy objects had left its mark.

He moved past it to the stairway and checked the layout. A steel door stood at the top of the steps. He turned the handle with delicate care, just enough to check that it was unlocked. It was. He left it and went to check out the lift shaft. But here his luck ran out; the dimensions of the shaft were too narrow and there was no handy inspection ladder to provide an alternative means of entry.

He walked back along the passage to the vent where he had come in, and slid back out. Carefully replacing the slats and the mesh, he walked away into the dark.

27

Riley felt strange entering the marble and gilt portals of Al-Bashir's flagship store in London's West End without shopping in mind. She stepped out of the early morning sunlight and was instantly absorbed by the warm glow of strategic lighting and soft music, and the near-hallowed atmosphere of one of Europe's best-known stores.

She approached the information desk, where a young woman in the company's sleek designer uniform and an ergonomic head-set was checking a computer screen. She was surrounded by a bank of phones and monitors with, Riley guessed, a panic button somewhere close to hand below the counter top. There were relatively few people about, and the day had clearly not yet begun in earnest in the field of luxury retail goods.

"I have an appointment with Mr Al-Bashir," said Riley.

The young woman smiled and glanced at the screen. "Of course. Miss Gavin, yes? I won't keep you." She touched the screen with her fingertips and spoke softly into her mouthpiece.

Riley looked around her. There was no overt sign of the Al-Bashir security system in sight, but she didn't doubt for a moment that it was in place. She wondered if she wasn't sticking her head unnecessarily into the lion's mouth. It would hardly be the first time. Coming here could be a huge mistake if Al-Bashir's fierce reputation was as it was rumoured to be.

A door clicked open in one wall, and she turned to see a tall man in a dark grey suit appear. He came over to her.

"Miss Gavin? My name is Koenig. I'm the security manager. Would you come this way?"

Riley followed him through the door and found herself in a small lobby. As the door closed behind them, Koenig turned and held out his hand. "May I check your bag, please? It's just a precaution."

Riley allowed him to take her shoulder bag. He produced a slim scanning wand and ran it over the outside of the bag, then flicked through the contents. His actions were precise and practised. He had the short hairstyle of a military man and the angular face and build of someone accustomed to keeping fit, and she guessed he was in his early forties. He reminded her of Palmer, only bigger and with a less obvious charm.

"That's fine. Thank you." He returned the bag.

"I'm surprised you don't do body searches, too," she said coolly. "Not that it's an invitation."

He smiled without humour and gestured at a metal frame-work surrounding the door they had just passed through. "No need. You were screened as you came through." He turned towards a small lift on the other side of the lobby. "We'll take this up to the third floor."

The lift was fast and smooth, and brought them to a narrow corridor lined with thick carpets and soft lighting. Koenig led Riley towards a set of glossy double doors. He ushered her through and into a long room furnished with a twin line of chairs around a boardroom-style table. More discreet lighting reflected off the polished wood, and a rich aroma of coffee hung in the air.

'Kim' Al-Bashir was sitting on the far side of the table.

He had a cup of coffee at his right hand, and looked chubbier in the flesh than Riley expected, with full cheeks and his hair cut close to the scalp. He was dressed in a crisp white shirt and a grey suit with a discreet check, and wore a diamond-pattern tie with a neat pin behind the knot.

Riley was immediately struck by how unremarkable he looked. For a man who always loomed larger than life in the headlines with news of his latest business deals, he appeared almost insignificant in the flesh.

But there was no mistaking the aura which sprang off him when he looked up.

Al-Bashir nodded at Koenig, who stepped forward and dropped a fan of papers on to the bare table.

The dramatic nature of the gesture wasn't lost on Riley. She stepped forward and looked down at them. They were photocopies of a selection of her past work going back several years.

"As you can see, Miss Gavin," said Al-Bashir evenly, "we know all about you." His voice was surprisingly soft.

Riley felt her heart thumping. The search and screening downstairs, the security guard at her shoulder, the sombre atmosphere, the display of control, power and now personal knowledge – it was all intended to dominate and intimidate.

"I'm impressed," she said, and spotted a typo on the top sheet. God, she thought, how humiliating. It was the first paper she'd worked for, long since closed down, where the desire to deliver local news fast had often taken priority over presentation.

"What do you want?" Al-Bashir twirled his cup with a faint squeak from the elegant bone china.

"What will happen if you win the Batnev network licence?"

Al-Bashir lifted his eyebrows in mild surprise. "Is that all you wish to know? My media department could have answered that question with a simple phone call." He frowned. "You said you had some information for me."

"I do." Riley breathed easily.

"Really. Then name your price." Al-Bashir already sounded bored.

"I'm sorry?"

"You have information to sell. Name your price and I'll judge if I wish to pay."

Riley felt a stirring of anger. He was treating her like a moneygrubber. Maybe it was because of the people he usually dealt with.

"You think that's what it's about?" she said. "Money?"

He shrugged. "That is what most people want. If you are different, then please say so." He glanced at Koenig, and Riley sensed the meeting was about to be cut short.

"I have reason to believe," she said, "that reports about your wife are shortly to be circulated in the foreign press."

Several heartbeats went by before Al-Bashir responded. "There are often reports against me," he growled. "How do you know this?"

"I've seen the notes."

"Notes? What do they say, these... notes?"

The door behind Riley opened and she realised Koenig had slipped out. She hadn't seen a signal from Al-Bashir; maybe he'd been summoned by thought control.

She took a calming breath before speaking. "They concern issues of a personal nature." Riley chose her words with care. Saying something to trigger Al-Bashir's legendary temper might do more than merely get her thrown out on her ear. Suggesting his wife was having an affair was bad enough; telling him she was doing so with another woman would likely result in a reaction she might not survive, professionally at least. Especially since she had no firm proof. But the mere suggestion would be something Al-Bashir could not ignore.

"Personal. When are they not?" Al-Bashir made a gesture of contempt for such things. But she sensed the tension that had suddenly entered the room. "What sort of personal issues?"

"Your wife's conduct. Alleged conduct."

28

"I beg your pardon?" Al-Bashir sat forward in his chair, his voice dangerously low. The atmosphere in the room had suddenly changed and Riley felt a shiver settle across her shoulders. Now, more than ever, she knew that making the allegations contained in the folder would be reckless in the extreme. It would be like poking a king cobra with a sharp stick. A short one.

"They claim," she said, carefully amending the words she had been about to use, "to have reports of activities unbecoming to the wife of a man in your position... and faith."

Al-Bashir crouched as if ready to spring out across the table at her. Riley noticed his fingers were pressed flat on the table before him, the skin white and bloodless.

"What 'activities'?" The words came out in a near whisper.

"Extravagance. A lack of modesty in her spending. That sort of thing."

After a few seconds, Al-Bashir seemed to relax. He sighed and sat back, lifting his hands from the table. He nodded slowly, then said, "So what? Asiyah is a wealthy young woman. Do these notes suggest she should not enjoy herself?"

"No."

"What, then? Is the press the moral arbiter of how my wife should spend my money? You think that bothers me?"

"Not that, either." Riley had struggled on the way over for a way of testing the water with regard to how Al-Bashir might react to the rumours. She didn't want to find herself faced with legal action – or worse, if the stories about his security team were to be believed. "There are implications," she continued, "that any stories circulating at this time might not be viewed in a good light by those behind you."

"Behind me?"

"Your backers. The investors you represent. Specifically, those you will be dealing with in the Batnev project." She saw he wasn't going to respond and continued. "They are going with you because the network will eventually spread far beyond the current proposed boundaries. They are banking – literally – on controlling the spread well across the Middle East, through India, Pakistan and beyond. Maybe even China." She waited to see if he would laugh in her face. He didn't, so she added, "Potentially, you'd be controlling the biggest telecoms consumer market on the planet."

"Really?" Al-Bashir smiled, and Riley felt the chill return. "And who told you that?"

She shrugged and said nothing.

Al-Bashir tapped a fingernail on the rim of his cup. "I don't know where you got your information, Miss Gavin," he said carefully. "But let me tell you this. There are no reports. There is no basis for anyone to have 'notes' about my wife or anyone else in my family. And if anyone – *anyone* – tries to suggest otherwise, they will regret it to their dying day." He lifted a hand and adjusted his tie. "Of course, if you were able to allow my security manager to have details about these notes you speak of, I would be most grateful."

He *knows*, thought Riley. She could see it in his eyes. In spite of his casual demeanour, a flicker of uncertainty hovered behind the bland façade, like smoke behind glass. And the chill in the room had not diminished in any way. No wonder he'd looked ready to leap out from behind the table. *The notes must be true.*

"I'm sure you would," she told him, her voice level. "But I didn't come here for that."

Behind her, the door opened and Koenig stepped up alongside her.

Al-Bashir didn't take his eyes off Riley. "So why did you come?"

"For the truth."

"Ah. The truth." Al-Bashir looked sour. "Not exactly what one looks for in your business, I think."

Except when it suits you, Riley wanted to say. "Maybe. What would be the effects if such reports came out?"

He didn't reply. Riley took it as answer enough, and wondered just how fragile this man's position really was. She was beginning to see how clever his enemies might have been.

Koenig leaned forward and placed a folded sheet of paper in front of his boss. Al-Bashir opened it. Inside was a photo. He read the note, then swept it to the floor with a sharp flick of his hand. It was the first clear sign of irritation.

"It seems you were followed here today," said Al-Bashir. He pushed the photo across the table so that Riley could see it. It appeared to have been taken from high up near the ceiling, and showed the area around the information desk downstairs. A man was standing nearby. He was short and heavily built, like a weight-lifter. "This man entered the building thirty seconds after you. He is waiting downstairs, pretending to study the floor plan, but not very convincingly. His name is Pechov."

Riley tried to remain casual. Followed? By whom? "Pechov? I don't know anyone called Pechov."

"Of course not. But he seems to know you. He was watching you all the way to the desk and only turned away when Mr Koenig went out to meet you." He nodded at the security man. "Mr Koenig is a very experienced security consultant. He can identify a bad tail at a hundred metres."

Riley began to feel queasy. In spite of the brief flash of temper just now, this man was far too calm. And now she appeared to have collected a follower.

"I still don't know who he is," she insisted.

"Then it's just as well we do, isn't it?" Al-Bashir smiled triumphantly. He nodded at Koenig, who cleared his throat and spoke for the first time since she had met him downstairs.

"Piotr Pechov is a former Russian military intelligence officer," he said calmly. "He's employed by an organisation affiliated to a network of organised crime across Eastern Europe. The current head of that organisation is believed to be a man named Fedorov. But he uses many other names."

"I've never met him, either."

"You should count yourself lucky."

"There still remains the question, Miss Gavin," put in Al-Bashir, "of how you heard of this... plan to discredit me through my wife. You didn't read about it on a London bus, did you? It was not something you picked up on YouTube." When Riley didn't reply, he pulled a mock-sad face. "Oh, don't tell me: you can't reveal your sources."

Riley said nothing. Either Al-Bashir was a master of control or he was superb at playing the part. But at least she now knew that he was aware of his enemies. And knowing that, she knew a lot more about the seriousness of the game he was engaged in.

"Never mind." Al-Bashir stood up. He was barely five feet six but his lack of inches clearly didn't bother him. "Thank you for your visit, Miss Gavin. I will take it from here."

"What about this Pechov person?" she asked.

Al-Bashir raised his eyebrows. "What about him? He was following you, not me." His smile was cold. "Perhaps you should ask him when you go back downstairs." With that, he left the room.

Riley followed Koenig back along the deserted corridor to the lift. He said nothing on the way down, but as the lift door opened, he held a powerful arm in front of her, blocking her way.

"Don't stop to shop," he advised her. "And don't come back. The boss was being polite. You won't be welcome here."

Riley felt her face flush. "I'm being banned? Why? That's unfair!"

He gave a faint sneer. "Maybe, maybe not. Don't worry – I'm sure the boss will cope with the drop in revenue."

"You know, don't you?" She decided to risk asking the question, although she doubted she would get an answer. "About his wife. What would happen if it came out. What would he do to prevent it?"

Koenig leaned closer, until she could see right into the depths of his eyes. He was so close, she could see individual hairs which he'd missed when shaving. "Drop it, Miss Gavin. Whatever you do, drop it." The menace in his voice was clear, and Riley felt a sudden desperation to get out of this place.

Before she could say anything else, he dropped his arm and allowed her to pass.

"More worrying for you," he said, "is that you've been in contact with Fedorov. He may have used another name." He held up a hand to stop her speaking. "Frankly, I couldn't care less. But you're lucky it didn't come to anything bad." He led the way over to the lobby door and held it open. "Stay well, Miss Gavin. It's a dangerous world out there."

Riley stepped through the door and walked out into the street.

The man they had called Pechov was nowhere to be seen.

29

It was mid-morning when Riley arrived home and found Frank Palmer waiting for her on the front step. He was looking sombre.

She led the way inside and poured a glass of wine.

"Don't say a word," she said, waving at his raised eyebrows. "I've had a trying morning." She told him about her visit to Al-Bashir's office.

"Sounds like a fun meeting," said Palmer, taking a seat. "What else?"

"You mean, apart from being followed by a former Russian spook named Pechov."

He sat up. "Who told you he was a former spook?"

"Al-Bashir's security chief, a man named Koenig. He reminded me of you. He advised me to stay away from Pechov. He also banned me from ever going back to the store." She scowled in irritation. "Bloody nerve of the man – I should sue him for discrimination."

Palmer laughed and looked up at the ceiling. "Yeah. I can see that must have added to your bad hair day."

"What about you?" Riley ignored the dig. "You've been very quiet."

Before he could reply, there was a knock at the door. Riley put down her glass and went to see who it was. She found DI Craig Pell on the landing.

"How did you get past the front door?" she queried.

He flashed his card. "The old chap downstairs let me in. He was trying to lure a large cat indoors with what looked like giant meatballs."

"That's Mr Grobowski. And the community cat. Couldn't you have rung first?"

"I would have, but I thought you might not be in." His smile faltered at the way that sounded, and he pressed on. "Anyway, I was in the area." He shuffled his feet uncertainly. "And I wanted to say sorry about the other night. I might have been a bit... abrupt."

"Were you? I didn't notice." She glanced over her shoulder at Palmer, who was giving her a snide smile, and felt her face flush. She didn't mean to give Pell a hard time; it was just coming out that way. "What can I do for you, Detective Inspector?"

"Um... right." He cleared his throat and said quickly, "Actually, I need to speak to Mr Palmer."

Riley threw the door open and let him in.

"I'm sorry to bother you, sir," said Pell, advancing into the room. "But I couldn't get you on your office number. Chief Superintendent Weller suggested Miss Gavin might know where you were." His voice had lost the tentative air and was all business.

Palmer digested that titbit in silence. For Weller to have suggested such a thing meant the senior policeman was in touch with Pell on a regular basis. He wondered if the lines had become slightly blurred between the murder investigation and Weller's role in SOCA. Unless, he thought, noting the way Pell carried himself in front of Riley, there was another reason for his being here.

"How thoughtful of him." He could guess what the policeman was going to tell him, and he was right.

"Someone turned over Helen Bellamy's flat," Pell announced. "I take it you haven't been there since our talk?"

"No, I haven't."

"I hope not. We're dusting for prints at the moment. You wouldn't care to provide some samples, I suppose?"

"Are you asking or instructing?" Palmer remained calm. The man was only doing his job, but he wasn't about to make it too easy for him.

Pell blew his cheeks out, seemingly undismayed. "Actually, I can't say I'm bothered, bearing in mind that you've been there before. I don't need to set us up for more embarrassment on flimsy forensics. I was more interested in whether you'd had any further thoughts about that photo Miss Bellamy sent you – the one of the office block."

"No. Like I said before, I think it must have been a mistake."

"Maybe." Pell sounded doubtful.

"Have you come up with anything at all?" Riley asked.

"We don't know who killed her, no. But we found a reference in her flat to a meeting three weeks ago with a man in a west London hotel. It could have been perfectly normal, but there's no trace of the man, unfortunately."

"What sort of reference?"

"A receipt for coffee. It was a slim hope, but the porter remembered her from a photo we showed him. He said she arrived early and had to wait. He thought she seemed a bit nervous and assumed it was a job interview. He vaguely recalled the man she met as a foreign national – possibly American."

"Anything on CCTV?" said Palmer.

"I wish. The tapes are turned over every week."

"You said American?" Riley echoed. She picked up a pen and paper and scribbled down David Johnson's number. "Helen recently did a piece on a US finance case here in London. He'll give you the details."

"Thank you. It all helps." He placed the piece of paper in his pocket. "Something else has cropped up. We received a formal request this morning from the Frankfurt Criminal Investigation Division. They're looking into the death of Annaliese Kellin and want a report on what we found."

"Can they do that?" Palmer wasn't sure where the boundaries existed now in the new modern EU, or how far a police force in one country could impact on a murder of a fellow national in another.

"Why not? It works both ways; we help them, they help us next time we have a query on their turf. It seems a former press colleague bumped into Miss Kellin in London, and she told her she'd got a new job, but she was thinking of jacking it in. The friend said she seemed unhappy – even distressed – and mentioned something about being asked to do something she felt was unethical. She didn't go into detail, though, so we're no further forward."

Palmer waited, wondering why Pell was telling them this. It was clear that Annaliese Kellin must have got herself into something nasty. Was her untimely death something to do with wanting to throw in her new job?

"Anyway," Pell continued, "I mention it out of interest. You'll let me know if you think of anything?" He nodded at them both, then turned and walked over to the door. As he went out, he looked at Riley. "I meant it – the apology, that is."

"Did your wife tell you to say that?"

He raised an eyebrow. "If I had one, she might've done." He walked down the stairs, humming to himself.

"What was that about?" asked Riley, closing the door.

"Just what I was going to ask," Palmer retorted innocently. "Wife, huh? Nice touch. Neat. He fell for it, too."

"You know what I mean!"

"My guess? He's taking his lead from Weller. Rattling our cages."

"Perhaps." She sat down and picked up her wine glass. "You still haven't said what you've been doing."

He looked surprised. "Me?"

"You. Where did you get to while I was at lunch with Richard Varley? Only, I had a distinct feeling you weren't far away. Why was that?" The look she gave him was cool, and it was obvious

159

she had been thinking about it for a while.

"If you must know, I followed your lunch date to see where he went." There was no other way of telling her. It produced the reaction he'd been expecting.

"I knew it!" she muttered angrily, slopping wine over her hand. "You've got a bloody nerve! Who I have lunch with is no concern of yours!" She stood up and stalked into the kitchen to wash her hand under the tap, leaving Palmer contemplating that it had been her idea to meet Varley in the first place. A cupboard door banged and a paper towel holder clattered as she snatched off some squares to dry herself. When she came back, it was without the wine. She went over to the window, throwing Palmer a furious look on the way, and stood looking out at the skyline.

"So where did he lead you?" she said finally, her shoulders tense.

Palmer told her about the trip across London, the visit to MailBox Services and the security men outside the hotel at Lancaster Gate. "And before you ask," he added not unkindly, "I admit I can't prove they were Varley's men."

Riley turned. "But you think they were."

"Yes."

"Maybe he's just paranoid," she said. "Or cautious."

"One or the other. We'll soon find out."

"What do you mean?"

He took a deep breath, aware that the next bit of information might also get a chilly response. "He's seen me, so I can't go near him. I'm having him followed."

"Good idea. Who by?"

"Ray Szulu."

30

Riley's mouth dropped open in shock. Palmer returned the stare without a flicker. He knew she still recalled with frightening clarity her first meeting with Szulu and the scare he'd given her, but he also knew she was tough enough to get over this.

"*Szulu?*" she echoed. "That idiot with the gun? Tell me you're joking!"

He shook his head. "I'm dead serious. The security men near the hotel didn't look twice at a couple of black guys who walked by. It's as if they weren't there. Don't ask me why… possibly making false assumptions. Everyone else got the full eyeball, men and women alike. Szulu's purpose-built for the job."

"What did you do – threaten to shoot him?"

"No. I offered him money." He was enjoying the moment. At least it had taken the anger out of the situation. "I also said if he didn't agree, I'd send you round. That seemed to clinch it."

"Very funny. What else?"

Palmer remembered the magazine he'd taken from the parcel in MailBox Services. He handed it to her. "Varley was taking a close interest in this. There was a box full of them in the shop." He waited while she glanced through it.

"Well, why wouldn't he be interested? It's his job." She looked at the cover. "This is the edition following the one he gave me."

"There was also a mailing list in the box. A long one."

"So?"

"Natalya Fisher said the circulation was three hundred, tops. The box and the mailing list must have been twice that."

"What are you saying?"

"It looks as if they distribute the magazines from London. It probably looks better than coming out of Georgia. The list, though, was only for the next two issues. I thought it was odd having such an inflated mailing for two editions."

Riley said nothing, so Palmer continued, "I think this first one – number 1572 – could be a mailing tester to flush out any problems with the list and to set up the next one."

"Or it's a simple marketing exercise to increase circulation." Riley still sounded prickly, but her tone wasn't quite so sure. She turned to the editorial page, then looked at Palmer with a sombre expression. "I think you're right." She handed him the magazine, pointing at an editorial piece at the bottom of the page.

In the next edition of **East European Trade***, we take you behind the scenes of the developing battle for control of the next-generation telecommunications network across the planet's largest land mass. What is the Low Earth Orbit BATNEV system? What does it promise for consumers in remote areas of Eastern Europe and beyond? Who will be the winners and losers in the forthcoming round of bids? Will it be the current giants of the telecoms industry expanding their business base even further, or is there room for newcomers in this exciting consumer market? We introduce you to one surprise bidder in this field –* **'Kim' Al-Bashir***, Egyptian-born London billionaire entrepreneur, who is staking his claim to a portion of this global business. He has the nerve, he has a formidable investment background, and an army of oil-rich Middle East fund-holders. But has he any weak links in his armour? Is there anything about Al-Bashir that might derail his plans at the last minute? His traditional and ultra-conservative Muslim backers are known to favour secrecy and a lack of anything approaching scandal in their dealings. But we ask, is this man, married to a beautiful young wife,* **Asiyah***, perhaps anything but conservative? To find out, you must read the next explosive edition of ETT!*

Palmer finished reading. "I don't get it."

"They're talking about my article," she said. "The article Richard Varley wants me to write. It's going in the next issue."

"But you haven't written it yet."

"Nor can I. This is a smear-job… it would be professional suicide. Al-Bashir would nail my skin to the doors of the High Court." She shook her head. "I mean, I knew there was some salacious stuff in the notes Richard gave me, but I didn't expect them to go for this kind of angle – " She broke off and paced the room, eyes flashing with growing anger. "They must have planned it this way this all along – and I stumbled right into it!"

They were both startled by the phone ringing.

Riley picked up the phone and listened, then glanced involuntarily towards the front window. "You're here?" She looked at Palmer and mouthed Varley's name.

Palmer jumped to his feet and pointed upwards. It was best if he stayed out of the way. He wondered if his visit to the shop in Camden had anything to do with it, although he couldn't see how. As far as Varley was concerned, there was no connection between him and Riley Gavin, and that was how he wanted to keep it.

Riley nodded and said, "Richard, just give me a minute, will you?" She put the phone down, a determined set to her jaw. "Good timing, really. I'm going to tell him I'm pulling out. I can't put my name to the sort of stuff he's talking about." She picked up the magazine. "You'd better take this with you. What are you going to do?"

"I want to see if he came alone."

"You're thinking of those security men."

Palmer nodded.

"And if he didn't?"

"Then we'll know what we're up against."

31

Riley went downstairs and opened the front door. Richard Varley was standing on the steps. He was as elegant and expensively dressed as before, and seemed to fill the doorway.

She led him upstairs. This time the roles were reversed and it was he who seemed ill-at-ease. She wondered what had happened to bring him here like this.

"Is there a problem?" She kept her voice level, wondering how long to give him before telling him to take his assignment away.

"Yes." He looked paler than usual and had cut himself shaving. She found it an oddly appealing sign. "I'm sorry, Riley, for coming round here like this… invading your space. But I've heard some unpleasant news."

"What about?" Riley had a sudden image of Palmer's face. Had they made the connection?

"I have," Richard began, his voice uncertain, "some… principals in the publishing business. Directors, shareholders, if you like. They have made substantial investments over the years and are very watchful about what we publish. It has come to my – their – notice… that you've had a meeting with Al-Bashir. Is that correct?"

"Yes. So?" Riley felt her gut react. If Richard or his 'principals' knew she had been to see the Egyptian-born entrepreneur, there was only one way they could have found out. She had been followed.

Pechov.

At the admission, Varley's expression underwent a change. A flicker of disappointment crossed his face. "That's unfortunate. It would have been better if you hadn't done that."

"Why? I told you when we first met that I do my own research.

And speaking to the subject of a profile piece comes pretty high on the list, don't you think? No ethical journalist takes someone else's notes as gospel – and certainly not with a man like him. What's the problem? More importantly, how do these 'principals' of yours know I've seen him?"

Varley shifted in his chair. "It came to their notice. How is not important."

"It is to me. Were they watching him? Were you?" She desperately wanted to ask him if they had been keeping *her* under observation, but it might be best not to let them think she harboured suspicions in that area. If he thought she was merely a working reporter trying to hang on to an assignment, he might say more than he'd intended.

He ignored the question. "By going to see him, and possibly alerting him to the fact that a story is circulating, you've made the whole project more... difficult, don't you see?"

Riley wasn't sure exactly what he meant, but opted to play dumb. "But I haven't submitted my copy yet. How do you know what line I'm going to take? If it's his Batnev bid you're worried about, it's already public knowledge. Al-Bashir is hardly a wallflower when it comes to his business intentions. The man's desperate for recognition."

"That's not the point." Varley's tone took on an almost desperate note. "Now he knows what's happening, he'll have time to prepare... to hide anything he doesn't want aired in public."

Riley very nearly blurted out that copies of the magazine currently being prepared for mailing would soon blow that hope out of the water, but she managed to control herself. And there had been no actual mention in the editorial tease of any scandal attached to Al-Bashir's wife. So what was the real problem?

Fortunately, Varley unwittingly supplied the answer.

"It's a question of timing," he continued seriously. "Too soon and Al-Bashir can brush off bad news. His PR people can work on his backers and supporters, and convince them that everything's peachy. Too late and… well, that's even worse…" His voice tailed off as if he had suddenly realised what he was saying.

Riley suddenly saw what he was driving at. She recalled what he had said at their last meeting, about how if Al-Bashir failed or pulled out right on the wire, it could drag everyone else down, too.

"But either way, he still wins," she said. "That's it, isn't it? *You don't want him to win!*"

"Riley, you don't understand. We're just a journal – we're right in the middle, here. We need your copy to go in urgently. We're simply trying to avoid being the cause of any problems, that's all."

"That's easy: delay the piece until after the bidding."

"We can't. It's too late."

"Why? What's the deadline?"

"It's very close. There have been… delays, and now we need to move along on this." He gave an unconvincing smile.

"What sort of delays?"

"I can't go into that. I know I should have mentioned this before, and I'm sorry. I thought you'd be able to put the piece together very quickly from the data we provided. There's a lot riding on it."

Riley nodded and stood up. She so wanted to believe him. "So you said." Then an unbidden, unwanted thought squirmed slowly to the surface. Something she suspected Palmer had been thinking about all along. "Richard, who else was on this project before you contacted me?"

His expression gave nothing away. "I don't know what you mean."

"Who gathered the material on Al-Bashir… the stuff about his wife?"

For the first time, Varley seemed unable to meet her eye. "Various people. Researchers… freelances – we went to several sources." He stood up and moved alongside her, his aftershave lingering in the air. "Are we OK on this?" The way he was looking at her was different, almost nervous, and she wondered how much he had riding on this business.

"I'll call you," she said. He was crowding her too close and she needed time to think. "Let me have until tomorrow."

Varley nodded, but with obvious reluctance. "The hotel where we first met? How about noon?"

"If you wish."

He nodded and walked out. It was only when Riley closed the front door behind him that she realised she'd been holding her stomach and felt sick with tension.

Palmer appeared a few minutes later, brushing dust off his sleeves. Riley suspected he'd slipped out of the landing window and shimmied on to the wall below to check the street. One look at his face and she knew.

"He wasn't alone."

"No. There was a black four-wheel drive at the end of the street, with two men inside. Sorry."

Riley didn't know what to say, so she said nothing.

"I did not expect this." The man known as Grigori stared through the window from the fourth floor of Pantile House. Another day was dying on its feet. He tapped a thumb on the plastic sill. The dull tattoo lasted a full fifteen seconds. "She has to be convinced. There is much riding on it."

"Perhaps," suggested Radko, "it would be better to find someone else."

"We don't have time to find another reporter with her credentials. She was the third, remember?" Grigori's words were savage with impatience. "If we continue this way, there will be no unattached credible reporters left for us to use. You think there is a bank of them, just waiting for you to work your way through like those sweets that idiot Pechov is always eating? We must have her name on that page." He drummed his fist on the woodwork in time to the words. "We've tried money; what else is there?"

"She's a loner. She has nobody we can use as leverage. It's the down side of why we chose her – like the others."

Grigori nodded. "That reminds me – what of the woman friend of Bellamy's? The one whose details Pechov discovered in her apartment? Have you dealt with her? Bellamy may have talked to her about us."

Radko looked defensive. "It was no good. I went to the address, but the house was empty, the milk cancelled." At his boss's look of incomprehension, he explained quickly, "Over here, milk is still delivered to many houses, especially in rural areas. When people go away, they leave a note to cancel deliveries." He lifted his shoulders. "It was cancelled until further notice."

Grigori gave a huff of irritation. A pigeon had flown. And they didn't have time to go looking for it. "That is unfortunate. You should have gone sooner."

The matter of blame was clear, and Radko shifted uncomfortably, but said nothing.

"We still have the Gavin woman." Grigori reached down and switched on the desk lamp, throwing a green-tinged glow across the room. "Since gentle persuasion isn't working, we must try other means."

"What do you suggest?"

"Everyone has someone," Grigori insisted, "or something. Friends, family, a neighbour, even… there's always a weak point." He looked bleakly at Radko, his meaning challenging. "I suggest you get out there and find out what Riley Gavin's weak point is."

32

Ray Szulu stifled a yawn and watched as a dull glow appeared in the fourth floor window of Pantile House. There were few other lights on, and he'd watched a steady stream of personnel drifting out of the main door and disappearing along the pavement or climbing into their cars.

He'd had no trouble following the men from Lancaster Gate. After waiting outside the hotel, which Palmer had told him was the start point, he'd latched on to them when they came out and climbed into the big four-wheel drive. The vehicle was easy to track, even among all the other Chelsea tractors around town, and sitting a steady hundred yards back in heavy traffic had been a simple task.

The tall one – the man Palmer had referred to as Varley – had come out first with another man in tow, and they'd been joined by two more. The security goons, Szulu decided. Palmer was right: they'd stood out like bouncers at a primary school picnic.

After Palmer's crack about the Russian mafia, Szulu had been in two minds about telling him where he could stick his job. He'd heard enough about their ruthlessness and didn't need that kind of grief. He knew the Russians were all over London like a rash these days; he'd driven enough of their women and kids around to know they'd made it their home from home. But how many were gangsters and how many were ordinary people, he had no idea. He'd heard a figure of four hundred thousand expatriates in town, but that could have been headline hype, tossed out to sell a few more papers.

In the end, he'd decided that working for Palmer and Gavin was better than sitting at home waiting for Ayso to call, so he'd gone round to a friend who ran a garage and told him what he needed.

"You doin' *what*?" Steadman was a wizened Rasta in his late sixties, for whom nature had traded in his dreads for a bald head. He was a dealer in used cars and bikes across south London. He'd listened to what Szulu told him and shook his head in dismay. "You daft, man, you know that? You *followin'* people you don' even know what they do? What you gonna do if they see you, huh? You considered that if this private dee-tective want them followed, they completely innocent men?" He huffed out his cheeks and wiped his hands on a filthy rag. "You growin' dafter every day, Ray. That bullet hole in your arm you so proud of, it must have let in too much fresh air and let out any brains you had."

Szulu sighed. As usual, Steadman was being an old woman, seeing danger behind every simple act. "It's nothing like that, Stead. I figured it out, see. What's the most common sight in London? Tell me that."

Steadman scowled. "Traffic wardens – they like fleas on a dog."

"Nah, not them. Transport."

"Taxis, then. Or buses. Don't tell me you want to borrow a Routemaster – 'cos you fresh out of luck, my friend. I sold the last two yesterday."

"No, nothing like that, bro. Scooters. There's hundreds every-where. Nobody sees them no more, they so common. Even those city boys are ridin' them. It's the new thing." He jerked his chin towards two scooters standing in the far corner of Steadman's yard. They were bruised and scuffed with dirt, but just what he had in mind. "One of them would do. They'll never see me coming. I'll bring it back, no problem."

Steadman looked across at the bikes, then sighed in defeat and waved him away. "Go, man. Take the Super 9 – the black one. It was a trade-in and I haven't done the papers on it yet." He waved an oily finger in Szulu's face. "But you bring it back without scrapes or record of wrongdoing, you hear? Else I come after you with a baseball bat. An' let me tell you, your hex-military friend, no matter how rough and tough he is, he won't be able to stop me."

Szulu grinned and clapped the old man on the shoulder. He reckoned he could stand the humiliation of riding a scooter around town for a while. As long as he wasn't spotted by anyone who knew him. "Great, Stead. Thanks, man. Hey, you don't have a bone dome to go with it, do you? And it needs to be big to go over the dreads, y'know?"

As soon as the men had parked outside Pantile House, Szulu had phoned Palmer and given him an update. Then he'd asked what was going on.

Palmer had kept it short, explaining that the men were using the building illegally, probably with the connivance of the supervisor.

"Stay with them," he'd told Szulu. "They might be there a while. If they leave, follow them and let me know. And stay out of sight."

Szulu had rung off and chained the scooter to a convenient lamp-post, then gone in search of a doorway where he could sit and keep an eye on the place. He'd settled on an empty shop. The porch was jammed with rubbish and old newspapers, and smelled like an old cat, but it was dry enough for his purposes and suitable for hiding in without attracting attention.

He'd been puzzled when the men had parked the four-wheel drive at a meter on the street, when there was a perfectly good car park at the rear of the building. When he'd taken a walk round the block half an hour later, he'd seen why: a CCTV camera up on the wall of the building was covering the car park.

If it was working, it would record every vehicle entering or leaving. Out on the main street, the nearest camera was pointed at a busy junction and rarely moved. He figured the men were paranoid and thought they might need a quick getaway. Szulu knew all about quick getaways; sometimes they worked, other times they went pear-shaped over a bus-pass holder with a bad hip and a supermarket trolley.

On one of his other recces, he caught a glimpse of a face up on the fourth floor. It was too far away to be certain, but he thought it was one of the security goons. Later, one of the men came out to feed the meter. Szulu stood up, shaking off his stiffness and ambling along the pavement towards him. There was something he wanted to try out.

Palmer had mentioned earlier that the men appeared to have a weak spot: they seemed oblivious to certain types of people.

"You mean black people, right?" Szulu had been unsurprised. "Most whites are, man. We the invisible ones, didn't you know that? We don't exist."

Palmer had given him one of his looks, and Szulu had quickly dropped the aggrieved minority act. Now, striding along the street, he kept his head down but a watchful eye on the man at the meter. Time to see if Palmer knew his beans or not. He loosened his shoulders, bouncing off his left foot and singing to himself as if he was out for a stroll, tugging loosely at one of his dreads. It was an act, meant to convince himself that he wasn't about to run into seven kinds of hell like the sort of grief Riley Gavin and her ex-soldier friend had put him through the last time they'd met. He shivered at the memory, hoping Palmer had told the truth about Mitcheson on the other side of the Atlantic. Best worry, he told himself, about the gunman you know rather than the Russian hard-face you don't.

Fifty yards ahead of him, the man at the meter was digging in his pockets for change. His jacket was pulled tight across enormous shoulders like a prize fighter's.

Szulu eased by, humming softly. He was invisible, he reminded himself. No way he can see me. The man glanced up as Szulu's shadow, thrown by a street light, fell across the pavement, then looked away again. Szulu shivered. It was just like Palmer had said: the man had clocked him, but he hadn't seen him. Weird.

When he thought about it he felt almost insulted.

He continued for a hundred yards and turned to cross the street. The man in the suit was returning to the building, his pace unhurried.

Szulu stopped at the next corner. It was good to change positions every now and then. Break the routine. He took out his mobile, intending to call Palmer with the car number.

Just then someone stepped up behind and prodded him in the back.

33

Szulu spun round. It was Palmer.

"Jesus, man – what are you doing?" Szulu thought his chest was going to explode. "How do you do that creepy shit?" He was annoyed at having had the former redcap sneak up on him so easily when he was supposed to have all his wits about him. He hadn't heard a sound. The guy wasn't normal.

"You've got a guilty conscience," Palmer chided him cheerfully, and peered round the corner towards Pantile House. "What's happening out there?"

Szulu told him.

"Where's your car?" Palmer scanned the street.

"I used something else." Now Palmer was here, he suddenly didn't feel like bragging about using a scooter for a surveillance job.

"Like what? A bicycle? You must have legs of steel."

"A scooter, all right? I borrowed a scooter." Szulu was angry at letting out the information so easily. But Palmer merely lifted an eyebrow.

"Really? That's neat. Who the hell ever looks at a scooter?"

Szulu smirked. "That's what I thought. Say, you still haven't told me what this is all about. You were kidding, about them blokes being Russian Mafia, right?" He smiled hopefully, but was disappointed when Palmer shook his head.

"Maybe not Mafia, but something close." Palmer felt in his jacket pocket and took out a small pair of binoculars. He looked around the street, settling on a building across from Pantile House. "See that place across there?"

Szulu nodded. He'd walked past it not long ago. The ground floor housed a travel agency and a print shop. The structure was old and of dull, red brick, falling behind its neighbours like a tired old horse with every new building project in the area and making it look more and more out of place. He'd bet it was on someone's list for demolition. "Sure. What about it?"

"If we can get inside, we'll have a nice view of the fourth floor." He glanced at Szulu. "Keep watch while I go find a way in. If they make a move while I'm over there, ring me."

With that, he slipped out of the doorway and made his way across the road, disappearing into the shadows behind the shops. Seconds later, Szulu heard a whistle and followed, keeping one eye on Pantile House. The light was still on.

He arrived at the rear of the building and found Palmer waiting, holding a door open.

"Man, how did you do that?" Szulu was impressed; he knew one or two guys who could open doors in a couple of minutes. But that was after checking it out first, not walking straight up to it like Palmer had done.

"Easy when you know how," Palmer replied, and closed the door softly behind them.

"In this dump, maybe. No way would you get through my locks that quick."

The sideways look Palmer gave him made Szulu instantly uncomfortable. "What makes you think I haven't already?" he said. Then he turned and led the way up a ratty set of stairs covered in mildewed paper and fallen plaster, leaving Szulu with his mouth open.

While the front of the building housed the shops, the rest seemed to have been abandoned to the elements and a slow, relentless decay. The treads were gritty and sounded hollow beneath their feet, and Palmer hoped the shopkeepers below were concentrating on cashing up and not listening for sounds of intruders overhead.

He stopped on the third floor. This was as high as the main

floors went, but from the doorway across the street, he'd noticed small attic windows sunk into the roof. There had to be another staircase somewhere, narrower than the main one and probably accessible through a single door. He found it at the end of the landing, nearly invisible behind a layer of ancient wallpaper and grime. A small number 13 in grubby plastic had been tacked to the door. Hoping it wouldn't be unlucky for them, he tugged it open.

A wave of damp, mouldy air hit them as they climbed a short flight of stairs into an open space with a ceiling angled downwards from the apex. Two attic windows looked out over the street, as did another one at the far end of the room.

Palmer checked this last one. They were in luck: they had an unobstructed view of Pantile House, barely eighty yards away.

The room they were in was long and narrow, probably a servant's quarters many years ago. It was stripped bare, and the rough wooden floor echoed with creaks and groans as the two men shifted their weight.

"Is this safe?" Szulu whispered, testing the boards. "This place is rotten as old grapefruit."

"It'll do fine," Palmer assured him, studying the building across the way through the binoculars. "Just breathe in and don't do any break-dancing."

He located the fourth floor and immediately saw Varley. He was standing at the desk, talking on a mobile phone. The glow of the desk lamp threw his shadow across the room, highlighting the strong features and athletic build. A second man was standing nearby. Smaller and balding, he had a pale, almost anaemic look. He was staring at the floor, waiting for Varley to finish his call.

Palmer lowered the binoculars to scan the building at ground level. Two men were walking around the outside. They looked solid and determined, and as they passed beneath the soft glow of a street lamp, he recognised the two security men from the hotel at Lancaster Gate.

"How many did you say left the hotel?"

"Four," said Szulu. "Why?"

Palmer shook his head. He'd have felt easier if he'd known where the third man was – the one who had checked the four-wheel drive. He shook off his disquiet; maybe they had a rota system and it was his night off.

Szulu moved up alongside him, breathing nervously.

"What you said about this thing," he murmured softly, as if the men across the way might hear him. "You said it was personal, right?"

"That's correct."

"So what did they do, these guys?" He nodded towards the light on the fourth floor. "It was something serious?"

Palmer didn't respond for a few moments. Then he said, "Somebody murdered a friend of mine. I can't prove it was the men over there. But if they didn't, they might know who did."

"Man, that's bad." *Bad for the men across the way*, Palmer's tone suggested. "Who was she, this friend – someone special?"

"You could say that. They tied her up, snapped her neck and dumped her body in a ditch." The words dropped into the silent room like slivers of ice, and Szulu felt the hairs move on the back of his neck.

"And you're going after them."

"That's the general idea." Palmer turned and looked at Szulu with a frown.

"What?" Szulu stepped back a pace. "What's up?"

"You said 'she.'"

"So?"

"Did I say my friend was a woman?"

Szulu looked away, unable to meet Palmer's gaze. "Man, the way you talkin' right now, you didn't have to."

For once, the cat was being halfway amenable. It had allowed Riley to scoop it up and hold it while she stared into the street outside, watching as car and foot traffic gradually dwindled with the passing evening. Late commuters looking for a parking space, shoppers with carrier bags hurrying home from the supermarket, even an early drunk – a short, squat man in a tight suit – holding up a lamp post across the way.

Riley wondered where Palmer was. She could have done with his steadying presence here. Maybe she would have to make do with the cat, purring like a small tractor and enjoying the rare occasion of shared comfort.

She still couldn't explain why she had shied away from telling Varley that she no longer wanted the Al-Bashir job, especially now she was certain that she wasn't the first person to have been hired to do it. That brought dark, unwelcome thoughts about who that might have been. But she wasn't ready to face them just yet. For now, all she knew was that on a professional level, going ahead with the assignment based on unverified information would rightfully incur Al-Bashir's anger. And that could be dangerous.

As she turned away from the window, the drunk in the street below let go of his lamp post and lurched away into the darkness. As he did so, his face turned up to Riley's window and gave it a last, searching look.

34

The pavement outside the hotel in Bloomsbury was awash with a coachload of Italian tourists when Riley arrived just before noon. They scurried around like minnows, resplendent in dark glasses and immaculate clothes, eagerly grabbing their bags as the driver slid them out from the luggage compartment.

Riley eased her way through and entered the hotel, walking past the reception desk. There was no sign of Varley in the front lounge. She walked through to the room at the rear, where they had first met. The corner table was empty.

As she turned away she came face to face with a familiar figure.

"Miss Gavin?" It was Varley's colourless associate, the man who had met her here last time. He was dressed in a plain grey suit and standing with his hands by his side, the image of a functionary waiting for orders.

Riley stepped back involuntarily, startled by a glint of steel in the way the man was looking at her. It was probably the coldest pair of eyes she had ever seen. "Where's Richard?"

"He has been detained." He spoke with deliberate care, his accent more obvious than before. Riley noticed beads of perspiration on his forehead, although the atmosphere in the hotel was cool. He gestured to the corner chairs. "But I can speak... on his behalf. " He gave a ghost of a smile and led the way, sitting down without waiting for her.

"And you are?"

"My name is of no importance."

"Well, man of no importance," Riley replied curtly, "I've decided not to proceed with the assignment." She took out the cheque Richard had given her and placed it on the table. "Under the circumstances, I'm returning this. I don't feel I've earned it.

Please pass on my apologies to Richard, but I'm sure he'll understand." She felt a sudden sense of relief at having voiced her decision, and of being free of any obligation by returning the cheque.

He showed neither dismay nor anger at her news. Neither did he attempt to pick up the cheque. Instead, he placed both hands together, resting his elbows on the arms of the chair. A buzz of traffic outside and a burst of laughter from the reception area sounded very distant, and alien.

"That is disappointing, Miss Gavin," he said softly. "You see, we need someone of proven... credibility to complete this assignment. You realise how important this is? How late you have left it to tell us?"

"I can't help that." Riley's heart began thumping at the coldly dispassionate way the man was looking at her, as if she were an unusual and mildly interesting specimen in a Petrie dish. "I told Richard I wasn't prepared to put my name to an article based on someone else's data. Neither do I like the slant of what he wants me to write. I thought he understood that."

"Perhaps. But I am not Richard." He reached in his jacket pocket and took out a square of thin, white card. He placed it on the table between them, reminding Riley of a similar move by Al-Bashir in his boardroom. "Is that your final word? You do not wish to reconsider?" He looked at her and waited, head cocked to one side.

"No. Why should I?" Riley began to rise, eager to be away from this man and his penetrating gaze.

As she did so, he flipped the card over.

Riley stopped dead, suddenly wishing more than anything that Frank Palmer was in the room.

But Palmer wasn't going anywhere fast. Stuck in an Underground tunnel near Tottenham Court Road with a few dozen other passengers, he felt the heat close in around him like a stifling blanket. Any trace of cool air drifting through the carriage was obliterated by the increasing body heat as passengers fought a rising sense of panic at the delay. Most tried to hide their feelings by fanning themselves with whatever came to hand. Others fiddled vainly with their mobile phones, frustrated at finding the networks unavailable.

Palmer breathed easily and stared at the ceiling, mentally distancing himself from the discomfort around him. He'd already scanned every advertising panel in sight, along with the backs of people's newspapers and magazines, and now shifted his attention to somewhere within himself, satisfied to wait until the train moved on. They had been stationary for twenty minutes, earning only a blandly insincere apology from a voice over the intercom system. Instinct told him that a delay of this length meant something serious had happened further along the line. A jumper, perhaps, or a bomb alert, it didn't matter which. They were stuck until someone got them out.

He'd rung Riley before boarding, hoping to catch her before she left for her meeting with Varley, but without luck. He'd wanted to fill her in on what he and Szulu had been up to the previous evening. Seeing Varley in Pantile House – the building Helen had photographed – still wasn't concrete evidence, but it was as close as he needed to proving that there was a connection between them. Unless it was a massive coincidence.

But Palmer didn't believe that. The one thing he had learned over the years was that where two or more even vaguely related points of information came together, coincidence could usually be ruled out.

Riley blinked in disbelief as she saw the reverse side of the card Varley's associate had dropped on the table.

It was a photograph of Mr Grobowski.

Why was he showing her this? The photo had been taken on the pavement near the house. The elderly Pole was walking along the street clutching a plastic bag and a large saucepan. He was probably returning home from the community centre where he served meals for his Polish compatriots.

"You know this man." The voice was flat, disinterested, a perfunctory question to which he already knew the answer.

"You know I do." Riley fought to clamp down on a rising sense of panic. "What's going on?"

"Miss Gavin, where I come from, if someone does not do what they have agreed, there are not many options open." His voice was calm and compellingly soft, his gaze intense and unsettling. "Here, you have your lawyers and your courts and the police. We have them, too, but they are not so… quick to help." He toyed with the photo, spinning it round and round on the polished surface. "Always they need paying. Sometimes lots of money. And they are not very efficient. So, we have been forced to develop other ways… a custom, you might say, of persuading people to do what they have promised. You understand what I am saying? It is simple. And it works."

Riley felt a tremor go through her. Was she really hearing this? Here, in this elegant London hotel, where tourists were excitedly rushing to their rooms, this… man with the coldest eyes she'd ever seen was quietly threatening her? Worse, he was threatening her through a lovely, harmless old man who wouldn't hurt a fly.

"Perhaps you do not believe me," he continued, in the same soft, flat tone. "That, I have to say, would be a mistake." He reached in his pocket and produced another photo, which he tossed on the table. It skidded towards Riley. She reached down instinctively to stop it falling off the edge.

This one was of Donald Brask.

"Why are you doing this?" Riley's voice sounded strange, even to her. She desperately wanted to pick up the photo and hurl it back in the man's face. But she couldn't.

"Why? Because I can, Miss Gavin. And because I have need of your services. Of your name on the article that you agreed to write." He studied his fingertips. "It is what I think you might call the law of supply and demand. I demand and you supply." He gave a brief smile, as if demonstrating that while he might have an accent, he clearly understood the subtleties of language. "You may resist. You may choose not to believe I will do anything. But in the end, you will do as I wish."

"Or what?" The words forced their way out through cotton wool.

"Or your friends will suffer."

Before Riley could say anything, he stood up and moved to stand close to her. He smelled of lavender, and Riley knew she would never come across the smell again without thinking of this man.

"If you doubt me, Miss Gavin, you should call home. You young people today – you are so careless with things. Especially your pets."

He stepped past her, patting her on the shoulder as he did so. The touch made her recoil, but he appeared not to notice. "Call when you are ready to submit the copy, Miss Gavin. You have the number. We will tell you where to email it. But hurry. Time is running out."

Riley watched him walk out of the lounge, a colourless little man in a plain suit, possessed of a manner that made her blood run cold.

What did he mean, she should call home? There was nobody there. So why –?

Her phone rang. She snatched it out and put it to her ear.

"*Miss Riley!*" It was Mr Grobowski. She had given him her number in case of emergencies, but this was the first time he had ever used it. He sounded distraught, and her thoughts went instantly to the man who had just left. "Miss Riley… you have to come urgent! Please to hurry! I so sorry!"

"Mr Grobowski?" Riley was shocked by the agony in the Pole's voice. His words were little more than a mad jumble, made worse by his heavy breathing, as if he had just run a marathon. "What's the matter?"

"Is Lipinski, Miss Riley."

"Cat?" The old Pole loved the cat just as much as she did. But at least her neighbour was safe. "What's happened?"

"I so sorry to tell you this things, Miss Riley. But someone, he has shot Lipinski…!"

35

Riley ran outside and saw a taxi depositing a fare. She jumped in and told the driver her address, then sat in mute impatience while he explained cheerfully about a problem on the Underground which had made taxis as scarce as hens' teeth. Riley ignored him, watching as each street sign and landmark reeled by in horribly grinding slow-motion.

She checked her watch, although time was unimportant, and was surprised to find that it was already past one o'clock. Had the meeting lasted so long?

She dialled Palmer's number repeatedly, each time getting an unobtainable message. He was either out of reach or his phone was dead. Thinking that word made her cringe inwardly, remembering the threats made at the hotel. But she told herself that the man didn't know about Palmer, or he would have produced a photo of him too.

When the taxi arrived at the house Riley thrust some money in the driver's lap, and was out and running before he had stopped.

Inside she found Mr Grobowski sitting on the stairs, cradling his head in his hands. The elderly Pole was moaning softly, rocking gently from side to side.

"Mr G?" She knelt down beside him, her heart flipping. "Where's Cat?"

He lifted his head and pointed towards his flat. His craggy face was puffed with anger and sorrow, and he tried hard to meet Riley's eyes. "The vet she is come… I could not take Lipinski to that place –" He wrung his hands together and shook his head. "I so sorry."

Riley grabbed him by both arms. "You did the right thing, Mr G," she told him firmly. "I wouldn't have been able to do it, either.

Tell me what happened."

"This man, he comes to the door. I think he is salesmans, or maybe a religious persons. I tell him we are not interested. But he a *buhaj* – a bull – and push past me like I not exist and ask where is animals. Without thinking, I say cat is in my flat, but why? He don't say nothing and go inside." He shuddered and took a deep gulp of air. "I follow, telling him to get out... and then I see he has a gun. Black and shiny... not very big. I can't believe it. Then he see Lipinski." He moaned softly. "Lipinski know he bad mans and show a fierce face. But the mans, he... he just shoot him and walk away. No words... just walking away. And Lipinski –"

Riley turned away and stepped through Mr Grobowski's front door.

The first thing she saw was a woman in slacks and a blue jacket, kneeling on the floor. Beside her was a black case with the lid thrown open. It contained a variety of instruments, boxes and sterile packs, and a roll of medical gauze, ripped open with one end hanging loose.

But it was the cat which drew Riley's gaze. Stretched out on the floor with its mouth open, it had a sticky-looking wet patch on its neck, the fur spiky and disturbed. There was no sign of breathing.

Riley dropped to her knees, a sob gathering in her throat. How could this animal be so long... and so *thin*, she thought distractedly, noting the length from battered nose to tabby tail. He'd always been such a bruiser. And with everything Mr Grobowski fed him, he should have died of over-eating, of a diet enriched by too many meatballs and other Polish delights, not... not *this* horror. She reached out to cradle him, certain her heart was going to tear its way out of her ribs. What evil bastard could have done this?

"Don't do that!" The vet spoke sharply, reaching out to stop

Riley touching the animal. "I need to get him to the surgery. He's lost a lot of blood."

"What?" Riley stared at the woman in confusion, wanting to tell her that her job was over, that she hadn't come in time, that it was all too late. "I don't understand."

Then the cat opened one eye and saw her. It mewed, his mouth barely open but the sound surprisingly deep and resentful, protesting about the indignity of what had happened.

"He's *alive*?" Riley was stunned.

"He's lucky." The vet replied pragmatically, pressing a pad against the cat's neck and skilfully securing it in place with what seemed like several feet of bandage. "He's built like a baby elephant or he'd have been dead. The slug wasn't a big one, but it looks like it went through the fat behind his neck and nicked the scapula."

"The what? What does that mean?" Riley tried to process her limited knowledge of anatomy into some sort of positive news. What the hell was a scapula? Wasn't it what doctors used to hold down a patient's tongue?

"It's the shoulder to you," the vet explained. "I won't know how serious it is until I give him a thorough examination and an x-ray. If there's no major damage or complications, he'll come out of this with nothing more than a nasty scar and a bald patch to show his mates. Just hope it hasn't hit the brachial artery." She finished off the bandaging with some adhesive wrap to hold it in place and jumped to her feet.

Mr Grobowski had heard the words and came rushing in to stand behind them. He moaned with relief, clearly having believed the worst had happened. "Is miracle! Lipinski…"

The vet gave them each a stern look. "Look, you two can do all that stuff later. Right now, we need to get him to where I can treat him. One of you hold the door, the other get my bag. My car's outside. I've put a pressure pad on to stem the bleeding, but we can't hang about." She looked first at the elderly Pole, but he was wringing his hands together, his face twisted with relief. She turned to Riley instead, indicating her black case. "Take a visiting card out of the lid and ring the surgery. Tell them what's happened and that we're on the way in. They'll get the theatre cleared and prepped." She bent and scooped up the cat with great care, then added, "I'll have to report this, you know. Shootings of any kind… the police have to be told."

"Of course." Riley grabbed a card and reached for her mobile, glad to be able to do something. The moment she got the chance, she was going to ask Mr Grobowski for a fuller description of the man who had done this, although somehow that didn't really matter. She already knew who was to blame.

36

"*Wake up, sweetie- it's Donald.*" Brask's voice penetrated the fog, jerking Riley awake. Dimly, she recognised the sound coming from the answering machine and rolled off the sofa, snatching up the phone while trying to shake off the lethargy. She checked her watch. God, she'd been out for three hours since warning Donald about the threats and telling him to get somewhere safe. It was probably a reaction to everything that had happened, but she felt guilty at having fallen asleep so easily.

"Donald? Are you OK?"

"Of course, dear lamb." His voice came through full and rich as usual. "I've got a simply *huge* man stationed at my front door, and another at the back, with orders to sacrifice themselves dearly for me."

Riley felt a smile tugging at her lips. Donald knew a lot of people with backgrounds not unlike Palmer's. He had assured her that he would get the best protection available.

"How's the cat?" he queried solicitously.

"The last time I rang, they told me everything was going fine and to call later this evening. They wouldn't let me go round and wait, though."

"Quite right, too. They're professionals, they'll do what they have to. Have you heard from Frank?"

"No. I'm getting worried. You?"

"Not yet. I'll keep trying – I've got his number on automatic re-dial. But I've just received something off the wires which might interest you. That magazine, *East European Trade?*"

"What about it?" Riley stood up and walked on shaky legs to the kitchen, where she poured a large slug of orange juice. She had a raging thirst. "Didn't I tell you, I've decided not to do that piece?"

"You did, dear, you did. But if you've still got the magazine Varley gave you, you might want to take a closer look. It will give you an indication of how they work."

"Just a second." Riley found the magazine and opened it. "OK, what am I looking at?"

"There's a piece about a man named Mustafa Tukel. He's a Turkish government minister and one of their biggest ship-owners."

Riley vaguely recalled the article, and flipped through the pages until she came to it. The photo showed a large man with a ready smile and a bushy moustache, posing against a background of a shipyard. The article was mostly about Tukel's planned bid to build a new deepwater dock on the Black Sea coast. It would have massive implications for the local economy and would soak up business in the area like a sponge, regenerating the entire region. The article, as well as outlining Tukel's plans, included some terse comments made by him about key members of the Turkish administration whom, he claimed, were trying to prevent him from winning the contract in favour of other, unspecified bidders. The comments had been highlighted in italics, she noted, for maximum effect.

"What about him?"

"He's just been arrested on charges of dissent against the state."

"That's serious, isn't it?" She recalled a writer who had been imprisoned on similar charges two years ago for criticising the Turkish administration, and was still in prison awaiting trial.

"It is. There have been calls for him to lose his ministerial job, and his bid for the shipyard has been disqualified. Interestingly, the contract has now been awarded to a company based in Ukraine."

"Why does this concern us?"

"Because *East European Trade* is the only quoted source of the information against him."

Riley sat back and stared in dismay at the magazine, the implications hitting home. "Another smear job?" she said dully. It was what they were planning to do to Al-Bashir. Given enough credibility, an article about his wife's lifestyle and a few carefully highlighted 'suggestions' or rumours would be enough to drive away his backers and sink his chances of ever winning the Batnev bid. Truth would be the first casualty.

She checked the name against the article. The piece was attributed to an unnamed staff writer.

"It's a clever technique," said Donald. "Not as final as a bullet, but just as effective. Be glad you're out of it, sweetie. Take care." He rang off.

Palmer arrived thirty minutes later. He looked hot and tired and spoiling for a fight.

"I spoke to Donald. He told me what happened." He took her by the shoulders and looked her in the eyes. "Are you all right?"

"I'm fine," she reassured him, and held up her glass, which she'd refilled. "High as a kite on vitamins."

"Yeah, I can see." He took the glass from her and drained it. "Nice. No gin. How's the cat and Mr G?"

"The cat's being treated. They think he'll be OK, but we'll have to wait until he begins to respond. Mr Grobowski's gone into defence mode downstairs. I had a job stopping him from setting up camp across my doorway. He feels guilty about what happened to Lipinski." She smiled weakly. "Listen to that – he's got me using the name now."

Palmer made her sit down. "Tell me everything. Donald only gave me a potted version."

Riley did so, from the time she had arrived at the hotel, through to the moment she had rushed back and stepped through the front door and seen the cat. As she talked, she wondered if she was doing an adequate job of describing the demeanour of the man at the hotel, and the way in which he had so casually and openly made his threats.

Palmer listened without a word. Then he stood up and prowled around the room, restless with energy.

"I think I know who he was," he said finally. "He was at Pantile House. With Varley." He shook his head. "I've been blind."

"How do you mean?"

"I looked right past him. I thought the goons outside were the only potential danger. I was wrong." He paused, then continued, "One of the security men from outside the hotel was missing yesterday evening. I never gave it a thought. I think he may have been here, checking out the area. Did you see anyone?"

Riley thought back. She couldn't recall anyone obvious; no strangers lurking in the bushes or canvassers with aimless lists of boxes to tick. The last time that had happened had been weeks –

"The drunk," she said, remembering the fat man leaning against the lamp post. "I was standing at the window, holding the cat. There was a man."

"What did he look like?"

"Short… fat. Bulky, anyway. A tight suit. That's all I could see – the light wasn't great and I wasn't really paying attention. He'd have seen me quite clearly." The idea that the man had been deliberately play-acting while watching her made Riley's skin go cold. Then something else came back to her. The photo Al-Bashir had shown her, of the man who'd followed her into the store.

It was the same man.

"His name's Pechov," she said quietly, appalled. "I just didn't connect it."

"Sounds like the one who was missing from Pantile House," Palmer said. "They must be getting desperate for this article to be published. A pity we don't know why it's so important."

"Actually, we do," Riley said. It all seemed blindingly obvious now, as if sleep and the threats and Donald's call had unleashed a torrent of connecting thoughts. She told Palmer about the article in *East European Trade* which had effectively torpedoed the Turkish minister's career.

"If the piece on Al-Bashir is in the same mould," Palmer said, "it must have taken some planning. You don't just come up with the idea of smearing someone on a whim. But why?"

"It probably goes back to when Al-Bashir first announced he was bidding for the Batnev licence. Until then the only ones in the running would have been the big international operators, and some local syndicates with the money to invest. The internationals are already being quietly ruled out by the federation David Johnson told me about, which just leaves the locals. Al-Bashir entering the fray must have been seen as a serious threat, so they decided to expose a scandal, hoping his fundamentalist backers would run for the hills rather than be tainted by association."

"Risky strategy. What if it hadn't worked? Money often talks louder than principles."

Riley shrugged. She wasn't entirely certain about her interpretation, but what else was there? "This could be a first option. They might have a more final one: remove the bidder altogether."

Palmer looked sceptical. "Difficult to control the outcome to that. Bumping off prominent types like Al-Bashir isn't as simple as it used to be. People talk. Sell out."

"But the end justifies the means, right? The rewards if it all goes to plan are eye-watering."

"You think the same people are behind this Turkish minister's downfall?"

"Why not? You'd be surprised at the connections that exist

across the commercial world. There are people with fingers in all manner of pies."

"But telecoms and shipping – are they connected?"

"They are when it comes to international business. Most of the big fortunes years ago were founded on shipping. It's still important, but the emphasis has changed since then to communications. Money is still the driver."

"So where does the magazine fit in to all of this?"

"There's only one explanation; it's used to get the information out there." She thought back to her conversation with Natalya. "Professor Fisher said EET has been in business for some years. They wouldn't have lasted this long if all they did was dish the dirt on people they didn't like. It would look too personal. But running the occasional exposé might seem like a normal day's work."

"And nobody obvious to take the blame."

"Apart from an anonymous 'staff' writer. Or, in this case, me."

"Or you." Palmer stared out of the window, his jaw set. His words were vague, as if his mind was elsewhere. Riley thought she knew where.

"You're thinking of Helen."

He nodded. "And Annaliese Kellin. It's beginning to make sense. Single, freelance, with no family and few close friends. Ideal candidates if things didn't work out."

Riley saw where he was going. "They both had the kind of track record which gave the article the credibility it needed. The Batnev project is a bigger prize than discrediting a Turkish minister, so don't take chances with an anonymous writer – get a named one to front the piece."

"But when they didn't like what they saw and decided to jump ship…" Palmer didn't need to finish.

Riley swallowed. What he had also avoided saying was that she might so easily have gone the same way. She heard the desolation in his voice, saw the stillness in his face, and felt guilty; guilty at surviving when the others hadn't; guilty at believing all the lies and being so easily taken in by Richard Varley's charm; guilty at having a friend like Palmer, something the other two girls had lacked when they had so needed it. She stood up and put her arms around him, needing as much to help him as to take comfort from his strength. "I'm so sorry, Frank."

He shook his head. "Don't be. It's they who should feel sorry."

She pulled her head back. As well as the anger in his eyes, there was an intense light burning deep inside, like twin lasers. She shivered and thought about the man in the hotel.

Her phone rang. She pulled away from Palmer and picked it up. When she replaced it, her eyes were wide and her face had a ghostly pallor.

"What's up?" Palmer asked.

Things were going from bad to worse. "That was Mark Chase," she said, her voice faint. "The supervisor at Pantile House – Goricz? He didn't clock in for work today. They asked an employee who lives nearby to check his house. He lived with his wife, mother-in-law and teenage son." She swallowed and shook her head. "Goricz is missing. The others are all dead. Shot in the head."

37

Riley's mobile was buzzing. She rolled over, kicking aside the bedclothes, disorientated by finding herself in a strange single bed. After hearing of the murder of Goricz's family, they had decamped the previous night, encouraging Mr Grobowski to do the same. It would only be for a day or two. He had gone to friends; Riley was in a small hotel north of the Edgware Road. Palmer was in a room just along the corridor.

Riley had been reluctant to let anyone drive her out of her home, but commonsense had prevailed, reinforced by the shock of the murders and Palmer's suggestion that the gunman who'd shot Lipinski – maybe one and the same man – might come back for another try.

She fumbled for the phone, expecting it to be the vet. To her surprise, it was Natalya Fisher, her voice unusually sombre.

"You were asking about a man named Richard Varley," the former KGB member said without preamble. In the background, a door slammed, a bell jangled and laughter echoed in a hollow corridor. School noises. She'd slept later than she'd thought. Her watch told her it was nine-thirty.

"That's right."

"I happened to mention him to friends of mine."

"People you used to work with?"

"Just friends. They know of him. They say Varley is nothing. A foot-soldier… a doer of deeds, not a decision maker." She coughed, the sound moving abruptly away from the phone. "Sorry – too many cigarettes."

"How would your friends know of him? He's American." Just for a second, Riley held on to the vague thought that Richard was nothing to do with the man who had threatened her.

She was soon disappointed.

"No."

"But he told me he was an army brat."

"An army brat, yes, Miss Gavin. But not American army." She paused. "Russian."

A ticking on the line was the only sound for a long time.

"*What*?" Riley finally managed to drag out a response. She felt something drain out of her.

"His real name," continued Natalya softly, "is Vasiliyev. He comes from Petrograd."

"No."

"Yes. He was a good student and worked very hard; he scored top grades in his class. When they discovered he had a facility for languages, he was recruited into the army where they placed him in a political section and polished off his rough edges, preparing for operations against the Americans."

"Spying?"

"Not directly. At the time, they had plans to use American-sounding officers to become friendly with their American counterparts. It was all part of a grand plan – a soft infiltration. Then everything changed and they had no use for men like him. No money, either. He left the army and went into private work."

"What sort of private work?"

"Mostly criminal. He uses other names from time to time. Men in his line of work often do."

Riley slumped against the headboard, waiting for more. She wondered if Natalya's friends had got the name wrong. Or maybe there was more than one Varley in publishing. Richard had seemed so smooth, so in charge, she had a hard time imagining him as anyone's gofer, still less someone named Vasiliyev. Then she recalled his manner when he had come to her flat. For a man normally so in control, he hadn't been exactly calm.

She'd attributed that to the pressure he was under from the shareholders of Ercovoy Publishing. Now she knew better. She felt a stab of something akin to shame at how naïve she must have seemed.

"You say he works for someone?"

"Yes. I am told a man named Fedorov."

That name again – the one Koenig had mentioned. "Who is he?"

"A man you do not wish to meet," Natalya replied bluntly. "He is well known in the country I come from. Fedorov has many friends and contacts across Eastern Europe. He is not a man to cross."

"He's one of these oligarchs?"

"An oligarch? I don't know for sure. Rich, certainly. Very rich. For that reason, maybe he pretends to be something he is not. But he is different. We have our career criminals, too, you know. They love money, like all crooks."

"Is he Russian mafia?"

"Perhaps. Probably. Nobody knows. They are not always easy to identify, these people. They belong to impenetrable factions, hiding behind various identities, their loyalties changing all the time. *Mafiya* is an easy title to put on men like him, but not always accurate."

"What's his full name?" Her instinct for detail asserted itself, dulling the disappointment of discovering that Richard Varley was not what he seemed.

"Ah, that I do know. He is called Pavel Ivanovich Fedorov. But he is not called Pavel by those who know him well. He uses the name Grigori. He does not care for Pavel, because it is from Latin, and means small."

"Great. A rich man with an ego problem."

Natalya gave a bark of laughter. "Tell me any man who has not. He was brought up by an uncle who was not successful with women due to his small stature. Because of this, he took out his frustrations on the boy."

"What happened?"

"One day the uncle disappeared. Fedorov was sixteen. He reported to the police that his uncle had gone looking for work."

"Oh."

"Later, Fedorov disappeared, too. When he returned, some years later, he was a different man. He was making money – doing what, nobody knows. But we can guess. He had moved up in the world and continued to do so. Now he has friends and wants more. It is said he is under investigation by the Interior Ministry in Moscow for illegal business practices and state fraud. This is very serious, but there are ways around it. He is looking for ways to make those investigations go away."

Riley remembered the analogy Natalya had used before, about exiled Russians. The boy going back home with the school prize. "Would that be enough, though?" she asked. "Ruining Al-Bashir's chances in the telecoms market?"

"It would," the professor confirmed, "if it meant control would stay in the hands of local organisations. Better that than going to a westerner." She sighed as if recognising that some things could never change. "As I explained to you before, some sins can always be forgiven if the price is right."

"What does this Fedorov look like? In case I should bump into him."

"I hope you do not, Miss Gavin, for your sake. But I think you will know him as soon as you do."

"How?" Riley felt a thud in her chest. Even as Natalya said it, an image, unbidden, had begun to swim up from deep in her consciousness. Suddenly, she knew without a shadow of a doubt: she *had* met Fedorov – and the next words confirmed it.

"Fedorov is short and becoming bald. He looks and dresses

like an accountant, and always stays in the background, where nobody sees him. My friends say he is a man to miss in a crowd. But most of all, a man to avoid... "

Riley switched off her phone. Her mouth was dry and she felt her heart pounding at the realisation that she had made a serious mistake. The colourless 'associate' was actually the boss. Which made Richard... what, exactly? According to Natalya, he was a soldier... a doer of deeds.

But did it also make him a killer?

38

Riley spent the day in the hotel, confined as much by her own feelings of disquiet, as by Palmer's advice to stay out of sight. The attractions of room service palled rapidly after the first two orders, along with daytime television, the video selection and the view across the rooftops and back gardens of Maida Vale. When she opened the window, she could hear the steady boom of traffic along the Westway, reminding her that life was still going on out there, in spite of and no doubt ignorant of death threats, Russian killers and wounded cats.

She called the surgery for regular updates on Lipinski, and found each one offering better news than the last.

"I don't know what you feed him on," said the receptionist at one point, "but that's a hell of a tough cat."

"Polish meatballs, mostly," Riley told her, and thanked her before hanging up.

Out of boredom, she soon found herself going over everything that Richard Varley had said, the files on Al-Bashir... and the threats uttered by the man she now knew as Pavel Ivanovich Fedorov.

And Varley. She was still having trouble coming to grips with the idea of him being someone called Vasiliyev. It was all too alien.

Then came thoughts of Helen Bellamy and the German reporter, Annaliese Kellin, and the part they had unwittingly played in this affair. And how she had come within an ace of sharing the same fate.

"You OK?" Palmer stood in the doorway. He'd just returned from a tour of the streets around the hotel. He was, she knew, unwilling to take for granted that the gunman who had come to

Riley's flat wouldn't find some way of tracking her down if those were his orders.

"Palmer, I'm going stir-crazy," she replied. "I need to do something. Can't I put on a hat and go out for a walk?"

"Maybe later, when it's dark. We still don't know what resources these people have got. All it needs is for someone to spot you. Shooting the cat was a warning. I doubt they'll leave it at that. Keep this door locked." He glanced at her mobile on the bed. "Any news?"

"You mean the cat? Yes, he's fine. Indestructible, according to the vet." She paused, unsure how to begin telling him about Natalya's call. She felt more than foolish already, and didn't need to suffer more humiliation over having been duped so easily.

"And?"

"What 'and'?"

He rolled his eyes, and she told him about Richard Varley/Vasiliyev and his master, Fedorov.

Palmer took in the news with little reaction. "Don't sweat it," he said evenly. "You weren't to know. But it answers lots of questions. This was carefully planned and financed. They're not here to fool around."

"Palmer?" Riley got off the bed and faced him.

He waited.

"Do you have something I can use?" She gestured at the room. "I feel naked."

"You mean a gun? No way. Forget it."

"No. Not that. Anything… I don't know." She shrugged helplessly, unsure about what she was asking. "Something."

Palmer's lips twitched. He reached into his jacket and took out a short black rod covered in hard foam. He gave a sharp jerk and it snapped into a tapered steel baton with a hard plastic tip. He pressed a release button in the handle and retracted it, then handed it to her. "Try it."

Riley was surprised by the weight. But it felt reassuring in her hand. She flicked her arm sideways, the way she'd seen Palmer do it, but nothing happened. She tried again, harder. This time she was rewarded with a satisfying click as the baton extended and locked out.

"Wow," she muttered, amazed by the feel of it in her hand. "Cool or what?"

"It won't make you bullet-proof," he warned her. "So take it easy."

"I will." She tried a couple of practice swings. "Where do I aim for?"

Palmer shrugged. "If you're mad enough at the time, any-where you can reach."

"What then?"

"Then you run like hell."

The long afternoon blended with aching slowness into the evening. Riley stood up from time to time, swinging the baton and getting a feel for its weight, snapping it out and back. Palmer was right: it wouldn't make her bullet-proof, but it might make all the difference if anyone came in here after her.

She eyed her phone and the time. It brought thoughts about John Mitcheson; it was probably morning wherever he was. They hadn't spoken in weeks. Months, actually. Should she give him a call, or would that seem too desperate? If she did, what would she say that wasn't going to sound pathetic? In the end, she decided against it. Boredom was insufficient reason to go unearthing something better left to take its own course.

In the end, she decided that enough was enough. She had to see the cat. And have a very strong drink or some fresh air, whichever came most readily to hand. She rang Palmer, but he wasn't answering.

She checked her watch. Nearly six o'clock. She threw on a

jacket and pocketed the baton, then slipped out of the room, half expecting Palmer to emerge from a doorway like a shadow and kick her back inside. She made her way downstairs and out through the rear entrance, which opened on to a narrow back street lined with skips, dustbins and a couple of bikes chained to some railings.

She decided to walk to the surgery, located on a quiet street in Westbourne Park. It wasn't far and she needed to feel the stretch in the back of her legs and the firm pavement beneath her feet. Soft carpets and sprung floors were fine for a while, but there were limits to the amount of comfort she could endure.

She arrived at the surgery and was ushered through to what the nurse called the convalescence suite, a room lined with cages, each holding a sick animal. The remainder of the space was heaped with an assortment of medical equipment, boxes of animal foods and pet paraphernalia.

Lipinski was sitting up, wearing what looked like a backpack with lots of strapping holding it in place. He looked bored and restless. She knew how he felt.

"He was lucky," the nurse told her, as Riley scrubbed the cat gently under the chin and he drooled over her fingers. "The bullet didn't hit anything vital, so there was no internal bleeding. He'll have a bald patch once the dressing comes off, but that will soon grow back." She eyed Riley cautiously. "The police said they'd be in touch. Sorry, but we had to report it."

Riley thanked her and wondered if they had already been to her flat to make enquiries. No doubt Craig Pell would have something to say when he found out, and she found herself smiling at the idea.

After ten minutes of talking to the cat, during which time he veered from looking interested on hearing her familiar voice, to grumpy when he realised she wasn't about to take him home, Riley decided she had better get back to her hotel room before

Palmer began scouring the greater London area in search of her. She gave the cat a final rub along his flanks and said softly, "Never mind, chum. When you get out, you can compare bullet wounds with Szulu."

With that, she told him to get well soon and left the surgery. She decided to take a taxi, in case Palmer was busy tearing his hair out, and set out towards the nearby Tube station, where the chances of picking one up would be greater.

She was only yards from the surgery when a large car pulled into the kerb ahead of her. A man jumped out and bent down to inspect a front wheel. He swore loudly and banged the wing, then stood up and looked around as if hoping a handy tyre depot would appear nearby.

As Riley drew level, he looked at her then looked away again.

Riley's antennae began to tremble. There was something about the man. He was tall and muscular, with a bullish neck and cropped hair. The way he had looked at her was just a little too deliberate, too focussed. She gripped the baton inside her pocket, her heart-rate increasing fast, and began to step away.

The rest happened very quickly. Riley heard one of the rear doors of the car click open, and from the corner of her eye, saw a second man emerging. This one was shorter and heavier. The first man turned in the same instant and stepped towards her, reaching out with big hands.

Whipping out the baton, Riley flicked it open and slashed the first man across the face. She felt the impact travel through her wrist and lower arm, and the man cursed but kept coming. The baton fell away, her fingers stinging and unable to retain their grip. Before she could retrieve it, the second man was on her, scooping her up in his massive arms and bundling her through the door on to the back seat like a sack of laundry. Following her in, he landed on top of her with a grunt, smothering any further resistance.

Riley tried to scream, to attract the attention of someone, anyone. She caught a glimpse through the open car door of a woman's startled face, watching from the pavement. Then a large hand was clamped over her mouth, the doors slammed shut and the car surged away down the street.

Frank Palmer tried Riley's room again. He'd already been up once but got no reply, and the receptionist had confirmed that the key had not been left. He tried her mobile, but there was no connection. He tried to think where she might have gone. Back to the flat to get some clothes? No, he'd made sure she had sufficient for at least three days. What other priorities did she have?

The cat. It had to be. He checked his watch. It was nearly seven-thirty. He went back down and asked the porter to get him a list of veterinary surgeries close to where Riley lived. He remembered her saying that the place wasn't far from the flat, which narrowed down the possibilities.

Eventually, the porter came up with three names, and he began dialling. The first two had closed for the day, and were on voice-mail. He struck lucky on the third.

"Miss Gavin left about an hour ago," the nurse confirmed, and Palmer instantly picked up something in the tone of her voice.

"What is it?" he said.

"Well, it might be nothing, but one of our customers came in and said she saw a young woman being pushed into a car by two men right outside the surgery. We called the police, but they haven't shown up yet. That's why I'm still here. I hope she's all right…"

Palmer thanked her and disconnected. He swore long and silently. Supposing it wasn't what the woman had thought? Maybe some friends messing around. An hour wasn't long –

Riley could have decided to stop off somewhere else, under-standable after being cooped up in the hotel all day. But instinct told him it wasn't that simple.

He began to dial DI Pell's number, then stopped. Pell wasn't the sort to mess about; he'd do the right thing, which was to mobilise all the resources he could muster. Especially given the circumstances and his knowledge of Riley's background from Weller. But going in with all guns blazing was the worst thing they could do. A blue light showing up within half a mile of anywhere Riley was being taken – if it had been her being lifted off the street – could only end one way.

He dialled Ray Szulu, who was still watching Pantile House, and told him what he wanted.

39

By Riley's reckoning, the journey couldn't have lasted more than thirty minutes, but it felt like hours. Once the man holding her seemed satisfied she wasn't going to kick and scream, he let go of her, but made her lie down with her head pressed into the back seat. To make sure she complied, he held a gun across her neck, buried under her hair. It felt cold and greasy against her skin, and she tried to recall what Palmer had told her about safety catches and the sensitivity of trigger mechanisms.

A stream of furious words in Russian and the occasional obscenity in English came from the driver, and Riley guessed it was the man she had hit with the baton. Eventually, the man holding her tired of it and said something short and sharp. The complaining ceased.

When the vehicle stopped, Riley was dragged from the car and marched across a short expanse of concrete. She had no opportunity to escape. Her captor kept one arm across her shoulders, his other hand holding her face in a vice-like grip and pressed into his chest. To an onlooker, Riley decided grimly, they might look like lovers, and she was as sickened at that dreadful irony as by the man's proximity and the smell of his unwashed clothing.

In the background, the car door slammed and the vehicle moved away.

Seconds later, a door creaked and she caught a brief glimpse of bright lights. When her feet echoed over tiled flooring, she knew instinctively where she was.

Pantile House.

The man let go of her face to palm the door open, and for the first time Riley managed to get a look at him. Her stomach went cold.

It was Pechov.

The lift hummed and the floor shifted. They were going up. The close atmosphere held nothing but the sound of the man's breathing and the creaking of the lift mechanism. When it stopped, Pechov bundled her out into a short corridor. One of her shoes came off, but he forced her on, making no move to retrieve it. He stopped at a door and kicked it open, pushing her through. She caught the sharp tang of disinfectant and saw more bright lights, and a row of sinks and several cubicles with thin walls. A tall metal rubbish bin stood beneath a hand drier. An extractor fan hummed, giving out an intermittent clatter. A tampon dispenser was fixed to one wall. They were in a women's washroom.

A hard chair was positioned ominously in front of the sinks. Pechov pushed Riley into it. He yanked her jacket down off her shoulders and produced a roll of gaffer tape; in seconds he had her taped to the chair with her hands immobilised behind her back.

When he was satisfied Riley couldn't move, he took out a mobile and dialled a number. He spoke briefly, then hung up and looked at her with an evil smile. "You in big trouble," he breathed thickly, and took a toffee from his pocket. He unwrapped it and popped it into his mouth, sucking noisily. "Boss is not happy man."

Footsteps echoed along the corridor outside the washroom door. For a brief moment, Riley hoped that it might represent rescue: that someone had seen what was happening and had come to take her away from this.

Then the door swung open and Grigori Fedorov entered.

He murmured to Pechov, who nodded and left, closing the door behind him. Fedorov walked across and stood looking down at Riley. Up close, she thought he looked slightly ruffled, the collar of his shirt slightly grey. Or maybe it was the lights.

"This is not productive, Miss Gavin," he said at last, his dry voice echoing off the tiled walls. "I have not the time for this."

"Tell me about it," she replied, surprised at how level her own voice sounded. She felt a tremor run through her left leg and fought to still it.

He stood for a moment, before turning away. Almost casually, he picked up the rubbish bin. Then, with a vicious surge of rage, he swung it in an arc over his head and brought it crashing down on the end sink. Shards of porcelain flew into the air as the front edge of the basin disintegrated, and a large piece fell to the floor and lay spinning raggedly, like a demented top.

Riley couldn't help it; she closed her eyes, stunned by the unexpected display of violence. When she opened them again, Fedorov was standing in front of her, breathing heavily, his eyes glittering.

"You did not call," he said quietly, a tremor in his voice. "I was disappointed." He stepped over to the sinks, his shoes crunching on splinters of porcelain, and studied his reflection in the mirror, turning his face left and right. Then he turned on one of the hot taps and let the water run. He tested the temperature, but turned it off again with a hiss of irritation.

Bending down, he picked up a sliver of porcelain. It was the length of a finger, with a razor-sharp edge. He ran his thumb along it. The skin opened as if sliced with a surgeon's scalpel, and a hairline of blood welled up. Turning to Riley, he touched the sliver to her face with almost gentle care, and drew it slowly across her cheek from one side to the other. It felt ice-cold to the touch. Riley froze, not daring to move or imagine what it might be doing to her skin.

Dreading what was coming next, she felt herself shrink inside.

Then footsteps approached and Pechov appeared. He was

carrying a steaming kettle.

"I wonder if you remember what I said to you, the last time we met?" Fedorov murmured. He sounded almost disappointed, as if a spell had been broken. He tossed the porcelain to one side and took the kettle, dismissing Pechov with a jerk of his head. "I believe I told you of the custom we have for people who do not do what they have agreed?"

Riley said nothing, her eyes fixed on the wisp of steam coming from the spout of the kettle.

Fedorov nodded. "Of course. How silly of me. You are a journalist, trained to remember things." His accent had become thicker, the final word pronounced as 'thinks'. He poured the boiled water into the sink, steam billowing into the air and clouding the mirrors. Then he dropped the kettle casually on the floor. Immersing his fingers in the water, he held them there, gently sucking in air through his teeth in a lengthy hiss.

Riley was stunned. She could see Fedorov's skin turning red with the heat, but beyond the initial reaction, it didn't seem to bother him.

"When I was young boy," he explained calmly, "I was made to stand out in the cold for hours, as punishment. No coat, no gloves. Arms above my head. It was very cold where I come from. My hands became numb. After a while, they lost most of their feeling. It never quite came back. What it taught me, Miss Gavin, was how to deal with extreme pain. How to close off the mind. How resistant are you to pain, Miss Gavin? Hmm?"

"What do you want?" she demanded, her voice shaking. "I'm not going to write that article, so you might as well let me go."

"Oh, I know that, Miss Gavin. I know that. But that is no longer the issue. Nor, sadly, is letting you go."

Without warning, he flicked a spray of water into her face.

Riley screamed as the hot liquid stung her skin. She saved her eyes only by instinctively turning away a split second before the water hit her. She kept her head turned, but Fedorov continued relentlessly, repeatedly flicking droplets at her, content to aim them at the side of her neck, where it burned into the soft skin of her throat and just behind her ears where the tissue was at its most sensitive. Riley clamped her teeth together, struggling as small rivulets began to run down inside her clothing, searing across her upper body and down over her stomach. The effect was like a line of fiery little ants scuttling over her skin, leaving her instantly chilled as the heat diminished. She tried not to scream, but in the end, could not prevent a low, agonised moan from escaping.

Fedorov examined his scalded fingers, which were a vivid red. One or two showed signs of blistering, and he blew on them gently, turning his hand, his intense stare on Riley as she fought in vain against the tape holding her.

"I can keep this up for a long time," he commented. "Hurting you slowly. Making you suffer. Or I can save us both a lot of unnecessary pain and effort." He moved round behind her and shunted the chair closer to the sink, making her recoil inwardly as his hips thrust against her. His stale breath washed over her as he leaned closer. Then, with slow deliberation, he placed a hand behind her head and forced her forward until she was staring down into the basin, the steam rising to envelop her face and hair.

"No… please…!" Riley gasped. She tried to resist, but the Russian was stronger than he looked. Her chest was pressing against the lip of the sink, and she knew that with one push, her face would be –

Suddenly he stopped. "Wait… I nearly forgot something." He stepped to one side and picked up a plastic bottle from beneath the sink. "A little… elaboration of mine." He unscrewed the top and dumped the contents of the bottle into the water.

The smell rose, harsh and acrid, and Riley gagged as her throat clamped shut against the familiar fumes.

Neat bleach.

Fedorov took hold of her once more, and began to push her face down to the water. "Now," he said softly. "Where were we?"

Vasiliyev barged through the front door of Pantile House and came face to face with Olek, one of the two tall security guards. The man was rubbing at his face with a more sullen expression than usual, and wincing. He had few conversational powers, but he knew what was expected of him and was unemotional in his work. It was Olek who had been sent to despatch the building's supervisor, Goricz, and his family.

Vasiliyev noticed a nasty red weal across the man's cheek. It was peppered with a line of blood dots showing where the skin had broken. "What happened to you?" he asked.

"I walked into a door," Olek replied sourly.

"You should be more careful. Where is the boss?"

"Upstairs. He's been waiting for you."

"Why? I've been waiting for him to call me." Vasiliyev wondered what was going on. Fedorov liked to keep a tight team around him, yet he'd ordered Vasiliyev to wait at the hotel until he was needed. But that had been hours ago. It had been an ominous development, following on Fedorov's earlier display of anger. In the end the waiting had become unbearable, and he'd come here to find out what was happening.

He turned towards the lift and found Olek right behind him. "Where are you going?"

"The boss said to show you up," Olek replied. He had a nasty smirk on his face. "Roychev will be along in a moment; he can watch the doors."

Vasiliyev shrugged, but felt a worm of unease in his belly. There was something going on here. Fedorov was unpredictable, mostly because he rarely took anyone into his confidence – not

213

even Vasiliyev. But this didn't feel right.

He stepped into the lift. Olek followed him, punching the button for the fourth floor.

40

Ray Szulu cruised the last half mile towards Pantile House, eyes alert for problems. Traffic was light and easy this late in the evening, the same on the pavements. The fewer people the better, for what he was about to do.

He was driving a white, unmarked Ford Transit, as common as a London taxi. It offered total anonymity and had good vision front and sides. The back he wasn't so worried about. He'd lifted the van half an hour ago from a deserted sales forecourt in Islington with a seizure notice on the front door. By the time anyone missed it, the van would be old news.

As he drew closer, he began drumming his fingers on the steering wheel. He couldn't help it; he was trying to convince himself that everything was cool, that he was OK with this. He could do it, no problem. So why, a niggling little voice wheedled in his innermost ear, was he acting like a virgin on her wedding night?

He gripped the wheel to stop the drumming, to cut out the voice. This, it was saying, was the stupidest thing he'd ever agreed to. Doing the surveillance job on the men and the building was one thing; it was easy money and entailed using his eyes, that was all. But this was going up another level. This amounted to direct action, which most definitely wasn't his thing.

He breathed deeply, forcing himself to calm down. What was he worried about, anyway? According to Palmer, Riley Gavin was the one in the fat-fryer. She'd managed to get herself lifted off the street by some Russian mafia types, and Palmer was sounding like he was ready to waste the entire north side of London to get her out. He could probably do it, too. Palmer was like a one-man search-and-rescue squad.

Szulu smiled suddenly, seeing himself as a Black Knight to Palmer's White. Gallant characters hadn't figured much in his upbringing, but now he thought about it, being any kind of knight felt pretty cool. And, if he had to be one, it might as well be black.

He looked down at the glove box with a sense of satisfaction. Palmer had told him he had to create a diversion at a specific time, and to use his initiative. It was an acknowledgment that he actually trusted him to do something without being told what.

"Be creative," the ex-army cop had said on the phone, in that lazy way he had of speaking. But beneath the calm, his voice had been anything but lazy. He'd sounded seriously pissed, and as cold as permafrost. "I need a diversion, and I'm relying on you to come up with something." He'd paused and added, "Make it loud. Just don't kill anyone. You know what collateral damage is?"

"Yeah, I know."

After telling Szulu precisely when he wanted it, he'd disconnected.

Szulu grinned at the memory and reached down for the length of nylon chord hanging from the glove box. He'd make it loud all right. This one was right from the Ray Szulu manual of insurance scams. The original idea had been tricky setting up, but he knew it would work because he'd used it a couple of times already. And best of all, nobody would be able to spot his handiwork. Fortunately, the mechanism was easy to put together and had taken only seconds to rig up.

He slowed his speed and checked the street either side. Palmer had said there could be watchers out, so look for anyone deliberately not doing anything. Like hard men in suits, he'd added.

Szulu shivered, in spite of himself. He knew what they looked like and didn't want to mess with them. He was just passing one of the doorways he'd used doing a recce of the place before. The building where the Russians had their base was along on the right, set back off a corner. Behind the building was a maze of narrow cross-sections filled with residential blocks and a few commercial properties. He'd taken a stroll earlier to see what was happening, but apart from a couple of small shops, some one-man-band businesses like printers and such, and a couple of pubs, there wasn't much activity and hardly any through-traffic. Best of all, there were plenty of dark patches between the lights. Ideal.

He drifted past the office block, ignoring it like Palmer had told him.

"Men like that," Palmer had explained, although Szulu didn't think he needed to, "can smell trouble. They've got senses most people don't have. Like radar. They develop it because of what they do."

Not just them, Szulu had wanted to tell him. I had that sense when I came out of the womb. It was part of the Szulu family DNA.

He glanced at his watch. Right on time. He pulled an about-turn and drove back, then turned sharp left and left again into the street behind the office block. As he did so, he lifted his foot off the accelerator and pumped it hard two or three times. The engine responded with a cough and a rattle, followed by a stutter as the fuel flow was interrupted, then did a kangaroo-hop as he repeated the process. He waved an apology to a car coming the other way and allowed the van to drift to a stop in the middle of the street. The engine stalled with a pop as he let his foot off the clutch. Simultaneously, he reached down and tugged hard at the length of nylon cord hanging from the glove box.

Under the bonnet, the other end of the cord was joined to a simple lever mechanism, then a flint and wheel from a cigarette lighter, and a cardboard Starbucks cup half filled with lighter fuel. A tug of the cord, and the flint made a spark over the fumes and splashes of petrol rising from the cup through the lid. He'd fitted a neat little spring since the last time he'd used it, so he could try again if it didn't take first time.

He swore. Nothing happened. He tugged again and began sweating. Damned if he was going to go back to Palmer and tell him it hadn't worked. He'd stick his head under the bonnet and strike the bloody lighter himself before that happened.

There was a *whump* from the front, followed by a thin plume of smoke curling out of the vent and up the windscreen like a soft lizard. He could smell lighter fuel. He counted to ten, then stamped on the accelerator. The engine flooded, as he knew it would, and he tried to re-start it. The starter motor whined noisily, but refused to catch.

Thicker smoke began seeping from under the bonnet, and he saw a faint flicker of orange in a gap in the bodywork. He checked his watch. Palmer must be counting, too, waiting for the bang.

The smoke became black and oily, snaking lazily out from all sides and lifting into the air. It billowed across the narrow street, gusting in the faint breeze and clinging to the sides of the buildings. Szulu could smell it now, hot and choking, making his eyes water. A voice shouted nearby, and someone laughed.

He jumped out of the van, leaving the door swinging open, and popped the bonnet. The heat surged out fierce and instantaneous, followed by a blast of flame and a curl of black smoke which seemed to reach for him like an angry monster. He dodged sideways and tried to locate where his fire-starter was lodged. If he could get the device out, all the better. There'd be nothing for any nosy accident inspector to find, should they come looking. But one look told him that his little plan had worked too well. The cup and lighter were gone, consumed by the flames. If he got any closer, he'd be roast meat. Best if he

218

bailed out and left it to burn. With a quick check to see nobody else was close enough to try any heroics, he turned and ran.

He was only fifteen yards away when the van exploded. A gust of hot air touched the back of his neck and something whizzed past his left ear and clanged off a Renault parked at the kerb. Glass smashed as something collided with a nearby window.

Szulu stumbled, his legs going weak, and hit the ground, his knees burning on the tarmac. He felt a momentary panic, enlivened by a sense of achievement. *Impressive or what?* He scrambled to his feet and turned to watch the van burn, the flames stained blacker than the night air as oil joined the mix. He checked the pavement again for pedestrians; Palmer didn't want anyone hurt by this. But there was nobody to warn away, the few onlookers still some fifty yards away at the end of the street.

He stood for a moment shaking his head, hoping to preserve the image of a distraught driver with his livelihood going up in flames before him. He rubbed smoke from his eyes, and grinned to himself. For the first time in his life, he didn't care what anyone thought. He'd done what he'd set out to do.

Up on the fourth floor, in the windowless washroom, the sound of the explosion barely registered, coming as a dull crump above the noise of the extractor fan. Fedorov, always acutely alert for any unusual sounds, glanced towards the door.

Riley heard it, too, and strained desperately against the tape holding her in place, hoping against hope that it would weaken enough for her to get free. Her face was already smarting painfully from the splash burns, and she was trying not to imagine the results if Fedorov did what he had threatened, and what effect the bleach would have on her skin, her hair. Her eyes.

She almost gave in and screamed, but she knew Fedorov would be on to her before the first sound was out.

"What do you want from me?" she demanded, coughing and heaving against the smell. A distant part of her brain was dredging up the constituent parts of bleach, recognised from the kitchen at home, the useless details filed away in her subconscious: Sodium Hydroxide and Sodium Hypochlorite. The words were almost harmless when she thought about them; mere chemical words to warn the domestic masses. *To be washed off immediately and kept out of the reach of children. In case of contact with eyes, seek medical help.*

"Who says I want anything?" Fedorov bent over and breathed in the fumes for a few seconds, as if relishing the purity and headiness of a fine wine. He turned his head and smiled, and she felt a cold chill run through her body. It was like coming under the gaze of a killer shark. She began to shiver violently and gritted her teeth, determined that this monster wasn't going to have the pleasure of seeing her grovel.

Then footsteps approached and Fedorov straightened.

The door burst open and slammed back against the wall. The noise echoed around the room, followed by the sound of a wall tile hitting the floor under the impact of the handle. A tall figure stood in the doorway.

For a split second, Riley felt elation as she recognised Richard Varley. Then, behind him, a vaguely familiar figure. This man had a vivid mark across his face. She realised with a sinking feeling that he was the one she had hit with Palmer's baton.

Varley looked stunned when he saw her. The colour drained from his face as he surveyed the scene, and he stared at Fedorov as if he didn't recognise the man.

He shouted something, the words making no sense to Riley, although the tone was full of anger. But the language reminded her that he was really a former Russian soldier named Vasiliyev, and any fleeting thoughts she might have harboured about him being here to help her turned to dust.

The outburst continued in a torrent, harsh and uncompromising, his eyes blazing. The veins stood out on his neck as he gesticulated at Riley and the sink filled with water; the smell of bleach in the air and the empty bottle amid the fragments of porcelain on the floor.

When he finally stopped, Fedorov replied. It was in English and addressed to the second man. "Olek. That noise outside. See what it is."

Olek nodded and disappeared. In the following silence, they could all hear distant shouting and a car alarm going off. There was no movement from Fedorov or Vasiliyev, who stared at each other as if they were figures in a ghastly silent tableau.

Moments later, Olek was back. He grinned nastily and jerked a thumb over his shoulder. "It looks like a delivery van caught fire in the street. The driver's running around like a headless chicken. It's nothing to worry about."

Fedorov nodded, then turned to Vasiliyev. When he spoke, his anger was quieter, more restrained, yet to Riley, even though he had reverted to Russian, so much more obvious. And menacing. As he finished speaking, he made a brief gesture.

And Olek, still in the background, produced a handgun and placed the tip of the barrel against Vasiliyev's head.

Riley sucked in her breath and closed her eyes, waiting in dread for the inevitable. When she opened them again several seconds later, she was alone.

41

Palmer felt the dull thump of the explosion vibrate through the floor of Pantile House. A trickle of dust rained down, silvery brown in the bulkhead lights. He winced. Whatever kind of device Szulu had used, he'd have made less noise with a pack of Semtex.

He stayed where he was. Give the men in and around the building time to react, to go to the windows and check the surroundings. It would be natural to look outside first, before assuming the noise had come from within. When they saw what was happening out in the street, provided Szulu had made it look realistic enough, they'd relax.

Earlier, after checking the outside of the building, he'd settled down to wait while the area had quietened down. The lights on the various floors had gone out one by one, all except for the lobby area at ground level and the dim glow from the desk lamp on number four. Still he had hung back, waiting. The move had proved to be a wise one; not long afterwards, a police constable had arrived with a civilian bearing a bunch of keys. They had left a few minutes later, the officer carrying some files and a cardboard box. The last remaining possessions, he'd surmised, of the late Mr Goricz. Hopefully, it was an indication that the police wouldn't be back for a while.

He watched as the two taller security guards appeared in turn, checking the front entrance and scanning the outside of the building. They moved about at random, keeping to the shadows, and were plainly accustomed to the conditions. There was no sign of the shorter man, Pechov.

Satisfied he was unobserved, Palmer waited until the guards disappeared before moving over to the louvred vent he had used before. He removed some of the slats, then pushed in the mesh and dropped stealthily into the basement. The familiar smell of cement dust and stale air rose to greet him. Replacing the outer slats, he squatted down and listened, allowing his eyes to adjust to the shadows and the dull glow of the passage lights.

He allowed five minutes to go by, ignoring the first signs of cramp in his legs. All he could hear above the hum and click of the heating system was the rumble of traffic outside.

Once he was satisfied it was safe to move, he stood up and flexed his legs, then walked slowly along the passageway, stopping every few yards to listen. He moved past the scaffolding and the cement bags, stepping over the spread of spilled powder. He was no longer bothered about leaving traces; everything had advanced too far for that. He reached the dark mass of the puddle he'd seen last time, now more of a small pool, and stopped again.

He was about to step past the pool when he noticed the curved edge of a footprint.

He eased against the wall, straining to hear a hint of noise in the dark. His options right now were limited. He could go forward or back. He studied the gloom along the passageway, searching for signs of movement. But it seemed to stare right back, unfathomable. Unfriendly. Someone had been down here recently. It might have been a maintenance worker, although that didn't seem likely, given the mess down here. And Goricz hadn't struck him as the sort to go out of his way to look for work. Maybe it was one of the security goons who'd come to check out the place. More likely, perhaps, but why bother? Had he left some sign when he'd come down here last time, alerting the men to his visit? Unlikely but not impossible. If they were already keyed up because of using the building illegally, they would be on maximum alert against anything out of the ordinary.

He squatted down and checked the area beyond the pool.

There were no prints on the other side, which meant that whoever had been here had been cautious enough to wipe their shoes before moving on.

He was concerned about Szulu's diversion out in the street. The fallout wouldn't last much longer; beyond the initial excitement of a vehicle fire and the arrival of the emergency services, there was little to hold people's attention for more than a few minutes. He could already hear the distant wail of a siren, but any attention drawn to the outside of the building would soon diminish, and all eyes and ears would turn back on the interior.

He stood up and was about to step forward when something else caught his eye. A couple of empty cement bags had been moved or had fallen, revealing an object which looked startlingly out of place. He leaned down to study it.

Lying half covered by the empty bags was a strip of leather with a buckle at one end. The metal glinted freshly in the light, sharply at odds with the dusty surroundings. The other end of the leather was torn, where the stitching had been ripped open as if by great force.

He held the strip up to the light... and felt something inside him go still. The leather was burgundy in colour, and the buckle was gold.

The strap from Helen's briefcase.

A pipe gurgled nearby, then died. A door slammed, distant and muffled. The high-pitched hum of the lift mechanism sang for a moment, then stopped. The living, breathing sounds of a building going on as usual.

Palmer took a deep breath to steady himself, and wrapped the strap absent-mindedly, yet with almost tender care, around his left hand.

Ten yards ahead, a bulky structure stood in the passageway. It was the aluminium ducting, part of the building's heating mechanism. Palmer checked the tunnel behind him. Nothing back there. Ahead, some way beyond the ducting, he could see the solid outline of the door to the service stairs leading to the ground floor.

As he drew level with the heating duct, he heard a faint rasp, followed by a whisper of moving cloth.

And something cold touched the side of his head.

42

A man was standing alongside him. His presence had been swallowed by the pool of shadow cast by the square ducting, the sound of his breathing hidden by the noise of the heating system. He had simply waited for Palmer to draw level, then reached out and placed the tip of the gun barrel against his head.

"Not to move." The man spoke softly. His breath was hot and sweet against Palmer's cheek. With his other hand, he reached out and patted Palmer down, flicking at Palmer's jacket and trousers to test for weapons. Satisfied there were none, he used the pressure of the gun against Palmer's head to force him across the other side of the tunnel, then spun him roughly until his back was to the wall.

Palmer allowed himself to be steered, conscious of the gun and knowing that down here it was unlikely the sound of a shot would carry far. The man was also strong, and clearly capable of handling any resistance. As he was forced back against the wall, Palmer felt the network of pipes and cabling digging into him.

In the light of the tunnel, the man was revealed as short and squat, with massive shoulders and a bull neck. His suit seemed to be losing the battle to contain his torso, and a tie knotted carelessly round his neck looked like a piece of string. His face was bare of emotion, like a wood-carving. He wore a Bluetooth headset in his left ear, the mouthpiece flat against his jaw like a character from a science-fiction movie.

Pechov.

He stared at Palmer and gestured with the gun barrel. "Put hands behind pipe." He pointed downwards.

Palmer turned his head. A four-inch pipe ran the length of

the wall just below waist level. It was held in place by metal brackets every six feet or so, leaving a small gap between the pipe and the tunnel wall.

He did as he was instructed. It was a tight fit. The pipe was uncomfortably hot against the inside of his wrists, and he guessed it carried oil or water. He worked his hands further down so his jacket sleeve acted as a barrier. This wasn't good. With his hands trapped like this, he was too vulnerable.

Even as the thought occurred to him, Pechov suddenly dipped one shoulder and delivered a short, brutal punch to Palmer's mid-section with his free hand. Palmer felt as if he'd been hit by a runaway truck. He gasped and sagged against the wall, all the air driven from his lungs, his back rubbing painfully against the pipes and cables.

"What you want here, huh?" the Russian demanded. He prodded Palmer in the chest with the gun barrel. Hard. "What you do here?" Without warning, he threw another vicious punch and more pain blossomed in Palmer's belly. The man laughed. He obviously enjoyed inflicting pain.

As Palmer fought for breath, he saw Pechov reach up to touch his earpiece. He was going to call someone.

"*Wait.*" Palmer could barely get the word out. If he didn't do something quickly, this moron was either going to summon help or beat him to death. Probably both. At the very least he was here to stop anyone intruding, and he clearly didn't care how he went about it, or how permanent his actions might be. Right now, Palmer didn't think his internal organs could take another punch.

Pechov leaned in close, breathing sweet air into Palmer's face. He followed it with a vicious prod of the gun. "Yes?"

Palmer nodded and coughed, then cleared his throat and spat wetly to one side. He allowed an agonised groan to escape from his chest and shook his head as a dribble of saliva ran down his chin. The man pulled a face and stepped back. Too far, thought Palmer. He had to draw him back in.

"I've got… got something for Fedorov," he croaked in between breaths. "You have to… to see it."

At the mention of his boss's name, Pechov leaned close. "What is?"

Palmer wriggled his left hand, and felt the briefcase strap uncoil and swing free. The buckle glinted as it moved.

Pechov saw it at once. "What?" He reached down and grasped the strap, lifting up the free end and staring at it, turning over the buckle to better study it in the poor light. Then he smiled in recognition. "Of course. Pretty lady. Very pretty. But not any more." He sniggered obscenely, his tongue pink and worm-like between thick lips. He peered at Palmer from piggy eyes and dropped his end of the strap with a gesture of contempt. "Your friend, perhaps?" he said softly, taunting, and made an obscene gesture with a stubby finger. "She good. Like lady upstairs."

Palmer felt a cold rage begin to eat into him like acid. The pain, the discomfort, even the presence of the gun, all slid away into the background as his focus centred on the man before him. Anger, he had always been taught, was a weakness. Anger can make you lose control. Anger can make you reckless. It can even get you killed.

But what Palmer was feeling went far beyond the brief red mist of mindless violence in a pub fight on a Saturday night, or the impulsive desire to hit back at a thoughtless insult. This was more like running towards an enemy when all good sense told you to stay back.

"It's a bogoff," he grunted, and braced himself. Pechov was closer, but he had to get him to come in just a little more.

Pechov frowned, his mouth opening a fraction. "Not understand."

"A bogoff," Palmer repeated. It was no good, he was still out of range. He sagged weakly against the wall and dropped his head, coughing, the reaction not entirely feigned. He began to think something might be broken and wondered if he had sufficient strength left to do this.

Pechov muttered impatiently and moved a step closer, his gun hand dropping to one side.

Thank you, God, Palmer prayed, and gripped the pipe in his right hand, ignoring the heat. Pulling his left hand out from behind the pipe, he flicked the strap away into the gloom. Pechov's eyes followed instinctively, drawn by the movement. It was all the opportunity Palmer was going to get.

Jamming his hand back behind the pipe for maximum purchase, he surged upright and swung his right leg out and up, using the full torque of his upper body to gain momentum. The pain was intense, but he drove through it, gritting his teeth.

He would not get another chance.

In the dim light of the tunnel, and with his head turned away, Pechov missed the movement. By the time he actually sensed something was happening, it was too late. Palmer's leg, straight as a board, whipped round in a vicious crescent kick, bringing with it all the desperation, anger and hatred he could muster, all the desire for answers and the shock of finally knowing where Helen had spent her last few minutes.

And most importantly, who had been here with her.

The edge of his foot slammed into the side of the Russian's head, mashing the brittle plastic of the headset deep into his ear cavity. The pain must have been immense, for Pechov squealed like a pig and fell sideways. Fragments of the earpiece went flying through the air, and his gun hit the bare concrete and skittered away. He planted a meaty hand on the ground, trying desperately to remain upright and scrabbling to retrieve the weapon at the same time. His other hand went to his ear and came away covered in blood.

"Bogoff," explained Palmer with chilling calm, "means you buy one…" He swung his foot again, this time high in the air, and brought it down as hard as he could in an axe kick, the sharp back edge of his heel aimed at a point a couple of inches below the man's unprotected neck. "… you get one free."

There was a sickening crunch as tissue and bone gave way, the vicious downward force on such a concentrated point too great even for Pechov's bunched muscles.

The killer grunted and lay still.

43

Ray Szulu huddled down in a doorway across from Pantile House. This time he was positioned near the rear of the building, where he could get a better view of the entrance and the car park. He was wondering what to do next.

After running down the street in the wake of the van blowing up, he'd found himself in the rare position of actually slowing down and then returning to a scene of a wrongdoing. This was entirely new to Szulu from another perspective: he was actually feeling the instinct to not run away, but to stay and help Riley and Palmer.

He hugged himself in indecision, eyes darting backwards and forwards, waiting to see if he was being watched or if the police had arrived. So far he hadn't seen any blue lights, but he could hear a siren getting closer and knew that if it was a fire appliance, a patrol car wouldn't be far behind.

He ignored the burning van, still spewing its cargo of black smoke, and concentrated on the building. Palmer was in there somewhere. And Riley Gavin, if she was still alive. He knew a thing or two about people being lifted; he'd seen the way men like Ragga Pearl, a south London gang leader and general psychopath, dealt with those who displeased them. Taking a hostage was usually only a preliminary to something far worse, and served as a terrifying warning to anyone else not to fall out of line.

Instinct told him these Russians were no different. If they'd taken Riley, it certainly wasn't just so they could have a nice chat over a glass of vodka and send her home again.

Palmer scooped up Pechov's gun and took a moment to regain his breath. His heart was pounding and the pain from his ribs intense. There was no time to stop now, but emerging from the basement panting like a marathon runner would be sure to draw attention, and he needed all the edge he could get. Before moving on, he felt Pechov's neck for a pulse. There was nothing.

He checked the weapon in his hand. It was compact and light, with a four-inch barrel, but no discernible markings. It was small calibre, probably .22, he guessed from somewhere in Eastern Europe. A close-proximity weapon; a killer's gun. He wondered if it was the one used to shoot the cat. If so, it nailed Pechov as the shooter. He remembered how Mr Grobowski had described him to Riley: '…*he a buhaj – a bull…*'

The door and the lift shaft at the end of the tunnel beckoned. The lift would be a quick way up and out, but risky because it opened on to the ground floor close by the front desk. It would also be noisy, instantly alerting everyone in the building to the presence of an intruder. But it was either that or the stairs – and either could be a trap waiting to be sprung.

As he passed another pile of maintenance junk, he spotted a short length of steel piping. He picked it up. It was heavy and felt good in his hand. A gun was good, but something blunt was quieter. He tucked the gun in his jacket pocket and headed towards the steps to the ground floor. After that, it was the main stairway or nothing.

He eased open the access door and edged out. He was at the rear of the lobby, opposite the emergency stairs. He stepped over and listened. The stairway was narrow and dark. Inviting. Maybe too inviting.

He backed up and risked a look towards the reception area. From here, he could just see the edge of the desk and a couple of chairs, and beyond that, a stretch of glass overlooking the rear car park. There was nobody in sight, but he thought he heard footsteps out by the door. At that moment, a figure strolled along the walkway outside. He ducked back. One of the security guards.

He waited for the man to disappear. It was tempting to wait for him to come back inside and use the threat of the gun to find out where Riley was being held. At the very least it would take another obstacle out of his way. But there was always the risk that the guard might be missed if he was supposed to report in regularly.

He decided to leave the man down here and do the one thing they probably weren't counting on: make a frontal approach up the main stairs. It was risky, but well lit and open, which gave him a better than even chance of sensing a threat before he walked into it.

He made it to the first landing and paused. His ears were pounding so loudly, he doubted he would hear anything. But he knew this was nerves. The moment anything moved, his training and instincts would take over.

Up to the first floor. No lights. All doors closed. Silence apart from the faint ticking of something in the heating system.

Voices were coming from somewhere overhead, probably a couple of floors up. He continued, taking the second and third floor flights at a run, ready to duck into the first available corner. Just ahead was the fourth floor landing. He stopped short of the top and waited, breathing heavily. There was a dull pain in his chest, but he ignored it. Time for medical treatment later.

The voices were louder now, and a faint glow of light came from along the corridor in the direction of the main office. He could also hear a hum from somewhere to the rear of the building. He doubted the men would use any of the other floors; that would be too risky if they were in this place illegally. So where was Riley?

As he turned his head to check the layout, he saw a woman's

shoe lying in one corner.

He stepped over and picked it up. He couldn't recall what shoes Riley had been wearing, but he knew it must be hers. He felt a drumming in his chest and bit down on the impulse to charge right ahead and confront whoever was up here. But getting his head blown off wasn't going to do Riley one bit of good. *Don't think the worst*, he told himself.

He looked around and considered the logic of the situation. If her shoe was here, so was she. Simple. But where had she been taken beyond this point? There weren't too many options, simply because most of the layout here was open plan. So start with the smaller rooms.

He cocked his head to one side. The humming noise was louder here, insistent and familiar. An extractor fan. Over in the corner was the door to a women's washroom.

Taking a firm grip on the length of pipe, he padded across and nudged the door inwards. A slight resistance, then the gap widened, and he was hit by a rush of hot, clammy air and a powerful smell of cleaning fluid.

The first thing he saw was an empty bleach bottle on the floor, minus the cap, and fragments of porcelain. A line of sinks – one smashed – stood against one wall, and above them a row of mirrors. The glass was misted by steam rising into the air. He pushed the door right back and stopped, the pain in his ribs instantly forgotten.

Riley was slumped in a chair by the sinks, bound by strips of what looked like electrician's tape. Her face and upper body were soaking wet, as was the floor around her, and the side of her throat and neck was a mass of blotchy, vivid red skin.

She was shivering uncontrollably, but struggling to fight her way out of her bonds and cursing fluently beneath her breath.

44

Ray Szulu watched as the firemen attending the ruined van packed up their equipment and got ready to leave. Their leader was hustling them along, shouting about a warehouse fire three miles away. They had expertly put out the small blaze in the engine compartment and shunted the vehicle into the kerb for someone else to tow away, leaving only a smell of burnt rubber and metal hanging in the air. A police car called to attend had also screeched off as soon as it was clear that there were no traffic problems.

As silence resumed, a squeal of tyres from his right made Szulu duck further into his doorway. A vehicle was approaching at speed. Szulu didn't know a whole lot about engines, but he'd been around Steadman enough times to know when he heard something race-tuned.

The bulky shape barrelled out of the dark, no lights showing, and skidded to a stop right across the entrance to the car park. It was a black van with sliding side doors. Even before it came to a complete halt, three shapes hit the ground running. The driver stayed where he was, the engine ticking over smoothly.

Szulu felt his mouth go dry. The three men didn't bother climbing the small brick wall around the car park, they hurdled it like Olympic athletes, their feet making almost no noise. As they flitted under one of the overhead lights, he saw they were dressed in dark clothes and soft boots. And each man was carrying a handgun.

Szulu swore long and hard. This wasn't good news. More bloody Russians? Had to be. Not police; they'd have had the place surrounded with lights and sirens and a risk-assessment team debating whether it was safe to go in or not.

He stepped out from his doorway, ready to take a run at the building and see what he could do. Maybe he'd find a weapon or something. Maybe he could pretend to be a cleaner arriving late for his shift. Maybe –

"That's far enough, pal."

No way! He'd forgotten the driver; taken his eye off the ball and missed the guy climbing out from behind the wheel. The man was dressed like his mates, all in black, and holding a handgun with a two-fisted grip, pointed at Szulu, his feet planted squarely. Shit, thought Szulu, this guy's not messing. He looked fit and hard, like he knew what he was doing, and the gun was big too. Szulu's legs felt like they were turning to water.

"You don't want to play Rambo," the man said, almost conversationally. "Best get back in your hidey-hole and wait. Your friends'll be out soon enough."

Szulu scowled at him, nerves forgotten as indignation asserted itself. "*Rambo*? Who you callin' names, man?" He stopped. Wait. The man didn't *sound* Russian. And what did he know about who his friends were?

The man chuckled. "No offence. Szulu, isn't it? Believe me, this isn't the time for heroics." He gestured with the gun towards the building. "You'd best get out of sight and stay down," he advised. "If any of the bad guys get out and see you, they might not stop to ask questions."

He turned and jogged back to the van and climbed in. Quickly reversing it back down the street, he tucked it into the kerb just out of the glow of the nearest street light. Now it was almost invisible: just another van parked up for the night.

Szulu had to admire the slickness of the operation. He swallowed and moved back to his doorway, wondering about something else which was a bit more worrying: how come a complete stranger – a gun-carrying stranger, no less – knew his name?

"You had her taken and brought *here*?" Vasiliyev was ready to burst. He spun round to face Fedorov as they entered the main office, ignoring the gun held to his head by Olek. "Are you insane? She is not going to help us – don't you understand that? This operation is over. What's the use of pretending? Why not simply put her name on the article and deal with whatever happens afterwards?"

Fedorov's eyes grew round at this open challenge to his authority. He was not accustomed to his underlings speaking to him like this. He had killed men for less. He made a chopping motion, cutting off further protest.

"*Enough!*" he hissed, a fleck of spittle appearing at the corner of his mouth. He reached out and stabbed his assistant in the chest with a thin finger. "You forget yourself, *Radko Vasiliyev.*" He placed a deliberate emphasis on the man's real name. "I brought you here... I can just as easily make you go away!" He snapped his fingers with contempt, the noise sharp in the sudden silence, and waited for an objection. When none came, he continued, "Now, get rid of the woman. And make it final. We are leaving this place as soon as we can and I want no traces to follow us. Do you understand?"

Vasiliyev licked his lips. He was shocked by the strength of Fedorov's reaction and the gun pointed at his head. His boss rarely demonstrated more than a quiet, contained anger when things didn't go right; it was what made the man so dangerous, as if he preferred to harbour his thoughts deep inside, using others to give physical vent to his emotions. But this was extreme. And the fact that he was still alive meant little; he was a realist and knew it might not last.

"But –"

"But nothing. Where is Pechov?"

Vasiliyev shook his head. He had lost track of Pechov long

ago, and it was now clear why: while keeping him out of the way, Fedorov had given the muscle-bound thug other jobs to do – the most significant of which was to take Riley Gavin hostage. And for what? A simple lesson in who held the most power? It was insane.

He tried to think. The other man, a tall, lard-skinned Ukrainian thug named Roychev, was downstairs, keeping an eye on the approaches to the building. "Pechov is not answering his phone. Maybe he decided to run." It was all he could think of to say. "I will find Roychev and get him to check the building."

Turning away from Fedorov was possibly the hardest thing Vasiliyev had ever done. But he had to move before his boss changed his mind and nodded to Olek to take him out. He felt the hairs on the back of his neck bristling all the way to the door, sure that a bullet was about to follow. He nearly gagged with relief when the door swung to behind him.

He walked down the main stairs, silently wishing that if Pechov had jumped ship, he had the courage to do the same thing. He wondered how much longer the other two would stick around. On the other hand, as they all knew, Fedorov's reach was long – very long. And his memory was extensive and vengeful, as Vasiliyev had witnessed.

Desertion, if that's what Pechov had actually done, was the worst kind of sin in Fedorov's book. Almost as bad as failure. It would attract shame and humiliation, and the derision of his peers, to have a man walk away. Few of them would allow Fedorov to forget such a thing, and the story would follow him wherever he went. Give it a few weeks and Pechov would turn up. But he doubted it would be a pretty sight.

He reached the ground floor and found Roychev standing by the entrance, yawning.

"Where is Pechov?"

Roychev grunted, sneering, bringing thoughts that he must

have been alerted by Olek to Vasiliyev's sudden fall in status. "I haven't seen him since he brought the woman here and took her upstairs." He sniggered nastily. "He's probably enjoying himself with her. I hope he leaves some for me."

"Pig," Vasiliyev swore. "Put a finger on her and I'll cut you into strips." The Ukrainian swallowed and stepped back, his already pale skin turning whiter at the realisation that he'd overstepped the mark, change of status or not. He was heavier than Vasiliyev and probably tougher physically, but until he received orders, he knew his place in the order of things.

"I was only joking," he said, and sought to make amends. "Maybe he's downstairs. He said he was going to check the basement doors to make sure they were secure." He stifled another yawn and grumbled, "I could do with some coffee."

Vasiliyev ignored him and made his way to the rear stairwell. In one corner was a single door bearing a NO ENTRY sign. He opened it and was met by a wall of warm, stale air and a steady hum from the air-conditioning system feeding the building. He stepped through and descended the single flight of concrete steps, treading carefully. If Pechov were down here, he might easily shoot first without bothering to identify his target. He reached the bottom and stopped. A patter of footsteps echoed overhead. He shook his head. Roychev, probably, stamping his feet to keep himself awake.

He edged along the passageway, eyes piercing the poor light, and wished he had a gun. Then he saw the body, lying in the spread of light from an overhead lamp. He recognised the bulk of Pechov's shoulders, and the suit. He bent down to check the man's throat. There was no pulse. He stood up and let out a lengthy sigh, wondering what they had brought down on themselves. He'd have bet almost anything against anyone taking Pechov – the man was a brute, and ferociously strong. Just not strong enough, apparently.

He turned and went back upstairs to the lobby. A feeling of impending disaster was growing in his gut and it wasn't simply because he had stood up to Fedorov – maybe for the first and last time. Something was seriously wrong here.

Roychev had disappeared.

Then he saw something in the shadows towards the rear of the lobby. He walked over to take a closer look.

It was Roychev. He had been shot once in the head.

45

Riley heard a sound at the door and struggled frantically. It could only be Fedorov coming back to continue where he'd left off. The only question was, how long would it last before he tired of his sadistic game?

"Hello, Cinders. Time to go home."

"*Palmer*?" She jerked her head up and saw him smiling down at her. He looked rumpled, his clothes dusted with what looked like grey flour, and he was holding a length of steel pipe in one hand and one of her shoes in the other. She was puzzled about the shoe, then memory flooded back and she remembered losing it as Pechov had bundled her along the corridor and into the washroom.

"Stone me," Palmer muttered, and coughed at the tang of bleach. "Did they have you doing some housework?"

Riley was choked with overwhelming relief, unable to reply. She felt a tear run down one cheek and turned her head away. If she broke down like a big girl in front of him, she'd never forgive herself.

Palmer put down the pipe and took out a small penknife. He gently cut through the tape and peeled it away, wasting no time talking but concentrating on the job in hand, his head cocked to one side, listening for the sound of footsteps.

As the final strip of tape fell away, Riley stood up and shrugged her jacket back into place, overcome by the sense of freedom. But she promptly cried out as the material brushed against the burns on her neck, sending her nerve-ends jangling, and her legs wobbled, the muscles unwilling as circulation was restored.

Palmer caught her before she fell.

"Pins and needles," she muttered quickly, hating the catch in her voice. She flexed her wrists to divert his attention. "If I ever meet Pechov again, he's dead meat."

"Too late. Been there, done it." Palmer's eyes were carefully blank. He could almost have been telling her he'd taken out the rubbish. "Who did this?"

"Fedorov. He probably pulls legs off spiders in his spare time."

"He's on my list, too. Can you walk? We need to get out of here."

She nodded, but the movement make her cry out again. Palmer put a gentle hand under her chin, studying her face and neck with care. She hoped she didn't look as scared as she felt. Palmer always maintained that fear wasn't so bad. Fear, he claimed, can make you run faster.

"You'll be fine," he said finally. "Hell – these people don't know who they're dealing with, do they?" His voice was calm, solid and reassuring, as always. Typical Palmer at a time of crisis – trying to deflect her attention away from bad news. Yet there was something in his voice, and she noticed he was standing between her and the mirrors.

"I don't believe you," she said softly. "But thank you." She felt some of the tension ebb away, his calmness reassuring and contagious. It was so good to know he was here, and on her side. "I'm good. Really."

"You will be, I promise." He stared into her eyes, willing her to take in every word, to cut through whatever she was feeling. "I've seen stuff like this before. It'll heal, I guarantee." He glanced towards he door. "Now, shall we break out of the asylum?"

"Yes, please. I've had it with this place."

"Good. Now listen. You're going down the emergency stairway. You'll be in decent light all the way, so don't stop, don't look back. When you reach the main lobby, head straight for the front door. Go out and keep going. Szulu is out there waiting for you.

Got it?"

She nodded dumbly, then reached out and took her shoe from his hand. She took the other one off and held them both. She could run easier without them. "What will you be doing?"

Palmer smiled enigmatically. "I've got some clearing up to do." He took a gun out of his pocket and inspected it. "It's a cheap bit of Czech rubbish, but for what I've got to do, it'll be fine."

"Palmer –" Riley wanted him to leave it, to come down the stairs with her away from all this. To leave Fedorov and his thugs for someone else to deal with. She'd never heard him talk this way before, and was frightened for him.

But he placed a finger against her lips and gently shushed her, and she knew there was no changing his mind. Since he heard about Helen, there never had been.

"No arguments, kid," he said firmly. "We don't have time. Don't worry – I'm not going to do anything daft. Well, not too daft, anyway. How's the cat?"

"He's fine. Built like he is, why was I worried?" She held on to his arm and flexed both legs in turn, the numbness and tingling gradually receding. If she could blank out the pain in her neck and face, she'd be fine. "Varley's here. Vasiliyev. And Fedorov has two other men at least."

"I know. Don't worry – I'll chase them round the building until they get tired." He led her over to the door and opened it a crack, listening. Then he glanced back. "You ready to roll?"

She nodded. Palmer opened the door and stepped outside. Silence. He motioned her forward, leading her towards the emergency stairs. When they reached the door, he pushed it open and pointed downwards, mouthing, "Go."

Riley hesitated for a second, then did as she was told. When she reached the bottom of the first flight, she glanced back. The door was closing and Palmer had already gone.

She turned and continued on down. Her breathing sounded harsh and loud in the confined space, and her head was pounding. The burns were a constant fire under the shifting clothing, each movement of her arms and shoulders bringing a further bout of torture. Too much noise, she thought, dully. Too much... *bloody* noise. They'd hear her coming from Belgium at this rate. On the other hand, she told herself fiercely, if anyone tried to stop her, they'd get a two-inch heel in the eye for their troubles. If only she still had Palmer's baton.

She spun past the next landing, sobbing against the fire in her skin, and kicked open the door. Too hard; the restraint was broken and it bounced against the wall, reverberating through the building like a twenty-one gun salute. *Damn.* Too late to worry now. She had to get out of here or Palmer would think she was a real wuss.

Down to the next floor. Bits of grit on the stairs, digging into her bare feet. She caught her ankle against a sharp edge, and felt the skin break. She ignored it. No time for pain. The alternative was far worse. Still no sounds of pursuit, but she had the ground floor to negotiate, the most dangerous part of the building. It would be like running across a bare, well-lit landscape.

She charged down the final flight of steps, through the fire door and saw the door to the basement facing her.

And a body lying bundled into the corner.

She couldn't see the man's face, but she guessed by the cheap suit that it was one of Fedorov's thugs.

She hesitated, momentarily forgetting Palmer's instructions. The words NO ENTRY stood out in big lettering on the basement door, a tempting invitation. Then his words clicked in again. Good advice, she thought; too many people in films went right up to the roof or down to the cellar, and promptly met disaster.

She turned and ran towards the main doors. And skidded to

a stop.

A tall figure was standing with his back to her. He turned.

It was Vasiliyev.

46

Riley felt a bitter stab of despair. Was this as far as she went? She had almost made it! Life really wasn't fair.

Vasiliyev looked indomitable, balanced evenly on the balls of his feet, like a fighter waiting for an opponent to attack. But there was a subtle difference. He seemed thinner, less sleek somehow, and his clothes, once so elegant, had lost their sheen. Or was it simply the man wearing them, she thought, his bearing now diminished in her eyes?

"I didn't want any of this, Riley," he said softly. Now, for the first time, Riley thought she could detect the faintest trace of another accent in his voice. Or maybe knowing his origins, and who he was – what he was – had begun to play tricks with her imagination.

"You didn't do much to stop it," she pointed out accusingly. Her breathing was laboured and she coughed as she stooped to put her shoes on. She winced as the pain in her feet and ankle blossomed to join the other hurts. It probably didn't matter any more whether she wore the shoes or not, but she was damned if she was going to stand here barefoot. As for using them as a weapon, it was a non-starter; this man was built like a tree. "What do you do now – finish me off and then vanish back to your *mafiya* pals?" Her voice dripped with contempt, and she wondered how she could have been taken in by him. Then she realised that maybe she hadn't; that deep down, there had always been something about him that had held her back. "Is this the end of the game – Vasiliyev? Or is that also a false name?"

A flicker of something touched his eyes. It might have been regret, she thought. Or surprise. Could men like him ever experience much in the way of emotion?

"It's Radko." He brushed a weary hand across his face. "Radko Vasiliyev. None of this was supposed to happen, Riley. I thought I had it all under control. It was… " He shrugged and gave the faintest of smiles. "Meeting you… I guess I forgot for a while just who I was dealing with. I doubt they'll let me make that mistake again." He sounded genuinely sorry.

A door banged overhead, the noise echoing down the stairs. It was followed by the sound of heavy footsteps. The newcomer was shouting something unintelligible. Riley guessed it must be Russian.

She looked towards the main doors, then at Vasiliyev. She wanted to suggest something – anything – that might offer a way out. To tell him to run, perhaps, to say he could give himself up or simply disappear into the night. But something wouldn't let her. If he was going to do anything, he had to decide for himself.

The footsteps came closer. Another voice called from higher up. Whoever the runner was, it wasn't Frank Palmer. He'd have moved a lot more quietly.

Then Vasiliyev shook his head, and a look of something approaching pain touched his face, as if he had reached an impossibly difficult decision.

He stood aside and gestured at the open door.

"Go," he said quietly. "Go quickly. Whatever you do, don't look back. Run for the lights – anywhere bright. The man coming after you won't stop at holding you. Go!" He waved her away with a fierce gesture of his arm, the snap in his voice jerking her into motion.

Riley ran past him and out into the night. Behind her, she heard the fire door smack back on its hinges as somebody burst out from the emergency stairway.

Vasiliyev waited calmly for Riley's pursuer. After hearing his given name on Riley's lips, he thought he was experiencing something like an identity crisis. The Varley persona had lasted longer than most he had used, and had meant more than merely a temporary name; it had, against his expectations, brought something of a revised outlook... and, thinking of Riley, even a new optimism, impossible though that now seemed.

He breathed deeply and forced himself to relax. It was too late for regrets. But it was good to be free of the pretence at last. The Varley existence had been a job, that was all. An act. But it was now over; it was foolish to pretend otherwise.

He had always known, ever since first meeting Fedorov and recognising him for what he was, that a day like this would come eventually. For men in their line of work, a cosy retirement and a villa in the sun did not figure high on the list of happy endings. Like moths to a flame, he thought wryly. After what had happened in the last couple of days, he knew that even if Fedorov didn't get away, orders would have already gone out to other associates, in Europe and further afield. Vasiliyev had made too many mistakes, and the loss of the Batnev bid, which he guessed was now inevitable, was the result.

For Fedorov, there would be no return to Russia with his future intact, no guaranteed place in his homeland. It would be his greatest humiliation. And somebody would have to pay.

He stood in front of the entrance and listened to Riley's footsteps fading across the parking area. He held the image of her face in his mind for a moment, and silently wished her well.

Olek appeared, breathing heavily.

Vasiliyev stayed where he was, blocking the doorway.

"Out of my way!" Olek spat, and charged, his shoulder bunched like a rugby player. At over six feet tall and two hundred and fifty pounds, with a history of military service and years in the gangs, Olek was a formidable person to take on. He was also utterly loyal to Fedorov, like a pit-bull to its master.

Vasiliyev was taller, with a longer reach, although not so heavy. But he was quicker on his feet. He swayed to one side just as the man's shoulder was about to make contact. Reaching out, he grasped at his opponent's jacket with a powerful hand and tugged viciously. As he did so, he spun on his feet, presenting his hip and using Olek's momentum against him.

It was too late for the other man to stop himself. He flipped off his feet and through the air, landing half on his back with a loud cry of dismay. The impact made a pot plant tremble over by the window. But Olek was strong and resilient, schooled in a hard arena of combat. He sprang to his feet and turned, eyes burning with pain and aggression. He stepped in fast and threw a wicked punch at Vasiliyev's head. But it was a feint; with frightening speed, he followed it with a spinning back kick, catching Vasiliyev full in the ribs.

Vasiliyev tried to curve his body away in a desperate attempt to lessen the damage, but it wasn't enough. The impact spread through his torso in a fierce wave and something cracked close to his heart.

He struggled to breathe, stunned by the power of the kick. All he could think of was to stop the man from getting through the door and going after Riley. As he edged around his opponent, his vision fading, he glanced towards the open door to see if Riley had disappeared into the dark. It was only for a split second.

But it was a fatal mistake.

Olek lunged in with frightening speed, his arm rigid. This time, he wasn't using his hands or feet. A glint of metal reflected off the overhead lights. He was holding a short commando dagger.

Vasiliyev, caught by surprise and paralysed by the increasing pain in his chest, felt a hollow drag of despair, and waited with knowing acceptance.

This was a fight he could not win.

Riley kicked off both shoes and sprinted across the car park. She swerved round the barrier, spilling tears of frustration and anger, and stumbled across the pavement. She ignored the pain in her feet, imagining the breath of a pursuer on her neck every step of the way and certain that Vasiliyev would have stepped aside to let his colleague do his job.

Then a tall shape rose up out of the darkness and wrapped strong arms around her, lifting her clean off her feet.

Riley screamed and struggled with rage, frustration and pain, and they both fell over in a tangle of arms and legs. Without thinking, she lashed upwards with her knee and felt the satisfying squish of full contact with something soft.

"Fuck's *sake*, woman… I'm tryin' to help you – ow!"

Ray Szulu rolled away clutching his groin and gagging. He coughed and spat as he struggled to his knees, hissing, "Dammit, Riley Gavin – why you always tryin' to hurt me?"

"*You!*" Riley jumped up, realising who it was. She turned and looked towards the building she had just fled. There was no sign of Vasiliyev, but another man had just emerged from the doorway, and was standing there looking around wildly.

"Where are the others?" Szulu grunted, getting to his feet, one hand clutching his groin.

"What others?" Riley was confused. "There's only Palmer."

"Three guys with guns. They went in earlier. You must've seen them."

"No, I –"

"Never mind. Come on!" Szulu grabbed her arm. "I ain't built for this hero shit. I want to live." He dragged her back into the darkness as fast as he could, and she stumbled after him, too tired to argue.

47

Frank Palmer heard a door slam below, followed by the heavy lumber of footsteps receding down the emergency stairs. He hesitated. Someone had gone after Riley. Probably the last security guard... or Varley. He hadn't seen the man anywhere, but he must have been here all the time. He briefly considered following, to try and head him off, but he knew he would never make it in time. Given the lead she had, Riley should be safe enough.

He walked along the corridor and stepped through the door into the main office.

Grigori Fedorov was alone. He was standing at the desk in the middle of the floor, stabbing impatiently at a mobile. He stopped when the door closed with a muffled thump, and turned. His face registered a brief flicker of irritation and puzzlement, but it was gone just as quickly.

"What ho, Grigori," Palmer said softly, advancing into the room. "There's good news and there's bad news. The good news is, all your goons are down and out. The bad news is, all your goons... well, I suppose you can guess the rest. It probably doesn't translate well into Russian, anyway."

"Who are you? What do you want?" Fedorov's voice was surprisingly calm, as if he had been interrupted in the middle of some boring but necessary paperwork rather than at a crucial stage of his operation to ruin a competitor's reputation and kill off anyone who got in his way.

"I want *you*, chum." Palmer's voice had lost any hint of humour. He stopped at arm's length from the man who had ordered the death of Annaliese Kellin, of Helen Bellamy and probably Goricz, the building supervisor, and his family. "I want you."

"Don't be ridiculous. You are nothing." Fedorov's tone was dismissive. He continued pressing buttons on his phone as if Palmer was a minor interruption who could be swatted away like a fly. He swore and tried another number, apparently without success.

"You can try 'em all," Palmer told him, "but they won't answer." He reached out and took Fedorov's phone and tossed it away across the floor. "Varley or Vasiliyev... whatever you call him... the two tall guys – I don't know their names – Pechov... I know *he's* not going to sit up any time soon... they're all out of the game." He jabbed stiff fingers into Fedorov's midriff, sending the man sprawling backwards, coughing with pain and shock. He thought he heard a sound on the landing behind him, and hoped he wasn't about to be proven horribly wrong about the diminution of Fedorov's forces.

"You are insane!" Fedorov snapped, struggling to stand upright. "You cannot touch me! I have diplomatic protection... I can have you arrested for this!"

Palmer stared at him, amazed by the man's arrogance. Or maybe it was something deeper than that. Perhaps in his own twisted world, he really believed he had done nothing wrong; that he could bully his way out of trouble; that he possessed some kind of diplomatic immunity. Maybe he was simply insane, having flipped over the edge into a realm where reality no longer mattered.

"Good try. But no peanuts." Palmer lifted his hand and studied the gun he'd taken off Pechov. It would be an irony for this man to die by the same weapon used by one of his men. He stared into Fedorov's cold little eyes, and saw something reflected in them: a flicker of something in the Russian's face which cut through the arrogance and self-belief.

It was probably a look Fedorov himself had seen in the face of his victims.

"I don't know what you are talking about." Fedorov's voice wasn't so certain any more. His eyes were flickering back and forth, looking for a way out. But deep inside, Palmer recognised the thin borderline that hovers between hope and fear – and Fedorov was slipping inexorably from one to the other.

"Annaliese Kellin," said Palmer softly. "Helen Bellamy. And nearly Riley Gavin."

Fedorov remained silent, his eyes burning with defiance.

"What you were going to do in the washroom," Palmer continued, his voice like cold silk, "with bleach and boiling water. She'd have been blinded at the very least." He checked the load in the magazine and flicked off the safety catch. He raised the gun, his arm straight out, body turned slightly to one side, the barrel centred on the other man's forehead.

Fedorov flinched visibly, and his mouth trembled.

Palmer felt no pleasure at seeing his fear. He was almost calm at the idea of what he was about to do. It wasn't legal and it was undoubtedly something that might follow him into the still dark hours of the night, when thoughts of deeds done began to intrude. But the alternative was to allow this monster to go free, to continue his lethal trade. And that was something he couldn't allow.

As his finger tightened on the trigger, Fedorov's eyes flickered away from the gun barrel and settled on the doorway.

Palmer relaxed the pressure on the trigger and slowly turned his head. Three men were standing just inside the room. They were dressed in dark, casual clothing and baseball caps, their eyes hidden beneath the shadows of the brims. Each man wore a slimline comms headset. The two on either side were solid and young. They looked like men who worked out regularly and trained hard. The man in the middle was taller and older, but with the lean toughness of someone who has lost none of the edge gained from years of experience.

Palmer hadn't heard them come in, and felt mildly annoyed at his carelessness. On the other hand, he knew instinctively who they were.

"Koenig," the older man announced, reading his mind, and stepped forward. He was holding a handgun down by his side, as were the other two. They had come prepared.

"About time you pitched in," said Palmer dryly. "I was just having a chat with this piece of rubbish."

"So I see." Koenig motioned to his men, who moved past Palmer and took hold of Fedorov, one on each arm. Koenig glanced at the gun in Palmer's hand, still trained unwaveringly on the Russian. "We're not going to have any trouble, are we?"

"That depends what you're going to do." Palmer glanced at Fedorov, who was looking even more agitated in the grip of the two men. He guessed it had finally occurred to him who Koenig and his companions worked for.

"We're taking him with us."

"To do what?"

"You don't need to know that. Sorry. I know what he did to your girlfriend. And the German girl." He seemed genuinely regretful. "I'd love to leave him in your care, believe me, but I'm afraid we have orders to assume prior rights on this one." He gestured at Fedorov as if the man were not human but simply a package, an object to be dealt with and delivered. "The boss has a tendency to go ape-shit if we don't deliver." He smiled genially enough but neither he nor his men looked prepared to back down.

Palmer sighed. He knew his limitations. There was no point in trying to fight these men; they were motivated and professional, and he had neither the resources nor the desire to prevent them taking Fedorov away. If he tried, he knew he might hurt one or more of them, but in the end he would lose. The fact that they were here right now meant one thing: that Koenig's boss, Al-Bashir, was taking steps to dispose of the threat to his commercial bid and to his wife's reputation.

"Fine by me," he said easily. He had already taken care of the man he believed was responsible for Helen's murder. The white heat that had allowed him to deal with Pechov was now beginning to seep away. He could leave the fate of the man who had given Pechov his orders to others. "There's just one thing."

"What's that?"

"You know he had this building's supervisor and his entire family killed?"

Koenig blinked. "I didn't." He glanced at Fedorov as if seeking confirmation, but the Russian ignored him. He shrugged. "So?"

"If you let him go, he'll come back." Palmer's message was implicit; men like Fedorov were ruthless and would do anything to protect their reputation. The murder of two journalists and the killing of the supervisor's family was proof enough of that. If he was allowed to get away, he would only go so far before re-grouping his forces. Then he would turn and come after them all. He had the means, the memory and the callousness to do it. Nobody would be safe.

"No worries. We've got it covered." Koenig did not elaborate further. "That it?"

"He also had my friend's cat shot. I'd like to blame him for the war in Iraq, but that might be pushing it."

Koenig looked at Fedorov with contempt. "I can't stand cruelty to animals." He jerked his head at his two men. "Take him down the stairs. Maybe we'll let him trip a few times on the way."

He backed towards the door in the wake of his men and their prisoner. "You did well, Palmer," he said. "With barely any resources, you did really well."

"I had enough." Palmer wondered if the man knew about Szulu. He certainly knew about Riley.

"The Rasta?" Koenig was reading his mind again. "Yeah, we

know about him. That was risky with the van, though; a touch too much bang, I thought."

"I'll be sure to talk to him about it. It worked, didn't it?"

Koenig chuckled appreciatively. "Yeah. It worked fine."

Something was puzzling Palmer. "How did you know about Fedorov and this place?"

"The day Riley came to see the boss? She had a tail. When a man like Pechov shows up on our radar, we like to know why." Koenig shrugged. "We had him followed. We've got one of the best trackers in the business on the payroll. In the end, he led us here."

"How long were you watching this place?"

"Long enough. We came in when we had to."

"The man in the lobby?"

"He got in our way. He went down." He gestured at his head-set. "I'm told there are two more down – one of them an own goal." He smiled as if it was all in a day's work. "Don't worry, we'll clear up before we leave."

Palmer remembered the sound of footsteps charging down the back stairs, and wondered if Varley was the own goal. "It might have helped if you'd done that first, don't you think?" He couldn't help it; with the other two men on the loose, getting back down the stairs with Fedorov in tow might have proved more of a problem than Koenig had imagined. Earlier intervention might also have helped Riley get clear and away.

"Sorry – we had our orders." Koenig gestured with his weapon. "Anyway, we had a man stationed outside to take care of any strays." He paused at the door and added, "Tell Miss Gavin she's welcome back in any of the company's stores, any time. That's from the boss."

"Gee, she'll be so made up."

"There's one condition."

"She stops using Tesco bags?"

"She destroys the notes. All of them. She'll know the ones I mean."

Palmer pursed his lips. If they were asking this, it seemed clear that the rumours must have some substance. Not that he thought Riley was going to do anything about it. "She might not agree."

Koenig looked sceptical. "She's not going to use them – if she was, she'd have done it already. It's hardly her thing, is it?" He smiled knowingly. "Anyway, we've already got the rest from the hotel at Lancaster Gate."

Then he was gone.

48

"Shh…" Szulu touched a warning finger to Riley's lips. They were crouched in the dark of the doorway where he'd dragged her after her escape from the building. There was a smell of rotten fruit and urine, and something scuttled away through a tangle of discarded paper. "Stay still."

Riley batted his hand away. "Don't shush me, you moron," she snapped, and felt instantly ashamed of herself. He hadn't exactly been forced at gunpoint to wait for her to come out. Well, not this time, anyway. He could have done his bit and simply disappeared back to his safer life of minicabbing.

She touched his shoulder. "Sorry. That was crappy of me. I always feel cranky after I've been tied to a chair and tortured. You did brilliantly. Thanks."

"No sweat. Did you say torture? Like what?"

"Boiling water. Bleach. That kind of thing." She said it quickly, preferring not to dwell on what might have been if Var-Vasiliyev hadn't come along at the right moment. And Palmer.

"No way!" Szulu sounded impressed. "Shit. They wasn't messin'."

"No, they wasn't." Riley gritted her teeth, trying to shut her mind against just how serious they had been. To add to it, now that she wasn't running for her life, the pain was kicking in again.

Suddenly an engine roared and a van took off from the kerb and swerved into the car park.

"It's those blokes I told you about," said Szulu excitedly. "They left a guy outside."

The driver stopped sideways on and close to the main doors of the building, just as all the lights on the ground floor went out. Apart from the faint wash of light from other buildings and passing traffic, it left the area around the entrance in near-darkness.

Szulu inched forward for a better view. "They went in after me and Palmer did our bit," he explained. "I don't know who they are, but they're on the same side as us." He looked around. "Must be something nasty about to happen."

"What makes you say that?" said Riley.

He pointed to a nearby street light, which was out. "They've disabled the lights. They were working earlier. How would they do that?"

"Maybe they shot them out."

Szulu scowled at her. "You obsessed with guns, lady," he warned her. "You need to talk to somebody about that."

Riley hissed a warning as a tall, slim figure stepped out of the main door towards the van and opened the nearest side door, moving briefly through the wash of the van's brake lights. She couldn't see his face, but she recognised something about the way he carried himself. It was Koenig, Al-Bashir's security man.

"Stay here," Szulu said. "I'm just going for a closer look."

"No way – I'm coming, too." Riley hustled after him, and they made their way across the road and skipped over the low wall into one corner of the car park. As they settled down to watch, two men moved quickly out of the entrance carrying something between them. They dumped the object in the van and went back inside. They came back with another load, then another.

On the fourth trip, as they moved through the lobby area, the driver, who had stepped out of the van, jumped back in and touched the brake lights. The glow was enough for Riley and Szulu to see that the load they were carrying was a man's body, with one arm hanging down.

Riley felt the hairs move on the back of her neck. "What are they going to do with them?" she whispered.

"They clearin' up the mess," Szulu replied knowingly. "No bodies, no proof." He sounded worried, though, and Riley caught the tension in his voice.

"What's up?"

Szulu shook his head slowly, the dreadlocks skimming against Riley's face. "That's four down."

"So?"

"I counted five. At the hotel and here. There's one missing."

"Are you sure?" She remembered the body she'd seen at the rear of the lobby. That must have been one of the four they had just carried out.

"Definite. There was a short one, like this monster body-builder."

"His name's Pechov. Palmer took care of him."

"Yeah? Cool. Then there was two taller guys, and a big dude in some fancy threads. I think he was the boss."

Vasiliyev. Riley didn't say anything.

"And there was a little guy with a bald head," Szulu continued. "I ain't seen no bald head yet."

"Or Frank Palmer." Riley felt sick. Wherever Palmer was, she had to believe he was still inside and safe. Palmer wouldn't give up easily. The always laid back, often irritating but mostly sweet former military cop just wouldn't let himself be overcome like that. He was indestructible.

The men ducked back inside the building, leaving the driver in the van, watching the car park and the street. For one moment, it seemed as if he was staring right at them.

Szulu gave a soft hiss and froze, his hand gripping Riley's arm in warning.

"What's wrong?" Riley whispered. "I thought you said they were the good guys."

"I did. But that don't mean they'd be stoked with anyone seeing them movin' a bunch of dead bodies around, does it?"

There was a movement at the entrance, and the other men re-appeared. This time, they had a figure sandwiched between them. He was on his feet, but seemed reluctant to go with them. For the last couple of yards, the men picked him up and carried him. They pushed him inside and closed the door.

Seconds later, they were gone, leaving just a wisp of exhaust smoke hanging in the air.

Riley and Szulu waited, both thinking the worst.

Then, from behind them, Frank Palmer's voice drifted out of the dark. "Are you two girls staying here all night? Only I'm gagging for a pizza."

49

Three days later, the pain from her burns slowly receding, Riley held a planning meeting with Mr Grobowski.

The surgery had called to say that there was a problem with the cat: he was howling so loudly, he was keeping the other resident animals awake. They would consider an early release, but on condition that someone would be able to look after him and change his dressings.

"Is not a problems, Miss Riley," the elderly Pole boomed eagerly when she told him. "You bring him homes and I be his nurses for as long as it takes." He paused uncertainly. "Is OK with you, of course?"

"Of course it is, Mr G. You know Lipinski – he's a free agent. If it hadn't been for your magic meatballs, he'd never have survived."

"Sure, I knowing that." He smiled shyly and rubbed at his craggy face. "You are very kind persons, Miss Riley. We are like little family, I think." He rushed away downstairs, suddenly overcome by emotion and muttering about having to cook more meatballs.

He passed Palmer and Szulu on the way. The two men had come in response to Riley's offer of lunch at the Belvedere in Holland Park, as a thank you for their help.

"You know, I never got into this sort of trouble before I met you two," said Szulu, slumping on to the sofa. It had been a recurring theme ever since they had left Pantile House. "Mind you, I never got taken to no fancy restaurants, neither." He grinned. "I am so gonna give the menu a pastin', man, I warn you."

"Suits me," said Riley approvingly. "You deserve it."

Palmer nodded in agreement. "I second that." He gave Szulu a stern look. "But you haven't mentioned any of what you saw to your girlfriends, have you? We've got too much to lose."

"Hey, man – what you take me for?" Szulu looked hurt. "I ain't no blabbermouth. I'm a professional – I know when to keep it zipped."

Before Palmer could say more, there was a knock on the door. Riley opened it.

It was DI Craig Pell. He was alone.

"I've been trying to get hold of you," he said sternly. His eyes flicked past her shoulder and fixed on Palmer and Szulu.

"I'm sorry," Riley replied, ushering him in. "I've been between the hospital and the vet's surgery. Neither of them like people using their mobiles." She smiled sweetly, daring him to call her a liar. "Would you like some tea?"

"No, thanks." His eyes widened when he noticed the reddened skin on her neck and lower jaw.

Riley nudged him along, to stop him asking questions. "Was there something else?"

"Uh, yes, actually. I got a report that there was a shooting on these premises. I need some details." He looked at them in turn, but Palmer was ignoring him and Szulu was pretending he was somewhere else.

"The shooting was downstairs," said Riley firmly. "I was out. It was probably a case of mistaken identity."

"Yes. The old bloke downstairs says the same thing. At least, I think that's what he said."

"Why are you investigating it? This isn't your area, is it?"

"My area is wherever I'm sent." He gave her a tight look and explained, "We have this new situations alert software that's been installed. It's pretty neat. Anything happening within a mile of a known address gets flagged for immediate attention." He smiled proudly.

"Known?" Riley's eyebrows shot up. "What do you mean known? This isn't a crack house!"

Pell's smile vanished in an instant. "I'm sorry. It's still in the trial stage and I entered your address as a test. I was… concerned." He puffed his lips and looked away, his face going pink around the edges.

Palmer exchanged a knowing look with Szulu.

"Oh." Riley was slightly mollified. "In that case, thank you. But I don't know anyone who'd want to harm a cat. Mr Grobowski said he thought the man may have been on drugs."

"Yes. Interesting man, Mr Grobowski." It seemed the nearest Pell was going to get to calling the elderly Pole a liar. "There's also a report pending about a kidnapping outside a vet's surgery. The same surgery where your cat was being treated for a gun-shot wound. That was also flagged on our new system. The only eyewitness is now having doubts. She thinks it might have been a prank."

They returned his stare with blank looks. He sighed. "I was told I'd have days like this. How is the cat, by the way?"

"He's fine. I'm bringing him home soon."

"That's good." He cleared his throat and addressed Palmer. "We don't have any new leads on Miss Bellamy's murder, I'm afraid. The foreign national she met in west London seems to have disappeared… if he ever existed. But we'll continue with the investigation, of course. I just want to warn you that we may never find out what happened. I'm sorry."

Palmer nodded without comment.

"You don't seem surprised." Pell's voice was dangerously soft. He waited for a few seconds, but when nothing was forthcoming, he shrugged. "I've got to go. Oh, one thing more: there was a serious ruckus in Euston three nights ago. Reports of shots, a vehicle blown up in the street and armed men inside an office building. No bodies, though."

"Really?" Riley forced the word out through a dry throat, not daring to look at Palmer or Szulu. Where was this going?

Did Pell know something or was he just fishing?

"Yeah. It took place at a building called Pantile House. Like the one in the photo you were sent by Miss Bellamy." He glanced at Palmer. "Added to that, the building supervisor is missing and his family are all dead. A nasty business."

Palmer returned the look with steady eyes. "What some people will do to get a cheap office."

Pell seemed to subside, his tone softening. "There's a possible link with a Serbian drugs gang. The dead man moved here to get away from them." He shook his head. "Obviously, it wasn't far enough." He glanced at Riley and gestured towards the door. "Could we have a word? In private?"

Riley followed him out on to the landing. She could hear Mr Grobowski singing in his flat, a mournful dirge which for him passed as light music.

The moment Pell's eyes settled on her burns, she said, "Please don't ask. I feel stupid enough already, without having it pointed out to me. I had an accident in the kitchen. It happens."

"Oh." He looked apologetic. "I didn't mean to embarrass you. But that's not what I was going to say."

"The answer's yes," she said, before he could elaborate. It was more for her sake than his, before she lost her resolve and shut herself away like a nun. John Mitcheson was out there somewhere, she knew that. And he might reappear at any time. But life was for living, and time was too precious to sit around waiting for maybes. "Dinner," she continued, "any time after today and anywhere you like except Korean. I tried it once and it didn't agree with me."

Pell grinned. "You don't mess about, do you? How did you know I was going to ask?"

"I didn't. Haven't you heard – we girls are doing it for ourselves these days." She looked at him with wide eyes. "Or am I being too forward? Only, if you're not interested –"

"I am. I am." He reached out and touched her arm, then snatched his hand back. "Uh, I'll call you. Later."

"You're not concerned, then?"

"About what?"

"About being seen fraternising with a member of the press. It might tarnish your reputation."

He pretended to give the possibility serious consideration. "Actually, I'm more concerned about your accident rate. I've been reading up on you. Gangs on the Costa, DEA rogue agents, Colombian drugs. And now shot cats and domestic accidents. I hope it's not catching."

"Well," she said, "you'll just have to find out, won't you?"

He fluttered his eyebrows, then turned away.

Riley watched him go back downstairs.

She was smiling.

THE PREVIOUS ADVENTURES OF
RILEY GAVIN AND FRANK PALMER
from
CRÈME DE LA CRIME
available from a bookshop near you

NO PEACE FOR THE WICKED

Old gangsters never die – they simply get rubbed out. But who is ordering the hits? And why?

Hard-nosed female investigative reporter Riley Gavin is tasked to find out. Her assignment follows a bloody trail from the south coast to the Costa Del Crime as she and ex-military cop Frank Palmer uncover a web of vendettas and double-crosses in an underworld at war with itself.

Suddenly facing a *deadline* takes on a whole new meaning…

ISBN: 978-0-9547634-2-8   £7.99

The excitement carries through right to the last page…

- Ron Ellis, Sherlock magazine

NO HELP FOR THE DYING

Runaway kids are dying on the streets of London. Investigative reporter Riley Gavin and ex military cop Frank Palmer want to know why. They uncover a sub-culture involving a shadowy church, a grieving father and a brutal framework for blackmail, reaching not only into the highest echelons of society, but also into Riley's own past.

ISBN: 978-0-9547634-7-3   £7.99

Gritty and fast-paced detecting of the traditional kind, with a welcome injection of realism.

- Maxim Jakubowski, The Guardian

NO SLEEP FOR THE DEAD

Riley Gavin has problems. Her long-distance love life seems set to stay that way, her occasional partner-in-crimebusting Frank Palmer has disappeared after a disturbing chance encounter, and she's being followed by a mysterious dreadlocked man.

Frank's determination to pursue justice for an old friend puts him and Riley in deadly danger from art thieves, black gangstas, British Intelligence - and a bitter old woman out for revenge.

ISBN: 978-0-9551589-1-9   £7.99

a nice, convoluted story guaranteed to keep you reading.
- Angela Youngman, Monsters and Critics

NO TEARS FOR THE LOST

For once, Riley Gavin and Frank Palmer are singing from different hymn books. As bodyguard to a former diplomat, it's Frank's job to keep journos like Riley at bay.

But the diplomat's dubious South American past is catching up with him. When he receives a grisly death threat, the partners-in-crimebusting stop pulling against each other.

Helped by former intelligence officer Jacob Worth, they discover Sir Kenneth has more secrets than the Borgias, and his crumbling country house is shored up by a powder which doesn't come in Blue Circle Cement bags.

ISBN: 978-0-9551589-7-1   £7.99

The crisp writing and fresh characters make this stand out from the mystery genre pack.
- Publishers Weekly (USA)

ALSO FROM CRÈME DE LA CRIME:
A CRACKLING DEBUT FROM
KAYE C HILL

DEAD WOMAN'S SHOES
A trip to the seaside suddenly got dangerous...

All she wanted was to get away – and suddenly it's raining cats, dogs and bodies...

Lexy Lomax has run away from her obnoxious husband, taking with her a cool half million of his ill-gotten gains and a homicidal chihuahua called Kinky. Holed up in a decrepit log cabin on the Suffolk coast, Lexy finds herself mistaken for the previous owner of the cabin, a private investigator, now deceased. Before she knows it she's embroiled in a cocktail of marital infidelity (possibly), missing cats (probably) and poison pen letters (definitely).

Oh, yes – and a murder or two...

ISBN: 97809551589-95   £7.99

From Gordon Ferris

THE UNQUIET HEART

Private eye Danny McRae battles with black marketeers, double agents and assassins in 1940s London and Berlin.

Lovers by night, gang-busters by day…

Danny McRae, struggling private detective. Eve Copeland, crime reporter, looking for new angles to save her career.

The perfect partnership…

Until Eve disappears, a contact dies violently and an old adversary presents Danny with some unpalatable truths.

His desperate search for his lover hurls him into the shattered remains of Berlin, where espionage and assassination foreshadow the rise of political terrorism. The ruined city tangles him into a web of black marketeers and double agents - and Danny begins to lose sight of the thin line between good and evil…

ISBN: 978-0-9557078-0-3   £7.99

Praise for *Truth Dare Kill*, Gordon Ferris's first Danny McRae adventure

… *a believable world of desperate people… will keep you turning the pages…*

- Catherine Turnbull, Dursley Gazette

…*dark atmosphere… a riveting read…*

- Gloucestershire Echo Weekend

… *populated with a carnival of misfits… an exciting debut*

- Crimesquad.com

From Roz Southey

CHORDS AND DISCORDS

Music may be the food of love, but it doesn't fill an empty belly…

Winter is not a good time for jobbing musicians in early 18th century Newcastle. The town has emptied for the season, and Charles Patterson, harpsichordist, concert arranger and tutor to the gentry, is down to his last few shillings.

But Patterson has another talent: solving mysteries. When an unpopular organ builder thinks his life is in danger and a shop-boy dies in dubious circumstances, the offer of a substantial fee persuades him to seek answers to some difficult questions.

Like, who stole the dancing-master's clothes? Why is a valuable organ up for raffle?

And will Patterson escape whoever is trying to kill him?

ISBN: 978-0-9557078-2-7   £7.99

Praise for Roz Southey's first gripping Charles Patterson mystery:
… points for originality… absorbing… unhackneyed setting
- Alan Fisk, Historical Novels Review

A fascinating read and certainly different
- Jean Currie, Roundthecampfire.com

… wonderful background… complex plot … the quality of the writing hurtles one along

- Amazon

From Maureen Carter

BAD PRESS

Detective Sergeant Bev Morris tangles with the media

Is the reporter breaking the news – or making it?

A killer's targeting Birmingham's paedophiles: a big story, and ace crime reporter Matt Snow's always there first – ahead of the pack and the police.

Detective Sergeant Bev Morriss has crossed words with Snow countless times. Though his hang-'em-and-flog-'em views are notorious, Bev still sees him as journo not psycho.

But a case against the newsman builds. Maybe Snow's sword is mightier than his pen?

Through it all, Bev has an exclusive of her own…a news item she'd rather didn't get round the nick. DS Byford knows, but the guv's on sick leave. As for sharing it with new partner DC Mac Tyler – no, probably best keep mum…

ISBN: 978-0-9557078-3-4   £7.99

Crime writing and crime fighting: Maureen Carter and her creation Bev Morris are the Second City's finest!
- Mark Billingham

Praise for Maureen Carter's earlier Bev Morris books:
Carter writes like a longtime veteran, with snappy patter and stark narrative.
- David Pitt, Booklist (USA)

Many writers would sell their first born for the ability to create such a distinctive voice in a main character.
- Sharon Wheeler, Reviewing the Evidence

British hardboiled crime at its best.
- Deadly Pleasures Year's Best Mysteries (USA)

MORE RIVETING READS FROM CRÈME DE LA CRIME

A KIND OF PURITAN by Penny Deacon　　978-0-9547634-11
A subtle and clever thriller…
- The Daily Mail

• **A THANKLESS CHILD by Penny Deacon**　　978-0-9547634-80
Penny Deacon has created a believable, hi-tech future world… In contrast to the electronic efficiency, interesting relationships(are) portrayed with genuine depth of feeling.
- Shotsmag

WORKING GIRLS by Maureen Carter　　978-0-9547634-04
A hard-hitting debut … fast moving with a well realised character in Detective Sergeant Bev Morriss. I'll look forward to her next appearance.
- Mystery Lovers

DEAD OLD by Maureen Carter　　978-0-9547634-66
Maureen Carter's work has a certain style, something that suggests she isn't just passing through. Complex, chilling and absorbing – Dead Old confirms her place among the new generation of British crime writers.
- Julia Wallis Martin, author of The Bird Yard and A Likeness in Stone

BABY LOVE by Maureen Carter　　978-0-9551589-02
Carter writes like a longtime veteran, with snappy patter and stark narrative.
- David Pitt, Booklist (USA)

HARD TIME by Maureen Carter　　978-0-9551589-64
Carter… leaves plenty of surprises for the reader to enjoy.
- Publishers Weekly, USA

BEHIND YOU by Linda Regan 978-0-9551589-26

… readable and believable… extremely well written…

- Jim Kennedy, Encore

PASSION KILLERS by Linda Regan 978-0-9551589-88

… confidently told and kept me hooked…

- Sharon Wheeler, Reviewing the Evidence

A CERTAIN MALICE by Felicity Young 978-0-9547634-42

a beautifully written book… Felicity draws you into the life in Australia… you may not want to leave.

- Natasha Boyce, bookseller

IF IT BLEEDS by Bernie Crosthwaite 978-0-9547634-35

Longlisted for the Pendleton May First Novel Award

A cracking debut novel… small-town atmosphere is uncannily accurate… the writing's slick, the plotting's tidy and Jude is a refreshingly sparky heroine.

- Sharon Wheeler, Reviewing the Evidence

PERSONAL PROTECTION by Tracey Shellito 978-0-9547634-59

… a book which isn't afraid to go out on a limb. It's a powerful, edgy story… the makings of a dark and challenging series.

- Sharon Wheeler, Reviewing the Evidence

SINS OF THE FATHER by David Harrison 978-0-9547634-97

…an intriguing protagonist… an accomplished debut and hopefully the first of many outings for Nick Randall.

- Karl Brown, Brokers' Monthly

BROKEN HARMONY by Roz Southey   978-0-9551589-33

... points for originality... different, absorbing, and with an unhackneyed setting...

- Alan Fisk, Historical Novels Review

TRUTH DARE KILL by Gordon Ferris   978-0-9552589-4-0

A gripping, if disturbing, read.

- Historical Novels Review

THE CRIMSON CAVALIER by Mary Andrea Clarke

978-0-9551589-57

... an ingenious plot line leading to a surprizing ending.

- Angela Youngman, Monsters and Critics